C.2

Hearon
    Hug dancing

DATE DUE

Also by Shelby Hearon

hug
dancing

hug dancing

Shelby Hearon

 Alfred A. Knopf New York 1991

C. 2

This Is a Borzoi Book Published by Alfred A. Knopf, Inc.

Copyright © 1991 by Shelby Hearon
All rights reserved under International and Pan-American Copyright
Conventions. Published in the United States by Alfred A. Knopf, Inc., New
York, and simultaneously in Canada by Random House of Canada Limited,
Toronto. Distributed by Random House, Inc., New York.

Library of Congress Cataloging-in-Publication Data
Hearon, Shelby [date]
Hug dancing / by Shelby Hearon. — 1st ed.
p. cm.
ISBN 0-394-58652-2
I. Title.
PS3558.E256H8 1991
813'.54—dc20   91-52735 CIP

Manufactured in the United States of America

Published November 11, 1991
Reprinted Once
Third Printing, December 1991

For my amazing, sweet children

Anne Rambo and
Reed Hearon

I am grateful for the support of the American Academy
and Institute of Arts and Letters.

hug
dancing

A thirty-two year old Texas woman tries to remake her life after a break-up with her Presbyterian preacher husband and to find love with her long lost high school sweetheart.

THEY LIVED HAPPILY *ever after*. Could it really be true? After three years (or ten years, or more than half our lives, depending on how you counted) of waiting?

When I saw Drew running across the Heart of Texas Fairgrounds, when he wrapped his arms around me right there in the middle of the field, when he waltzed me around and around, shouting into the air, I knew he had done it.

"I told her," he crowed. "I told her I was leaving."

When he whirled me around again, lifting my feet off the ground, I kissed him, full on the mouth, right there in plain sight of anyone. Oh, Lord.

We'd talked about it—his leaving, my leaving, us, Drew and Cile—about almost nothing else, since that first time we made love with hail big as walnuts beating down on the roof of his old farmhouse. Or, really, since that first time we'd got back out on the dance floor again, amazed that nothing at all had changed since high school.

It was Wind Day, and everyone in our part of town, our part of the world, was flying kites. My two girls, middle-school Amazons, were far across the grassy expanse, letting theirs rise into the blue of the March sky. They'd brought homemade, ecologically sound newspaper box kites, tied with twine, anchored with rag tails made from scraps of old shirts and pajamas. Beyond theirs overhead were hundreds of brighter, newer kites: taloned see-through dragons; segmented fish; wide-winged butterflys in paint-box colors; sleek Mylar sharks; Czech, Japanese, Indian, Chinese, Mexican, German, Korean banner kites of spinnaker nylon; tissue paper and balsa wood throw-aways. All diving and dipping like sea gulls into the surf, like ships' sails snapped by sudden gusts. Like dancers leaping against gravity.

The faces of the children, gazing upward, were as multihued as the kites themselves. Here in central Texas near the confluence of two rivers on a faultline, it was easy to believe the school district's statistics: that by the turn of the new century a scant fifth of all our students, K through twelve, would be white.

I'd been looking for Drew, knowing that on Wind Day he'd be there with his sweet boys, the three of them flying model planes on another part of the Fairgrounds. I'd heard the loud aggregate hum of small motors like Judgment Day locusts, and strained for the sight of him, longing to see him.

Wind Day was a happy time for us; we loved the kite fliers all trying to get their hopes airborne. We joked that the Saturday got its name from the fact that it was the one day of the year in this town I called Weather, Texas, when the wind was calm enough not to rip kites to shreds and splinters, or blow topsoil under your eyelids, or spiral your car right off the ground and land it in one of our dammed-up lakes.

We'd come every year since we'd found each other again, every year when the sky was this fine cerulean blue, and the gentle nudging wind pushed at our shoulders and legs, shoved us into one another, tumped toddlers on their behinds, sent dogs scurrying off, coats ruffed as if chasing rabbits, blew hair into wide-open mouths and ice-cream scoops off cones, tugged strings from slippery little fists, sent plastic killer bees and yellow happy faces into high wires and treetops, dumped biodegradable tatters into vacant lots.

We waved to my daughters, who were looking our way. They waved back, pointing to their recycled kites bobbing like corks high in the sky. They'd be fine, about the news. His mild-mannered sons would be, too.

"Where are the boys?" I asked him, looking toward the whirring sound that reached us from the athletic field.

"They said I was old enough to fly my own model planes now." Drew looked momentarily glum. "They don't mingle with the masses anymore. They've got a tennis match. Besides, their momma thinks they'll get Pasadena tick disease standing in the grass."

"Oh, don't do that." I hated it when he got down on his two. We went a long way back together, his boys and I. Back to when they were almost lap babies; back to "Ring Around the Rosy Rag." They were different from their tall, long-legged daddy in his stovepipe jeans and boots, his heavy longhorn belt buckle reaching my rib cage. They were a smaller, more gentlemanly breed.

"Yeah," he said, giving me a casual public arm around the shoulder. "You get on with them, Cile."

"Should I tell Eben tonight?" I was, in truth, hesitant to tell my husband I was leaving him, not so much because, a pastor, he had the authority of the church behind him and the approbation of his flock, rather because I knew from long experience that he'd put his prying fingers on my news. He liked to appropriate my surprises; to confiscate my secrets. I'd have preferred to say nothing to him until after Drew and I had moved to the farm together. But that was wistful thinking: another name for cowardice.

"Sure, tell him you're gone." Drew looked up at the sky and shouted out, *"She's gone,"* and then, *"She's mine,"* amazed at the utter wonder of saying it right out loud, his voice blown away on the wind with hundreds of others, parents calling their young, kids calling to friends.

"Maybe I should wait until after Easter? You know Easter in the church."

"You've got to tell him, honey. I did it. I told her. The rest of them can wait. His whole congregation doesn't need to know yet; most of all my mother, the preacher's biggest fan, sure doesn't need to know yet." He looked anxious just talking about her. "It's going to take a while, anyway, to get my things cleaned out of that half acre of carpet, to move everything up there."

We'd planned this for so long—our living together in his tin-roofed old farmhouse, north of Waco and east of West, on the rolling blackland acres that had been in his family as long as there'd been a state of Texas. On the plot of ground where his bones felt at home.

That was as far as we ever got making plans. Then he'd start talking about how his great-granddaddy had almost lost the farm to flooding, his granddaddy to drought, his daddy to the tornado of '53, which wiped out the downtown here and cleared a path up through the countryside. How he, Drew, was damn sure not going to be the one to lose it, no matter what kind of bribe the federals came up with next as an excuse to grab the grasslands for themselves.

"I can't believe it yet," I said, joy sinking in. "That we're really doing it." I looked at the lightness of shapes scudding the sky.

"Believe it," Drew said, grinning, scratching his cropped red hair as if he was just getting used to it himself. He looked the way he had at seventeen, back when we used to dance our legs off to country music on sawdust floors. "Believe it."

"And the kids?" I asked him, looking off toward my big girls. "They'll be okay, won't they?"

"They'll be great, honey. Every last one of them will be great. Nobody will even notice we're gone."

THE GIRLS HAVING decided to come later with friends, I drove home alone in the old clunker of a Pontiac for which Drew foresaw a great future. It was a vintage model, he said, the '74 Firebird, a real muscle car; fixed up they were fetching fifteen gee. Not fixed up, in the meantime, it had that sound old cars make in high gear on city streets, as if their underbellies were loosely wired on, liable to drop out on any dip in the road, not so much without shocks as without even the memory of springs.

It wasn't far through the Lake Shore section of town from the Heart of Texas Fairgrounds to the parsonage: down Loch View to Lago Vista, then up Laguna Vista to Lake View, our street. Our neighborhood of family homes, primary schools, playgrounds and churches sat, as did Waco proper, between two rivers—to the east, the wide Brazos, which alternately watered and flooded the countryside, and to the west, the forking Bosque with its white chalky cliffs—on a faultline that ran from San Antonio to

Dallas and attracted weather the way a magnet attracts iron filings.

The faultline dividing the city divided also the loamy farmlands to the east and the grassy prairies to the west, and, more recently, served as a line of demarcation between the past and its cotton and the future with its particle physics. (It was a sign of the times that the nearby community of China Spring, originally named for its stand of chinaberry trees, was now home to Chinese researchers who were building a science corridor connecting the supercomputers to the south of us with the supercollider to the north.)

On a more daily level, the faultline divided the rice belt from the potato belt. Waco was essentially a rice-eating town, what with the old Deep South boiled white rice, the Mexican rice-bean dishes, the Pacific Rim influx of brown rice, plus a touch of Cajun dirty rice. I had, for some reason, sided with the potato people, mostly Germans and Czechs, a minority in the church, and through the decade I'd been here in service to Grace Presbyterian, I'd developed a small repertoire of dishes: potato soup for the family on weekends, potato dumplings with company turkey, potato fritters and casserole potatoes for congregational meals. There was even Cile Tait's Potato Bake in the new church cookbook.

Pulling the dragging Pontiac into the driveway, I reckoned how much I would miss the house, if not the marriage, despite the fact that it had always been, being a parsonage, only on loan to us. It was an authentic 1920s ranch house, in a city of a hundred thousand ranchstyles, and had (small tidy world of the faithful) once belonged to Drew's mother's parents. Across the front ran a large, spacious gallery room, divided into dining and sitting space. We had half a dozen cane-bottomed chairs and a cane-backed sofa whose cushion held the original horse-hair. These could be arranged in a circle for company, or the chairs pulled up to the old trestle table for meals. Or, when needed, pushed out of the way to make a fine polished meeting room. The girls' bedroom and bath opened off a long hallway as did a small former nursery with desk and phone which each of us used when in need of a bit of privacy. At the end of the hall was the room Eben and I shared, and our small bath fashioned from what had once been a second linen closet.

The only restriction on the house was that nothing could be hung on the walls; the plaster was not puncture-friendly. When we moved in, the one exception had been two heavy gilt-framed mirrors that had hung by guy wires set in the molding at the ceiling. I hadn't been able to live with that—seeing myself going in all directions, serving plates and tea glasses, making guileless smiles, seeing Eben's too attentive, too hopeful stance. I'd packed the mirrors away in the back of the remaining walk-in linen closet in the hall, and hung cow pictures instead. One, by a local artist, was a stand of black and white Holstein with soulful eyes and doglike ears, gazing out in front of a milking shed. The other was a nineteenth-century primitive (a gift from Drew's mother) of a flat orangy Guernsey, broad-backed and small-headed, who possessed both a jutting horn and sagging udders.

It wasn't only the parsonage I was thinking about missing, of course; it was my big, beautiful daughters. I tried to tell myself, I had to believe, that they were so grown-up now, so responsible, so independent, that they would have no trouble with their father and me living in different locations. That they'd quickly expand into the extended space, flourish, even, at the change.

I'd take it a step at a time. Let them get used to the

idea of my leaving until school was out; then, when I really packed to go, they'd be free to help me, to come with me, to get me settled. To make a place for themselves that they felt was home at the old farmhouse. Choose a bed; argue about the bath. Get to know the land, the grassy blackland acres. We'd have long hot lazy months to make our gradual transition. They could come into town on the weekends to help Eben at the church, he'd expect that; come back to the farm on Mondays. Have the best of both worlds.

Then, by September, we'd have a surer footing, a comfortable routine to continue in reverse, for trying out our school-day separations. I'd be in and out of town; we could have a Dr. Pepper in the afternoons, catch up. I could run errands with them; teach them to drive my old beat-up Pontiac.

(Although what I was going to do about sharing them with Grace Presbyterian when I moved, I couldn't think about now. They could not be asked to absent themselves from the heart of Eben's life; my moving would be disruption enough.)

Right now, I ached at the prospect of not seeing their faces on a daily basis come fall, at the idea of not being able to reach up and brush a young cheek with my hand in passing, a mother sort of touch. But it would all work out fine, I told myself. They'd be fine. I had to believe that: they'd be fine, and I'd be fine, too.

Tying an apron on over my shorts, I put pared potatoes, sliced leeks, chicken fat and skim milk on the stove to simmer. Turning the burner on low, I took off my Reeboks and checked the clock. Plenty of time to move a bit. I put Willie Nelson on the record player that dated back to university days—time stood still in parsonages—letting him sing his gospel numbers: "Shall We Gather at the River,"

"Will the Circle Be Unbroken," "When the Roll Is Called Up Yonder," "Whispering Hope."

Thinking of the potato, going through the reflex and comforting work of changing its raw starch into our meal, I considered that the church might retain my recipe but it would soon no longer have the taste of *my* potato bake. Because like most cooks, I'd left out the one ingredient which gave it that special flavor. I'd listed the potatoes, the leeks, the heavy cream, the black pepper, the hot oven, but had made no mention of the tablespoon of anchovy paste. Just as, in giving out freely my recipe for the German potato fritters—grated raw Idahos and raw onions, raw apple, egg, baking powder, nutmeg—I'd never mentioned that I cooked each batch of six in a stick of creamery butter. Old cookbooks were rife with similar omissions. The ancient granny did not reveal that her dark rich giblet gravy contained half a cup of strong black coffee; the bride, that her chocolate pie which tasted like Hershey's kisses had two teaspoons of real vanilla.

This exclusion was an instance of the oldest fight between Eben and me. He found my secrecy grudging and withholding; I found his scrutiny invasive, intrusive. He accused: You hold back. I accused: You usurp. I suppose it stood to reason that the basic discord of a marriage should spill over even into such a minor matter as a recipe in a church cookbook.

As I added a tablespoon of Parmesan cheese to the bubbling soup, I wondered how he would handle the more serious secret of another man.

WASHING MY HAIR in the shower stall of the small bath, I was getting myself ready to tell Eben. Preparing myself for what we'd really be talking about when we talked about my leaving.

The custody fight between us was not going to be over the girls, who'd want to stay here close to the schools on weekdays, or over the house, since it belonged to the church, or money, because even in a community property state, neither of us had much for the other to claim. No, the painful tug-of-war was going to be over Lila Beth Williams, a woman who had been the mainstay of Grace Presbyterian, an elder, my husband's good right hand, and who had also been for ten years like a real mother to me. Like a fairy godmother who'd waved her wand and brought all manner of kindnesses upon me and my daughters.

She'd come into our lives back in Baby Days, back when I slept light as a cat, able to hear the tiniest gurgle or fret a room away, back when the short people, as I called my children, played patty-cake and Where's the baby? and wore those sturdy cotton snap-on clothes. Back when every place we lived, even the lovely new parsonage with its polished floors, dripped with dresses, panties, little socks, nighties, drying on doorknobs, hanging from doorjambs, so that you had to duck to go in and out of every room.

I met her the very first Sunday, or the first official Sunday that Eben presided as the new pastor. I'd got our two out of the nursery and stood with him at the door of the church, shaking hands with the congregation as they looked us over. I'd dressed the girls all in white, to make a good impression, in those angelic smocked things with the rosettes and puffed sleeves and gathered fronts that floated out over little bellies in search of grape juice, dirt, finger-paint.

This nice woman, lean as Presbyterians always are, very weathered in the way of women who garden, came up and took my hand in hers. "Cile—may I call you that, dear?—I have two grandbabies just the age of your two, little boys they are, and a daughter-in-law who could use a nice friend like you. She's a Dallas girl and hasn't put down roots yet in our little city. Will you come for tea, well, nobody has tea anymore, do they, come for something Wednesday afternoon? I know Mary Virginia is free on Wednesdays. We'll get the children together, and you two girls as well."

"Williams," Eben had murmured to me as I shook the hand of the tanned woman in the straight gray silk.

"Thank you, Mrs. Williams," I said, "we'd love to come." I hated being so obviously prompted; he did it all the time. Did he expect me to know every one of them the first Sunday? I imagined perhaps this woman I had never met before, with the name that had an echo of an earlier time in my life, might have preferred to introduce herself to me. Let me know what she'd like to be called. Surely she'd already planned the rest of her speech, hardly an invitation that had occurred to her on the spot. Maybe she wanted to say that her name was Lila Beth and before her marriage had been Jarvis, and can you imagine how much kidding she'd got, in Texas in those days, having LBJ as her monogram? She must have planned to say some of that at church, because she said it all when I did arrive for tea, and that was what she had after all, spiced tea in tall frosted glasses filled with crushed ice.

I'd lost my own mother at eighteen, in one of those too quick and awful accidents—a flash-flood drowning—that replayed for years in my mind, leaving no chance to say the unsaid things, to get to know her, grown. When she was alive (and I remember most how alive she was), I'd had my mind, as kids do, on school. The spring she died, in fact, on Drew (Andy he was to me then). One day she'd been there, a beauty I thought I could never equal, and the next she'd been gone. I'd missed her steadily, but most fiercely after having babies of my own.

Lila Beth's house was not near ours, but in the old part of town where the streets were named for Texas's founders, high on the bluffs adjoining City Park, above the meeting of the two rivers at Lovers Leap. Inside, her house aroused total awe in me with its stretch of Aubusson rug between George Something chairs, marquetry cabinets and bureau bookcases flanking one another and the mantel. Long-skirted end tables with tiny boxes and silver bud vases. So many things that children could wreak destruction on, it quite took my breath away. But when she produced lemonade in paper cups for them, saying lemonade didn't stain the way fruit juices did, I could see we were going to get on fine.

She thought my calling the girls short people was amusing, and at once began to refer to the four children in that way, watching unruffled as the two sets of toddlers took to each other like ducks to—the Gobi Desert?

Mary Virginia turned out indeed to be a Dallas girl. Although it's hard for anybody outside the frame of reference to understand, if you saw her in a restaurant or airport you'd say to yourself right off, Dallas girl. Glossy hair cut just right, a generally turned-out, put-together look. Wearing more different items than the rest of us possessed. A couple of rings, but casual, lapis and coral, plain gold circles in pierced ears, an expensive belt, the lightest of cotton sweaters edged in silk ribbon over a silk blouse over a cotton camisole, pale hose and espadrilles. Friendly but not too friendly, this brunette Dallas girl, sitting on the George Something sofa, dragged out by her mother-in-law to meet a preacher's wife.

I was scared of her, truth be told. Girls like that in school had always made me feel unpolished, lacking. My mother, Celia—even then, ten years ago, already forgotten by everyone else on earth but me—had never taken too well to what she called *ladies*. "Ladies are a pain in the neck. It's hard to believe I'm descended from an unbroken line of them back to the Ark. Promise me no one will ever accuse you of being one," she'd said. I doubted anyone had.

Anyway, that afternoon, that Wednesday, I walked across Lila Beth's elegant room, in my wraparound skirt, T-shirt and tennis shoes, and sat down by this Dallas girl I'd been invited over to meet, while together we watched my daughters, built like Tonka trucks, begin to beat up on her frail surprised little boys, who yelped exactly like puppies when you stepped on their tails.

It didn't seem the best start to a friendship.

TO MY SURPRISE, not only did Mary Virginia not mind my rowdy girls punching up on her amenable boys, she welcomed it. A week later she called to invite us all to her house. "Me with boys?" she said on the phone. "Right there you know I'm going to make a fine mess of it. What do I know about boys, growing up with a sister? Boys don't tell you one thing about themselves when you're dating; you're the last person they want to know anything. Husbands, you can double that. I always envied girls with brothers. They knew everything. What went on in their heads, never mind the bathroom stuff and all the unmentionable business.

"When they handed me the first one in the hospital, I said, you must have made a mistake. The worst of it is that my husband was pleased as punch. He worships the memory of his dad—he was killed in that awful ice storm of '78. He has this image of him as this big outdoor man in boots and Stetson, his face brown as an old briefcase. So now he has these boys and he expects them to be like that. Forget it, I tell him, it's another world now. But I can't stand it if he's disappointed in them. So if, you know, playing with your girls—I don't see how you even keep up with them—toughens them up, that would be the grandest thing in the world for me, Cile."

Her house, in the scenic part of Lake Shore off Lago

Lake, had more rooms than I could count. One of those big rambling ranches with a lake view, and each room had its own bath, even the little boys' rooms did, at their age, plus each had a big double closet and all kinds of features built in for when they were older. Everything was in these mossy colors, gray-green in one boy's room, gray-blue in the other, and there was wall-to-wall carpet everywhere, acres of it, all looking as soft and clean as the day it was installed. In the living room there were love seats in bisque gray, brocade chairs in cream gray. The master bedroom was beige gray with a bed the size of a football field.

There was a maid, white and Swedish, silent as her footfalls on the turf, who brought us Dr. Peppers outside in a fenced yard filled with trikes, scooters, push toys of every sort, plus rocking horses and racing cars that ran on small boys' feet.

It was March, the week of Wind Day, and there was a nice steady breeze blowing off the water. It made me think of kite flying and roller-skating, all those aimless, harmless occupations of grade school. I thought I might move in. The maid appeared with thick slices of hot banana-nut bread for us and oatmeal cookies for the children. I remember letting my breath out slowly, wondering if it would be rude to slip off and take a nap on the big beige-gray king-sized bed in that quiet and spotless, immense and private room.

The fact was, I had to keep an eye on my watch; Eben was expecting me in an hour at the church, to greet and go eat with another pastor in the synod who'd helped him get the appointment at Grace Presbyterian.

"Ruth and Martha are nice names," Mary Virginia said to me. "Different. I mean I haven't met one preschool female in this town who isn't named either Sherrie Lynn or Lynn Cheryl. I mean it. Aren't yours Bible names? I know

they are; even Episcopalians read the Bible sometimes.
Ruth is the one who goes with her mother-in-law to her
country, 'Whither thou goest, I will go,' right? And Martha, that's New Testament, Mary and Martha."

"That's right." I gave her a big smile for knowing all
that. Keeping to myself a very old secret, that while this
was her assumption and, of course, had been Eben's, too,
my daughters' names, to me, were those of dancers leaping
free of gravity, names to grow into.

"How about Trey and Jock?" I asked her, returning her
interest. "Are they nicknames?"

"Sort of. Trey is the third. He's named for his daddy
and granddaddy. Jock is named for Lila Beth's daddy, the
other granddaddy. Actually, Mr. Jarvis, who I didn't
know, was named Jochem, which I couldn't do anything
with. Nobody was ever going to say it right or spell it right.
And my sister had already got our daddy's name. So we
decided on Jock. And Lila Beth likes that okay." She looked
doubtful, breaking bits off her banana-nut bread. "Your
husband is Eben, is that right? That's an unusual name."

"Eben Tait, the original one, was a Scot clergyman,
way back. He's a namesake."

"What do you call him, I mean his title? We say 'rec-
tor,' Episcopalians. I mean I know you never call them
'reverend,' that's an adjective, but I don't know if you say
'preacher' or 'minister.' "

"Probably Lila Beth knows more about that than I do."
I smiled at my slight disclaimer; I'd only been in the church
five years then. "She probably knows more than Eben. But
I say 'pastor.' 'The whole congregation ministers; the pastor preaches' is what they say. We say."

"Do you like it? Seems like it would make you nervous.
Being a preach—oops, a pastor's wife."

"I try not to think a lot about it." I laughed. "What

does your husband do?" My hope was that he'd be somebody Eben could like, so that we could be friends, the four
of us. I was thinking that if I helped turn her placid boys
into little hoods then maybe we would see a lot of them.

She stopped to smooth the hair and hurt feelings of her
smaller son, Jock. She wiped his blue eyes and set him back
in his play car that my Martha was trying to push him out
of. "He's in agribusiness. Isn't that the worst word in the
world? The paper here is always talking about agribusiness. He says he's a farmer; he likes that, calling himself a
farmer. I can't say I do. I don't know why but *rancher*
sounds a whole lot better. You know? I mean there's as
much oil found on people's land in east Texas as in west
Texas, but people don't know that. They think oil, they
think ranch. That's Hollywood, I guess. If they're going to
do a farmer, they put him in a straw hat with a stick of
grass in his mouth. You'd think people who had oil on their
property could think of another name to call themselves."

"It sounds nice and private to me."

"Do you like this town?" She made a face, a Dallas girl
face, which meant she closed her eyes and lifted her brows.
"But then you just got here, didn't you? I've been in Waco
since we got married. Actually, before that I went to Baylor. That's where we met. That's been about a hundred
years ago, and I can't get used to it yet. It's so antebellum
that sometimes I think it's antediluvian." She looked
pleased with herself for making a biblical reference to me.
"It's just so set on itself. I mean nobody in the whole place
can mention Waco without reminding you that it has produced six Confederate generals and three Texas governors.
And Dr. Pepper. I mean you don't go to Atlanta and hear
how they invented Coca-Cola, do you? Maybe you do; I
haven't been there. And cotton. Don't forget cotton. How
they supplied the whole Confederacy with cotton. 'When

Cotton was King, Waco was Queen.' I can't believe people still say that. And brag on how they had a suspension bridge before the Brooklyn Bridge, and the first skyscraper west of the Mississippi, south of Kansas City? Doesn't that just slay you? Don't you wonder what town up there is bragging it had the first skyscraper west of the Mississippi, *north* of Kansas City?" She shook her head as if amazed. "At least Dallas knows there's other places on earth."

At that exact moment, Ruth barreled into my legs, spilling the Dr. Pepper all over my lap—my lap being my one good skirt, a pink lined linen, which I'd worn with my one decent blouse, also pink. No accidents are small in the lives of pastors' wives. I would have snatched my daughter up on the spot and spanked her, except for the audience. I looked at my wristwatch, trying to decide whether or not I had time to go home before meeting Eben and the visiting clergyman. Trying to recall what, if anything, was hanging in my closet to wear if I did get there.

"Come on, Cile," Mary Virginia said. "I'll fix you up. My fault for serving anything but water with four little kids around."

Leaving the redoubtable Swede with my terrorists and the boys named for grandfathers, she led me into her dressing room, where in two minutes flat she had me in a rose silk shirt and matching skirt with flapped pockets and a self-belt. About ten times as nice as what I'd arrived in. Her skirt, several inches longer on me, gave me a nice conservative look that Eben was sure to appreciate.

"Lila Beth would never forgive me," she said, "if I returned you to her church a mess. That place is her whole life. You know the house you're in, the parsonage? It belonged to her family. When they died, she gave it outright to the church; it wasn't touched when the tornado of '53 tore down the town, and she thought it must have been spared for a purpose. Can you imagine?"

I thanked Mary Virginia, gave her cherubic boys moist kisses on their placid cheeks, gathered up the pair of rowdy ruffians I'd come with, and headed for my new second-hand Pontiac. "My time next week," I told her.

IT TURNED OUT what Mary Virginia wanted was not really a new friend, but a weekly dose of rough-and-tumble for her boys.

"You don't do churchy things on Tuesdays, do you?" she'd asked at my house the next week. "What do Presbyterians have? Prayer meetings? Covered-dish suppers?" She'd waved a hand in the air vaguely, as if mainstream churches were beyond her with their confusing ways. Episcopalians were like that. I wondered if Lila Beth had minded dreadfully when her son went over to his wife's church. Decided it had broken her heart.

"Tuesdays are fine," I said.

"My mother and sister got me in this exercise class up in Dallas—they live up there, in the Park Cities part—and it's practically hereditary, getting in. Someone practically has to die. It's fabulous; I never miss it. It only takes me two hours door-to-door, less if I go early." She'd got down on the polished floor of the parsonage and demonstrated an impossible posture, hands on the floor, chest up, chin out, one leg crossing the other in the back, then kicked toward the sky. "Amazing for the thighs," she said, smoothing her cuffed, belted shorts, worn no doubt be-

cause the parsonage had ceiling fans but no air conditioning. "Then we have lunch and shop. It's the only time I
get to see them. It's my one day in Dallas, and wild horses
couldn't keep me away."

I told her that trading days was a wonderful idea. And
after my initial disappointment at seeing I was not to be
her new friend, I saw that it was. It meant no more worrying about what mine were going to do to hers. No more
watching while my Tonka truckers tore blocks and push
toys and moving vehicles from the hands of her mild-
mannered boys. That would now be a problem for her all-
purpose Swede.

I knew having them here all on my own, the four of
them, would be grand. Would be cake. Because I knew
that she might have all the equipment of an amusement
park on the patio of her enormous place, but that I knew
the secret of short people: they loved to move.

So once a week from that spring until the youngest of
them, Martha and Jock, started kindergarten, I had Play
School at the parsonage every Tuesday from seven-thirty
in the morning to five-thirty in the evening. Then on
Thursdays, I left mine at Mary Virginia's from nine until
seven, so that Eben and I could have some time alone before the weekend, which was always hectic and public.

My days with the four children were wonderful days.
The best of the best. The first thing I did was move everything out of the way, the bench sofa and cane-bottom
chairs and the long trestle dining table. Then I put Arlo
Guthrie on the turntable, the same record every time, and
we all held hands in a circle and danced up and down over
and over to "Ring Around the Rosy Rag." It would have
made sense to make a tape of it, but I had no player. Besides, it seemed part of the ceremony to get to the end,
sagging and gasping, and then put the needle back at the

start, with all of them giggling, and dance through it all over again.

We developed little routines: a kick with the left foot here and a kick with the right there. Sometimes we kept our feet on the floor and bounced up and down, and once, when the music was just right for it, we dropped hands and turned all the way around, catching hands on the next note. They loved it. They never got tired of it. They probably—as is the way with babies of two and three—could have repeated it for the whole ten hours. But when we'd done it four times through, we stopped, all sat down on the floor, and had the first of zillions of tea parties. This one being cocoa, because it was still breakfast time for them. (In fact, the boys were often delivered in their robes and jamas—imagine small persons owning robes and piped pajamas, with buttons and belts all extant and in place!— with a change of clothes packed in their little campers' backpacks.) I tried to see to it that every wild routine was followed by some refreshment that would have been impossible in their, the boys', carpeted spotless universe.

Sometimes we played our own version of tag, a sort of "thimble, thimble, who's got the thimble." For this one they stood with their hands behind their backs and their eyes closed, and I put something tiny in the palm of one of them. Then everybody ran around and tried to guess who it was. It was too silly and they all knew at once because of the closed tight fist and erupting shrieks, but there was always a lot of suspense while they waited to see who got it. And once in a while I fooled them and tucked a piece of bubble gum into every hand, and that was an irresistible joke causing them to laugh so hard they fell into a heap on the floor. Or we had musical chairs, lining up four little cane-bottoms that my children had with a small wooden table in those days.

hug dancing

After lunch, which was always sticky, squashy peanut butter and banana sandwiches, we had run-and-touch. In this game they lined up in a row, with their feet all exactly even, which took a lot of pushing and shoving and squealing about who was out of line, and usually one or all of them had to stop and go to the bathroom, and then we'd have to start all over again. By this time I was a heap on the sofa, my feet propped up on its curved arm, and I'd call out the name of some spot or piece of furniture and they would all run to it, to see who could touch it first. "Front door." "Big table." "My tummy." "Fridge." "Back door." "My feet." It didn't matter what it was as long as the object wasn't something likely to be destroyed when the four of them ran the length of the house and crashed into it.

We ended, the last thing in the afternoon, after their naps on mats on the floor, with nice totally indelible grape Popsicles which could drop and melt and mess all over the place. For this we sat back in our circle, on sheets of newspaper, with bibs made of ScotTowels pinned on with paper clips. And everybody laughed when everybody else grew fat purple lips and mustaches.

Why was that all so wonderful?

Maybe because my life, already beginning to stretch the tightly fitted skin of the preacher's wife, felt ground-bound and constrained, every muscle longing to peel out and let go.

Or maybe I simply wished that I were one of those babies, holding hands, bouncing in place, doing "Ring Around the Rosy Rag," over and over and over again.

WHEN, THREE WEEKS after she'd come up to me at church, Lila Beth invited us all for Easter Sunday—yellow and purple straw baskets for the children lined in a row on the dining table, crinkly pretend grass and a stuffed bunny in each—I thought I'd found myself a real family at last.

Although we gathered at her house after the eleven o'clock church services, ours and Mary Virginia's, she served us breakfast: mounds of apple crisp and peach coffee cake, platters of deer sausage, special oven-scrambled eggs with cream cheese, homemade biscuits no bigger than half-dollars, a bowl of fresh strawberry butter. She'd decided against the traditional lunch because I'd confided to her that the only thing church, the church life, had taken from me was the leisurely Sunday breakfast. (Actually, my daddy had always been up at Lake Travis bait fishing and my mother off working the birth control clinics in south Texas. It was the imaginary Sunday mornings I'd missed that Lila Beth provided.) She'd said graciously that it had been the custom when she was a girl to have the Easter breakfast and egg hunt after church, and that I'd simply reminded her of it.

The daddies of Play School had not joined us before, and by then I was really curious what sort of man could be at one and the same time the husband of a Dallas girl and the son of a dedicated church elder. I imagined, to be fair, that Mary Virginia was also wondering what sort of person could be married to someone like me and yet so charm her formidable mother-in-law.

Then, just after we'd all arrived, through the archway into the dining room appeared this familiar-looking redhead on long cranelike legs whom I'd last seen in high school. I looked around at everyone, wondering how on earth he'd got here: someone from the wrong town, the wrong time in my life.

"This is my son, Drew," Lila Beth said.

"Andy?" I stared in astonishment.

"Cile." He stared, too, as if seeing a mirage.

"Lord," I said, laughing in disbelief.

"God," he said, rubbing his eyes.

We started to fling our arms around each other, then stepped back, embarrassed.

Mary Virginia said, "I changed his name. I wasn't going to be Mrs. Andy Williams all my life."

I hadn't seen him since we'd been crazy mad sweethearts twelve years before. The May of our senior year my mother had got swept away in the flash flood south of Wimberly, and by the time that got settled and I'd looked around, come back to life, Andy's family had picked up and moved to wherever they'd come from. But in those days that seemed the way the world turned: people you loved to pieces vanished; you grew up.

"How do you do, Pastor," Andy/Drew introduced himself to Eben, still looking at me, scratching his head, trying to find me under the church clothes. He said, "Hey, you were going to be a schoolteacher. What happened?"

"Something changed my mind." I couldn't take my eyes off him. "How about you? A man of property now. Who would have thought it? You were going to run a weather station. Whatever happened to all that stuff? 'Birds fly lower before a storm because the barometric pressure hurts their ears.' " Lord, just thinking about that, our big dreams, made me homesick out of my mind. "Bugs—what? Slow down? Speed up?" I grinned at him.

"Bugs are more active," he said, grinning back, "just before a storm. They like the moist tropical air."

"That's it."

We stood, our feet here, our heads back there.

"I was sorry about your mother," he said.

"Me, too."

"Whatever happened to your dad?"

"He remarried." I wasn't about to mention in that rarefied company that my father, who ran a hardware store, had married my least favorite high school English teacher. That she'd all but walked him down the aisle the week after the funeral, and that she was the one who'd made wanting to be a schoolteacher seem like a really trashy idea.

Lila Beth came and stood by her son, slipping her arm through his. "*You* were Celia Guest?" she asked me, dismayed.

"I went by Cile; my mother was Celia." I wondered if her finding out I was the old girlfriend was going to be the end of our Easter Sundays, just when they'd begun.

She made a gentle smile, as if it cost her a lot. "The one who liked to go dancing?"

"That was me." I'd never met her or even been to their house in Austin; Andy'd been scared to death of her. We'd planned that we'd "run into each other" at graduation, so he could introduce me then.

"It's a pleasure to finally meet you, dear," she said in a kindly tone. Then, still recovering, she'd taken Mary Virginia's hand and introduced her daughter-in-law to her esteemed pastor.

The kids had a glorious hunt. Wonderful eggs dyed in

primary colors easy as pie to find lying right out on the lawn for the two-year-olds, who got a head start. Harder ones tucked in the monkey grass and flower beds for the three-year-olds, whose fat baskets dragged the ground. Ruth found the golden egg hidden in the low branch of a tree; Martha got a prize for finding the most; Trey got a special birthday egg; and Jock got the chocolate one with the rabbit inside.

That was eons ago. By now, the Williams boys had grown into polite tennis players, already working on their manners and grades against the day when they had to make the choice between Princeton and Baylor. My athletic girls, bent on saving the planet, were already making plans to go to Texas A & M.

The reason I'd wanted to wait until after Easter to tell everyone our news had nothing to do with the church, everything to do with Lila Beth. I hoped that in time, after Mary Virginia had gone back to Dallas, and one of the many widows in the church had started courting Eben, Drew and I could have our egg hunts and those wonderful breakfasts at her house again. But I'd wanted one last Easter with nothing changed, one more of those special family Sundays that stretched all the way back to Baby Days.

M Y WHOLESOME GIRLS sat in the dining room with me, eating an early supper of potato soup and warmed-up corn bread. They were poised on the edge of their chairs, waiting for their friends the Bledsoes to show, so they could all go out and hang around. I had someone else on my mind, too, and was wishing I could tell them my news.

I'd named them for dancers (Ruth St. Denis, Martha Graham), wanting to embed in their very bones from the start the lightness and grace that I'd longed for myself. Then watched, bemused, as—generously overshooting the mark—they'd grown instead into towering, leaping athletes. I had also, missing my mother so terribly when they were small, felt it my bounden duty to pass on to them her fervent social consciousness, aware that in some way I had not been what she wanted, my passions too private, too personal, too *local* for her. So that they, her graceful granddaughters, had learned to soar into the air to score, to spring across the courts, all the while carrying the world's worries with them. Runners bearing the torch. The result was that they were stuffed with the dreams of two lifetimes, packed with the bulging hopes of two generations. No wonder my fair daughters were larger than life: they'd been raised on the anabolic steroid of wish fulfillment.

As usual, I felt dwarfed and plain in their company. It reminded me how my mother used to say—when I complained about being so short and about how my mousebrown hair was always blowing in my face—that she'd given me the best heredity she could manage and to be grateful for my straight hair, straight nose, and straight teeth. My girls were a more robust and vibrant breed than I. Not dark like their father, having my lighter coloring, they took after him in height, being already, at twelve and thirteen, five seven and five eight. Ruth, the older, my serious ecologist, wore her sandy hair in two thick clumps, one sticking out over each ear, and over ample breasts which her sports bra failed to bind wore a green T-shirt that urged SAVE THE WETLANDS. Martha, the younger, my animal lover and future vet, had a fat French braid down her back, two deep dimples she tried to ignore, and a chest message proclaiming FUR IS DEAD.

As usual, they were talking cows.

Today, N'Damas.

Martha, looking milk-fed herself, and to my motherly eye as if she should still be wearing pajamas with feet in them, was arguing with the stubbornness of younger siblings. "We're mapping their genes. To increase milk production. They're tsetse resistant, even though they don't give much milk, the N'Damas are, their cows. But ours, that do give milk, they die like flies from those flies over there, the same as people. So we're *mapping* their *genes*, see?"

Ruth tugged at her clumps of hair, holding them out like antennae. "That's evil. That's really *evil*, Mart. You know that, don't you? That it's evil? There are already two billion cows in the world, plus one and a half billion goats and sheep, plus one million pigs. What they ought to be doing, instead of using stuff like bovine growth hormones to engineer cows for bigger burgers and better cheese spread, is to get rid of them all. Do you have any idea how many people in the world could be fed on the grain that livestock eat?" She leaned across the table and waved a spoon at her sister.

Her kind face crinkling in frustration, Martha raised her braid and her voice. "You don't even listen. You never pay any attention to what I'm saying. What we're doing is mapping genes, and that's *good*. I'm writing a paper on it. So those starving people in Africa can have milk. The reason they don't have protein over there is not because the cows are eating the sorghum in the Sahara, Ruth"—she leaned forward, her earnest dimpled face intent—"since there isn't any, but because the cattle they have, the N'Damas, don't give enough milk."

"What you need to be writing a paper on, Mart, is on plans for a livestock eradication project."

Martha stood up, looking as if she might burst into tears. "You're like those farmers in the dairy states objecting to everything. To gene mapping the same way they objected to the steel plow and barbed wire and the mechanical hay baler. I did a paper on that—"

"Do a whole Ph.D. on it. Or on your fly-proof N'Damas. Or on that wrinkled old Asian cow you love with the lousy meat."

"The Wagyus, for your information, have the kind of meat that if you eat it, it actually lowers your cholesterol. For your information, that happens to be a very important scientific research idea. I may do a—"

Ruth sighed, stuck her spoon behind her ear, made a face.

How beautiful she was with her deep-set eyes and wide mouth, growing to look more like my mother every day. How proud she, Celia, would have been of these girls, with their passion for the whole world, their unflagging concern for every mouth unfed, every avenue of rescue unpursued. They must have got it straight from her, by a sort of osmosis in the womb, as if she'd implanted an incubator just for the likes of them in me, a nest destined to produce her heirs.

"The trouble with you, Mart"—my eldest tried to wrap up the argument; it was time for the Bledsoes to show— "the trouble with you is, you just parrot what you read. Don't you know that all that gene mapping stuff is just McDonald's financing bovine somatotropin McBurgers?"

"You thought it was a big deal, last year, when they were mapping *corn* genes—"

"Because it was. It is."

"Well?"

It made me happy to listen to them, thinking that soon, so very soon, I would be able to offer these daughters of mine a farm where they could have their daily debate surrounded by the very four-stomached, ruminating milk cows they so adored/abhorred. Nice rich pastureland filled with live slow-moving, cud-chewing, shade-loving specimens to study.

And it rushed over me to tell them about Drew. Girls, I'm running off with this dear gentleman farmer that I've known since before you two were born or even thought of, and we're going to live out there on the land, happy as Herefords at the State Fair. And you can come anytime and have Cow's Party in the bluebonnets. You, Martha, can stuff long stalks of bluestem into the gentle rubbery-lipped mouths of heavy-lidded Holstein, lay your dimples against their thick necks, and you, Ruth, can breed hybrid maize in rows behind the barn, where the soil has been turned and furrowed for a hundred and fifty years.

And if I'd already talked to Eben, I might have told

them then and there. I had a need to reassure myself that although I'd be leaving them on weekdays until they could drive, I'd still have them in my life. More, that I'd have something new and fine to offer them; someplace that they, in their easy independence, might grow to love and consider home.

I must have looked at them with the words near my lips, the wishing on my face, because both girls turned to me.

"What do you think, Momma?" Martha asked, trying to read my expression. Wanting to keep peace.

"I wanted to say—"

Ruth held her clumps of hair straight out to receive my message. "Attention," she said, with her tolerant elder-child smile, "a bulletin from the short people."

I caught my breath; my news would have to wait. It wasn't fair to their father to tell them first. "While you're having this cow fight," I said, lightly, my throat choking slightly, "don't forget you're eating soup that has half a cup of milk and a pat of butter per bowl. Not to mention a secret spoon of Parmesan cheese."

"Momma!" Ruth made a strangling sound, staring at her bowl of white liquid in horror, as if she might have recently contracted bovine spongiform encephalitis. "I thought this was potato soup?"

"It is. But if it didn't have anything else in it, it would be mashed potatoes." I laughed.

Ruth's debate over whether to push her bowl away and get up from the table or finish her meal was solved by the sound of the Bledsoes' car, honking out front.

I walked them to the curb, waving at the departing mother behind the wheel of the big new Olds.

The Bledsoe girls, in racing shorts and running shoes, with their amazingly long legs and high behinds, were taller even than my girls. The older, named Rosa by her mother but called Sugar at school, was five ten at least, and the younger, named Phillis but known as Baby, looked to be five nine. It was hard to tell for sure, because their shoes seemed to have lifts and they wore their hair, cropped close in back, in high wiry tiaras in front, adding at least three inches to their height.

The two pairs of siblings had met during their sixth-grade year when all the schoolchildren in the city were bused to separate and equally inconvenient schools. The older girls now played basketball together; the younger two, volleyball.

The Bledsoes' nicknames, Sugar and Baby, had been dreamed up by school paper sportswriters who needed a good tag. In the case of mine, their last name provided a wealth of leads concerning what one or the other had done to the opposing team in citywide games: devasTAITed, irriTAITed, decapiTAITed. (Or, when the writers were reaching, obliterTAITed, annihiTAITed, elimiTAITed.) I could see that in a couple of years when my daughters were playing on the same teams in high school, the headlines would herald their rat-a-TAIT-TAIT offense and their TAIT-à-TAIT defense.

In a couple of years, also, these four would all be taking Japanese, a new course that had come into the curriculum without a murmur, giving a new twist to the term *bilingual education*, which once had meant English as a second language for Spanish-speaking students, and now meant Japanese as a second language for English-speaking students. The earth turns; Waco had become part of the global village. The school district wanted our youth to be ready to deal with the Pacific Rim, which, in this case, meant the corridor of scientists settling along the interstate. Baylor University, that Baptist bastion which still offered a vigorous course of studies in the separation of church and state, had led the way and now taught—in addition to Japanese—Chinese, Thai and Indonesian to its fresh-faced, drug-free students.

In response to this same brave new world, the district was also putting into effect an accelerated prep school imbedded right in our existing high school. And although the Bledsoes did not live in Lake Shore but in Oak Hurst (on Oak Wood off Wood Oaks off Forest Oaks off Oak Forest), they went to school with my girls because Barbara, their mother, taught gym at the middle school. They were eligible for the program anyway, because selection was to be citywide. Modeled on the best preparatory schools in the East, it was going to give every student a shot; there was to be no test screening or teacher selecting. *Those who can take it can take it* was the slogan.

The school system was trying to promote it as the Academy, harking back to the time when Waco, because of all its early educational institutions, had been known as the Athens of Texas. But the kids had already coined another name for the would-be Academicians: nesters. An old term around here for those small homesteaders whose farms were tucked within the spread of larger landholders. Besides, Athens to most of the kids was just the name of an east Texas town. They were concentrating now on the glory that was Kyoto and the grandeur that was Jakarta.

But right here in the mild breezy tail end of Wind Day, the foursome was debating whether to go run or stop by the school and shoot baskets.

While they talked, bouncing up and down on the balls of their feet, Baby was slowly drumming on Sugar's back with her fists, doing a little jivey dance, as if making music.

Sugar whirled and glowered at her sister. "I wish you

would stop acting like a dark continent, dickhead—" The
tall athlete looked down at me and made a polite apology.
"Pardon, Mrs. Tait, that's peer group parlance for 'seventh-
grader.' "

I laughed with them. How transparent they all were
in their feuds. Each needing constant attention, approval,
from her one true peer, her sister. Maybe, I thought, that
was who we always cared the most about, the ones we
grew up with.

Maybe that was the cement between Drew and me: we
went all the way back to the good old dumb old days.

I SAT ON the side of the bed, in a
white cotton gown and an old white
terry-cloth robe. My thinking was that I
didn't want to be wearing only a nightgown when Eben
came in, as if everything was the same; on the other hand,
if we had bitter words, I didn't want to have to excuse
myself to go get undressed. I was nervous as a cat. There
were no guidelines for telling someone you shared a double
bed with that you were no longer going to be the wife you
were right that minute being.

It was curious, unlikely really, my having married
Eben. He'd come from a Calvinist background that
stretched back to Calvin himself, at least in thinking.
Grandfathers far before him, and then his illustrious old
missionary father, fifty when Eben was born, grappling

with the heart of the church doctrine, the kernel of its paradox: can there be free will if our actions are predetermined?

Eben had been the old son of an old father who'd spent his life disavowing the legacy of the Victorian world: its hysterical warnings against morbid desires, spermatorrhea, novel reading, lascivious thoughts. Eben's mother had died in childbirth with him, a fact that had been presented to him as foreordained. Surely, I'd often thought, this death was the seed of Eben's faith in a Calvinist God, a God to whom all things are known, all outcomes decided. Perhaps, I also suspected, it was the origin of Eben's inability to handle surprises, his insistence on knowing everything in advance of its occurring.

He'd gone into the church expecting to battle crises of faith; instead, he'd faced its banalization. When we moved to Waco to Grace Presbyterian, Eben had found himself, rather unwillingly, an authority in ecumenical circles on mixed marriages, concerning which he complained bitterly that the battle was never over the liturgy or the ceremony—matters for which the couple's forebears had gone to their deaths—but only over the wedding reception. The Baptists refusing to allow hug dancing or alcoholic beverages; the Presbyterians seeing strength in moderation. The bride crying: It won't kill him to have a dry reception. The groom sulking: She won't go to hell in a handbasket for dancing with her daddy in her wedding dress.

In his private pastoral counseling, he'd handled nondoctrinal matters of an even more disheartening sort. For instance, there were the three regulars who'd appeared in the past year. First was Boyd, a skinny high school math teacher, who'd come in because, he said, he was so lonely he'd bought a ring to marry himself, and oughtn't he to have some sort of ceremony before he consummated the relationship? Then there was Blanche, an elderly woman who'd lost first her husband and then most of her hair. (Eben had got so excited, thinking how marvelous, that the body would reenact the response of the grief-stricken widow tearing out her hair!) She'd come, she explained, because she'd had a stress reaction to her husband's death, and the doctor was giving her antidepressants and the hairdresser, protein packs, but she wanted to know if Eben thought it would look all right if she took to wearing hats to church again, the way they used to? Then, more recently, he'd been having weekly sessions with Jae-Moon, a Korean woman whose family had been converted by missionaries back home, who knew of his father and therefore felt she had the right to point out to Eben where in each of his recent sermons he'd been sexist, racist and classist.

I hadn't been a religious person when Eben and I met. We'd been introduced by the younger Mrs. Dr. Croft, a woman whose son and daughter I'd successfully tutored for the SAT, back when I made my living that way. She'd been on the lookout for someone nice for me, and he'd shown up, the assistant pastor at her church. What he and I had in common from the start was that we were both textualists of a sort. I spent my time wrestling with the exact meanings of words, just as he wrestled with the more ambiguous texts of the Testaments, Old and New. He'd seemed, at the start of our marriage anyway, to find it pleasing, gratifying, that I never tired of talking over with him the smallest passage, listening as he squeezed the last drop of meaning or promise or prophecy from it.

For instance, tonight, I knew, he was working on a sermon for tomorrow titled "The Garden in the Desert; the Desert in the Garden." He'd said, when he began it earlier in the week, that he was using the Gospel of Matthew. It being three weeks before Easter, I knew then that he would be doing Gethsemane and Peter's denial. That he would read, for the lesson, Jesus saying, "This night before the cock crows thou shalt deny me thrice," and Peter protesting, "Though I should die with thee, yet will I not deny thee." And I could hear already in my mind Eben's reasoned exploration of the question: If it was prophesied, could Peter have done otherwise? And, Did the fact that he could not have, lessen his responsibility for what he did?

In truth, it was my knowledge of the Scriptures that allowed me to keep my deepest secret from Eben: the real source of his daughters' names (St. Denis, Graham). Allowed me to present them with these promises for their future. I'd had no trouble with calling the first baby Ruth, Ruth's story in the Bible being one many times retold from pulpits, a lesson in unselfish love; her promise to her husband's mother, "Thy people shall be my people, and thy God my God," many times quoted. But I'd had to cite chapter and verse to get his agreement on calling the second child Martha. I used a parable in Luke in which one sister, Mary, sits at Jesus's feet while the other, Martha, complains that she has to do all the serving while Mary gets all the attention. To which Jesus responds with the lesson of grace and works that is at the heart of church doctrine. When I pointed out to Eben that had Martha not pushed the confrontation, the lesson would have been lost, he accepted my point, and agreed to that name for our second child.

I'd not been entirely happy, when we married, to quit my SAT tutoring; it had been satisfying, every student a success, every parent gratified. And the money was grand. But in those days, fifteen years ago, churches still expected a preacher-plus-wife for their salary. Now, at least, when so many divinity students were marrying each other, that was changing. It wasn't that congregations were any more

eager to have a spouse working out in the community—
risking the possible leakage of church confidences—but
rather that they'd become willing to pay the price of joint
preachers, husband and wife, two for the price of two. In
fact, a couple of Waco's big downtown churches, First
Methodist and First Presbyterian, now had joint married
pastors, a parity situation satisfactory to everyone.

No doubt I was thinking all that, here on the side of
the bed, in some effort to reassure myself that to Eben my
defection might seem only one more example of the general
dispiriting changes within the church. The preacher's wife
who packed and left.

'D BEEN QUITE awed to be asked
out by Eben Tait. *Awe:* wonder mixed
with fear, and I guess that's what I'd
been. He wasn't my image of what a preacher would be
like. I'd imagined that we'd, oh, see cultural things, or sit
and drink a lot of hot tea and talk about religion—my lack
of it, his obvious excess of it. That he'd ask at the door,
the way they did in old books, if he could kiss me good
night. Not at all the way it turned out.

We had our first evening together with the younger
Mrs. Dr. Croft and her sister-in-law, then the next night
we went out alone to a café, connected to a bakery, in an
old part of Austin, and had falling-off-the-bone chicken
and homemade bread. Eben asked me quite a lot of ques-

tions about myself, seeming to know all the answers in advance, which had seemed clairvoyant and flattering. Then he asked if I'd come back to his apartment for the evening, with an option to spend the night if we both agreed matters were headed in that direction. Was I—he hesitated—*prepared* to do that? Me, he was asking, the daughter of Celia Guest of Planned Parenthood. All I said was yes, yes I was, and that all right, yes, I'd like to do that.

I have no memory of the rest of the meal. Whether we had dessert or whether he'd ordered wine or even whether we split the bill as we always did later. I was in sort of a daze at his moving so fast. He was older by what seemed to me then at least a generation (being thirty-two to my twenty-four) and certain of everything. That was my first impression, that this man, dark, tall, serious, attentive already, had the confidence to come right out and ask me to stay the night with the church looking over his shoulder. Quite different, his style, from the awkward, taking-what-was-available men I'd been with. (Not that many, but some, anyone with long legs who liked to move, anyone who reminded me of Andy.)

Eben drove my car to his apartment—a small place over a garage in a nice fading neighborhood near the church, not far from downtown—so that he wouldn't have to give directions, he said. In fact, he drove my car whenever we were both in it until he got the church in Waco and a (Korean) car of his own. That should have been a warning: that he could never be a passenger. But I was not looking for signs at that time.

His apartment had floor-to-ceiling shelves of books, mostly theology, and a double bed, with an iron frame, that was covered with texts and typed papers, and so high off the floor it somehow gave the impression of a work space. There were two chairs by the upstairs window, easy chairs that belonged to the landlady, and we sat there and had, after all, our tea. Many cups of tea, while he told me about his father, about the tradition of missionaries in his family, about the strong connection with Korea, about the decline of faith in the church.

I bit the bullet and said, "I'm not really what you'd call a believer, Eben. I guess I'm more of a—heathen." I knew, although I didn't know if he did, what the word actually meant: someone on the heath, an outsider.

"Grace," he'd said, quick as a wink, as if he'd prepared for this, "is not at your disposal but God's. The whole point of Calvin's reformation was that he created a place in the church for the solid, pious, educated layman."

"Pious," I said. "Faithful to the duties naturally owed."

"Exactly. I am not interested in a wife who professes great faith and makes a show of her religiosity."

"We've only met," I said faintly.

"I'm not an expert at the trivial," he said. "If we are interested in pursuing this, if this should go further, shouldn't we clear the air from the start?"

"Tell me about the Presbyterian church," I said. And was given a copy of the Westminster Confession to take home, plucked from the stack of books and papers on the bed, as if placed there in advance for me.

When it was late, he simply cleared the bed, pulled back the spread, turned out the light and reached for my hand.

It was quite the most thrilling lovemaking I'd ever experienced. There, without our clothes, with no fumbling around, he kept himself aroused with one hand and stroked me with the other until he brought me to orgasm, slowly, kissing me the while, and then, mounting, quickly came himself. Early in the morning, when I stirred slightly, he indicated that he would like to repeat what he had done before, and did.

It was a year before we married; I had a lot of reservations about taking on the job of pastor's wife—which I saw before me in capital letters, Pastor's Wife, sort of like Goody Tait. I had read by then my histories of the church in America. Knew that Jonathan Edwards had been turned out of his pastorate at forty-seven with ten living children because he changed his view regarding admission of the unconverted to take the sacrament. That Henry Dunster, the first president of Harvard, had been removed from his post for deciding that infant baptism was wrong. That Anne Hutchinson had been driven from the church, delivered unto Satan, and accounted to be a liar for accusing her clergy of preaching salvation through works not faith. Was it any wonder I was fearful of incurring the enmity of my newfound church "family"?

Eben soothed me when I talked of it, saying that it was one's duty only to act as if one was a member of the elect; that one could do no more. That in time the roots I was sinking into the Scriptures and the Confession would bear far sweeter blooms for the rocky soil they grew from.

At first I wondered why he had chosen me. What did he want? Surely there were meeker girls, filled with sanctity and probity, who were eager for the job. Later, I grew more secure that he had not wanted someone to receive his sermons by rote and cant; that he had wanted a careful reader. And this I had been for him from the start. Faithful to him always in this way if in no other.

A T LEAST TONIGHT I would not have to deal with his wanting to make love. He approached me only on Sundays after his sermon and on Wednesdays after his evening of Bible study. This was a routine he had had since the first, except for the brief years of Play School when our Thursdays were free.

I'd thought then, in Baby Days, that things might change between us with the sudden gift of a day alone. Anyone who has had small children knows that immense erotic feel of an empty house with no one in it. No one asking for anything, or interrupting, or needing you. Lord, my whole body felt a rush of desire up my legs at just the space and vacancy of the empty parsonage. I'd thought that Eben would feel this, too, would rejoice that we didn't have to have our intimate moments soundlessly behind the closed doors of our bedroom, or whisper together as far from the babies as possible, letting our oatmeal get cold while we talked over the schedule of the coming week.

But it was as if Eben retreated more because there was no one about. He'd agreed to free his schedule on Thursdays, to spend the mornings through lunch at home, perhaps a part of the afternoons. But the first day my Tonka-truck girls were safely off in the firm hands of the Swedish contingent at Mary Virginia's, he'd gone straight to the private room with his sermon notes and closed the door, staying in until lunchtime. After that, when I suggested a nap, he'd agreed, not meeting my eyes, and we did that, just that, lay on top of the spread and slept an hour with the blinds down. It was restorative, he said, a good idea. Turn it off for a while.

I tried what I knew to do, my body thrilled with being slim again, unpregnant, very needy for attention, having spent the better part of three years being myself primarily a nourisher. The next week, Thursday, when Eben was in the bedroom, dressing after the children were gone, pulling up his braces, getting that disappearing look on his face, I threw my arms around him from the back, pressed my face against his shoulder, and touched him through his trousers, feeling him stiffen. He turned on me, red-faced and angry. "It cheapens you and therefore us, Cile, for you to make such an—out-of-character gesture."

The next week, I tried once more. When we were lying down for our nap, shades drawn, a wind whipping them against the screens, the whir of a lawn mower down the street, I rolled over and put my tongue in his ear, something I recalled from my single days as the gentlest, clearest kind of invitation. Perhaps it seemed too practiced to him. He sat up, again almost blinded by his anger, or maybe panic at having a response he had not himself orchestrated. "This is not some film, Cile, that you can parody. We have our way of doing things which is grounded in who we are."

It was clear to me then, just freshly freed from birthing and nursing, that my body, wild to be fed, was going to go hungry here. I saw that I was not going to be allowed to arouse him ever, to touch him ever in order to begin things, ever to straddle him, ever to move beneath him for my own pleasure, ever to bring him to orgasm in my own ways.

I let a week go by, and then I asked him to talk to me, sitting with my hands between my knees, anxious, on the footstool in the bedroom while he pulled on his socks.

"What is it, Cile?" he asked, his full attention to fitting the black hose firmly over his toe and heel. He looked up, to show that he was not avoiding listening to me, that he was available to me.

"We have been given a gift of this free day once a week. I'd like it if you could see your way clear to changing our schedule because of this. Giving us a chance to do on Thursdays what we have always had to crowd into your busy Wednesdays."

He paused, put on his other sock, fitted it carefully to his foot. Put on his shoes. Reached in his pants' pocket for the tiny calendar he carried with him always. "Your point is well taken. Perhaps we could go over the order of the service, the texts that I am considering, our schedule, on a day that was less structured, after the Bible study evening is behind me."

Feeling as if I were walking on eggs, I held my breath, and sure enough, he thought it through in his head, in his own way and his own good time. He worked in the study in the morning, then took off early for talk over lunch, going over the schedule, discussing with me—what we always did best—which verses of Scripture might most ably make the point for the week. What sort of overarching structure should be imposed on the five Sundays after Easter before the start of Trinity. What sort of pentateuch he should make of them. I knew that *pentateuch* meant vessel and that he must know I knew that, know that I heard him say not only what quintet of scriptures must he construct but also what vessel for his message must they be. We smiled over our plates, he with his cup of tea, drained, me with my coffee. We were at our best with texts.

Perhaps, he said, he would do all the New Testament readings from John, his favorite Gospel. Starting with John 10:1–10, then John 12, John 14, John 20, John 21. What did I think? I knew that the first verses said that he that entered by any other way but the door was a thief but that he who entered by the door was the shepherd. It was Jesus's saying: "I am the shepherd." And the other scriptures were explaining who Jesus was also, and the last was a command to feed his sheep. I considered all that while Eben waited, and then I said, "So that you explore what the risen Christ knew himself to be and how he explained himself to his disciples. Not prophecy any longer, but the task at hand."

"Yes," he said, digesting my summary, looking it over in his mind, seeing if that was right. "Yes, that will be something I can work within and around."

Then, after we'd washed up our bowls, we went back to take a nap, and, the shades down, sun raining a deep yellow stripe on the boards of the floor, Eben made love to me on a Thursday afternoon, out of his trousers, in the daytime, in the harbor of an empty house.

WHEN EBEN CAME home, we sat together in the bedroom alcove between the bathroom and the closet. It was a comfortable space we used in the evenings because it was as far as possible from the common wall with the girls' bedroom. I sat on the footstool, pulled so I could lean against the wall. My hands were tucked, palms together, between my knees. A sign of nervousness.

He was in the armchair in his undershirt, his braces dangling, his trousers rolled, massaging his feet with his black socks still on. From time to time, in an unconscious gesture, he reached a hand down for his cup of tea, remembered it was empty, set it back.

He had a full day on Saturday, visiting the housebound, making hospital and rest home calls (the Presbyterian population was aging as well as shrinking), and preparing his sermon. I let him collect himself, turn his attention to the fact that he was home.

I hadn't done much to this room, with its polished floors and white plaster walls, but there was a basket of dried grass on the wicker chest at the foot of the bed, a row of blue willow pitchers (my mother's) under the windowsill, and an old will and testament box (his father's) we used as an end table by the chair.

"Where did you eat supper?" I asked him.

"At the hospital cafeteria. We've two in there"—he gave their names—"on respirators. Another in ICU with a bypass. It's been a hard spring. It's as though they can make it through the ice storms and winds of winter, and then as soon as the weather turns warm and the days grow longer, they have trouble. The perennial situation."

"Yes," I said. Spring and bad times had an echo for us both. For him, because he'd lost his old father to a stroke at eighty-four the March after we married. For me, because I'd lost my young mother, just turned forty, to a flash flood the May of my high school graduation.

"Then I had the mixed wedding. This time the groom was a Baptist, hard-shell. The bride said if they couldn't have champagne she wanted Dr. Pepper, be up front about it. His family did not take kindly to that; they wanted spiced tea and petits fours. Such are the theological hurdles of our day." In reflex, he lifted his empty cup, discouraged.

"The Bledsoes came by to see the girls after supper," I said.

"Do you think the elder one—"

"Sugar."

"Do they go by those names all the time now? Do you think, I was asking, that she will attempt the Academy?"

"I'm sure she won't have any trouble. She's very verbal." I remembered but did not repeat Sugar's definition of 'seventh-grader.'

"Ours should bring their friends to church sometime."

"The Bledsoes are Baptists."

"I meant as visitors, not to proselyte." He kneaded the ball of his right foot in a rolling motion.

"How did the Garden go?"

"Well. As you know, passages I have read a hundred times can come alive. When He is in Gethsemane, it says, 'He began to be sorrowful and very heavy.' How many times I've skipped over those words. Yet how telling they are: He sees the prophecy before Him. And in the here and now He already experiences it physically."

"So you made changes?"

"You will be interested in what I've done with it."

"I always am."

Finally, looking at me, he indicated my hands pressed between my knees. "What's on your mind?"

I exhaled and inhaled. "Eben, I am moving out." I paused to be sure he heard, watching his face. "The girls may stay here with you weekdays, in order to walk or bike to school. To their schools," I added, realizing that next year Ruth would be in Waco High.

"Well." He leaned forward, working on the instep of his left foot. "I see. Well." He wore his sagacious face, the one he put on when something had gone wrong—the hot-water heater blew up, wind damage to the church—and he was acting as if it was part of a plan whose outlines he'd seen all along, a detour whose signposts he'd been following, not a pothole he'd hit flat bottom before he knew it. He lifted his teacup, set it down. "Is it one of your secrets, Cile, or may I know why you and Drew have picked this particular weekend of this particular year to come out in the open?"

My hands knotted into fists. I could feel my anger rise like a flood on the Brazos at his acting as if Drew and I were old news to him. "He told Mary Virginia today," I said.

Eben placed both feet flat on the floor, unrolled his trousers. "I assumed that. I was conjecturing why now. Most probably because the price of the land the government is considering annexing has gone up from five hundred to seven thousand an acre."

I twisted my fingers, not wanting to say anything I'd regret.

Eben returned my silence.

"Trey is going off to prep school in the fall." I didn't know if he'd make any sense of that, but he was playing know-it-all, so he could try. There was some truth to it. Drew and I had promised ourselves we'd wait until our older two got drivers' licenses, which you could do in Waco at fifteen, with a "hardship" waiver, claiming that some parent needed you to drive. That was so they could come to see us or come to town without an adult having to fetch and carry. But when Trey decided to go East next year, with Jock likely to follow the next, there didn't seem to be any point in waiting anymore.

"He's not opting for the Academy here at home, I see."
Eben slipped on his shoes.

"No." I retied the belt of my frayed terry-cloth robe.
We were both dressing, unwittingly, as if now we must
take cover from one another.

Eben slipped his braces over his shoulders. After a moment he stood and stretched out a hand to me. "Come into
the kitchen. We'll have a bowl of oatmeal."

I followed him down the hall, past the girls' closed
door, wearing the white socks I used for slippers.

In the kitchen he put on water, got out bowls, moving
around while I sat on a stool at the counter.

Pouring boiling water on instant oats, he asked,
"What's the timetable?"

I aimed for a matter-of-fact tone. "I'd thought after
Easter, for telling the girls. For telling everyone. June for
moving out."

He stirred in wheat germ and skim milk and handed
me a spoon. "If you're set on doing this, let's see it done in
such a way that my congregation at least does not feel
deceived." He showed a thin edge of resentment, his lips
tight, and I knew he was thinking of Lila Beth.

"Of course, Eben. Lord, handle it however you want."

He stopped eating. Put down his spoon. "Just this once,
Cile, just this one particular time, do not take His name in
vain."

"Sorry." I almost said, Lord, I'm sorry. Old habit, a
wringing of the hands, lordy, lordy, not intended as blas-
phemy. But he knew that; and I knew how it annoyed
him. It was one—one more—sore spot with a well-worn
callus.

"Easter, you say?" He fished his tiny weekly calendar
from the pocket of his trousers. "I'm going to use Luke this
year." He glanced at me, knowing I loved that text best:

"O fools, and slow of heart to believe all that the prophets have spoken." Last year he'd used instead the verse from John: "Cast thy nets on the right side of the ship and ye shall find." But he was at his best with prophecies: the heart of predestination after all.

"That's good," I said.

Easter in Eben's church was always a fine service, with Christ rising again, lilies banking the pulpit, children carrying their six-foot cross of flowers down the aisle (the smallest ones loudly whispering claims to that daisy, this pansy, that rose, the bloom they'd brought from home and poked through the rolled chicken wire with their own fingers), the triumphal music rising in hallelujah.

"I plan to ask Jae-Moon to help with the service, not only in order for the congregation to see how varied their number is, but also so that she can monitor in advance the pitfalls I apparently continue to create." He lifted his thin black hair with his fingers, as if to make it stand up, be bountiful.

I smiled, feeling an enormous relief at being back on familiar ground, going over the service.

"There is a Korean church in town now," he continued. "I don't know if you are aware of it. A mix of denominations, primarily Presbyterian, of course, some Baptist, some Methodist, with a bilingual service. I thought we'd have them as our special guests this year."

"That's good." The church here always had outsiders at Easter, a way of extending the message beyond the "family." One year they'd had the entire congregation from an all-black church in east Texas. Last year, they'd invited a group of handicapped adults from the Riverbend Living Center. Brightly dressed middle-aged men and women excited and giggling like five-year-olds, putting their quarters in the collection plate, some able to follow the hymns. A

few of them had got up and moved with the children and
their flowered cross to the front, beaming and patting each
other while it was presented.

Eben studied his notes. "Next week is daylight
saving."

After a minute, I nodded. He'd said it as if daylight
saving were some lesser Lenten occasion, but then I knew
what he meant: the crowd would be small. People who
made the effort to set their clocks; people who didn't mind
getting up at what would seem an earlier hour.

"Then the next week is Palm Sunday." He closed his
calendar and tucked it back in his pocket. He rinsed our
cereal bowls and set them in the drainer.

I let out my breath. It was going to be all right. He
would shower and we could sleep without awkwardness,
from long habit. Then it would be another day. It would
be Sunday and the schedule would take over. The hard
part, getting it out in the open, was done.

He turned out the kitchen light. In the dark he said,
"You like Palm Sunday, don't you?" His tone was gentle.

"I do," I admitted, grateful. "I like the fickle mob
shouting hosannas and waving palms."

MY OLD FEAR of being pillo-
ried by the congregation swept
over me in the Fellowship Hall,
where we gathered after Eben's sermon for the covered-
dish lunch. This was a fine big room at the back of the
church, with tables along one wall, and smaller school-
sized tables and chairs scattered about, a piano for when
the Sunday School classes met here to sing or put on pag-
eants together. A nice sunny room which looked out into
the primary play yard with its two large willow trees.

For a moment, as the crowd closed around me, I was
back in Eben's first church in Austin, being embraced by
Mrs. Dr. Croft and her mother-in-law and her friends, in
awe of their powers to see into my uncertain soul. Now,
fifteen years later, I still had not been brought over, turned
around, converted as the church said. To which I had
added yet another transgression: adultery. (Which, in an
earlier day, would surely have been a lesser sin compared
to lack of faith.)

The congregation here, much the same as that earlier
one, were mostly in their late sixties and seventies, all old-
line Presbyterians descended from old-line Presbyterians
back three hundred years, all trim, neat, nicely bred, and
sober. Light on their feet, with youthful voices, they looked
like students (as they once were) hosteling abroad, ruck-
sacks on their backs, seeking their fortunes and those of the

world. Students dedicated to the YM-YWCA, the Experiment in International Living, the American Friends Service Committee.

Eben was robust in their midst, the sort of pastor that such thin-chested, narrow-nosed parishioners elect to serve them. Clergy, men and now women, too, with the general look of athletes who have heard the call on the road to their own Damascus. Clergy like the young Scot running for God in *Chariots of Fire.* Surrounding Eben, the congregation resembled schoolchildren who had not yet got their growth, eleven-year-olds longing to cross the finish line to adolescence. The church, I thought, had not been so much a family as I had hoped; rather, it functioned more like a scout troop—a leader surrounded by eager tenderfeet. And I was not quite either.

As always, everyone was in good spirits at the sight of the long plank tables heaped with food: rice and beans, rice fritters, rice cakes, stir-fried rice, rice molds, my potato bake, fried chicken, sliced turkey, hams baked with pineapple and cloves, yams, Jell-O salads heavy with Bing cherries, sweet carrot cakes, peach pies, peach turnovers, peach cobblers crusted with cinnamon sugar.

The talk buzzed around the newly arrived hymnals which we had used for the first time that morning. Adopted by the national church, they came to us a blue-bound multilingual surprise. Languages by the dozen were represented. The waltz "Amazing Grace" appeared not only in English but also in Kiowa, Creek, Choctaw, Cherokee and Navaho. Here—firm arms held out hardback royal blue copies to friends—was "Holy Night, Blessed Night" as "Sheng Ye Qing, Sheng Ye Jing" in Chinese; "Silent Night" as "Stille Nacht" in German; "Christo Vive," an Argentinean version of "Christ Is Risen"; "De Tierra Lejana Venimos," a Puerto Rican version of "From a Distant Home."

Transliterated Korean songs such as "Whak Shil Hahn Nah Eh Kahn Jeung" (an old favorite, this one, "Blessed Assurance, Jesus Is Mine"); the African "Kum ba Yah"; the Israeli "Shalom, Chaverim"; the Filipino "Awit Sa Dapit Hapon"; the Hispanic "A La Ru"; the Japanese "Hitsuji Wa" and many many more.

Gray heads with tanned clear faces nodded in astonishment, read aloud phonetically—here a verse in Dakota dialect, there a Latin American folk hymn. All sharing the beaming faces of lifelong believers raised on the old hymn that promised: "Red yellow brown black or white, we are precious in His sight. Jesus loves the little children of the world."

But what transfixed, amazed them most, one and all alike, was seeing that in the front of the hymnal even the Order of Worship appeared in three languages. So that, for example, we could all say together the Lord's Prayer in English, "Our Father who art in heaven," or Spanish, "Padre nuestro, que estás en los cielos," or in Korean, "Ha neul eh geh shin oo ree ah buh jee," as the Spirit moved us.

"Well, my dear, what do you think?" Lila Beth stood at my elbow, in soft gray, looking, with her deep weathered cheeks, as she always did, not only like a gardener, which she was, but like a rancher. The sight of her, Drew's mother, made me start, happy but uneasy. I was grateful to have her near and pressed my face to hers. Don't you, I longed to say, don't you turn on me. They may all hurl stones when they learn the news, but not you. To you my heart is vulnerable.

"About the hymnal?"

"Yes," she said. "Not the food, which is too sweet for my taste, as always."

"It gives a new meaning to 'speaking in tongues,'

doesn't it?" I smiled at her. I'd noticed that all of Willie Nelson's gospel songs that I played at home were gone from the new songbook: "Will the Circle Be Unbroken," "When the Roll Is Called Up Yonder." But on the whole it was cheering to see this congregation of Calvinists trying to pronounce their faith in the strange utterances of other voices.

"It's often the case, isn't it," she answered, "that the language precedes and in some sense creates the situation. I'm thinking of the courts, certainly, but here, too. You'll see, even here in time it will be one world."

Eben, talking with a group of other elders, beckoned to her then, and she touched my arm and left. His face revealed nothing of our last night's talk, but a slight chill swept over me. These were his people, the sheep of his flock, and under his eyes I felt myself shut out of communion with them already.

T HAT SUNDAY AFTERNOON, late, Drew called, bold as could be. "Hi, honey," he said.

I waved to the girls, who were going out the door with the Bledsoes, and sat at the desk in the private room. "Lord, it's good to hear you. How'd you know he wasn't here?"

"Drove by. Saw his car at the church; saw that beautiful Pontiac in the drive."

"I wish you'd stopped."

"Same here."

"How're you doing?"

"Come up to the farm tomorrow? I'll tell the office here I'm up there talking to the federals. I figure we don't have to be so careful now. Everybody's going to know before long anyhow."

"Sure. Sure I can. I'd like to be there now. I miss you like crazy."

"Did you tell him?"

"Last night, when he came in."

"And—?"

"I was scared to death. But it was okay. He agreed to wait until Easter to tell the girls and the congregation."

"How about letting your folks know?" he teased.

"Please, Daddy and my former teacher can hear it on the grapevine."

Drew laughed. He liked to get a rise out of me about my father and his wife, who now lived here in town, whenever he could. It took his mind off his mother.

"You know what I found up there yesterday?" he asked.

"A '57 Chevy, in mint condition. Green and cream."

"Close. Very close. I was rooting around in the old shed, after I saw you, thinking about us being up there all the time, and I found us a couple of totally vintage bikes. I mean they were just sitting there, on racks even, behind a mower and some shovels. One's a Schwinn Phantom, that must sell for around two-gee-plus fixed up, and the other's an old Western Flyer, fifties model, that you can't get anywhere anymore, period, except from collectors. When you're up here, when we're living here, we can bike around on these old roads. I did a little WD-40 on the chains—but I didn't have time to try them out. Maybe we'll get married on them." He sounded happy.

"Can you believe we've done it?"

"When I was up there I could. Back here, it's like nothing has changed, zip. I guess that's why I called. Make sure I hadn't dreamed the whole thing."

"But you told her. You told her yesterday."

He made some kind of noise in his throat. "I did. Right. I told you. I told her first thing in the morning, broad daylight, in the breakfast room, while the boys were at their tennis lesson. Told her straight out, said I wouldn't tell them until she said. But then last night, I don't know, honey, it was like it had never happened. She was going on, on the phone, to my mother about my birthday, what they were going to do for the big Four-Oh in May, you know, like I hadn't said a word. I don't know if that's just her way of getting used to the idea, or what. I've only known Mary Virginia since Adam put his long johns on and I still don't have a clue how her mind works. Anyway, so I kind of coughed and she waved and went on talking.

"Then, when she got off the phone, she was talking about Easter and then my birthday some more—she's got a calendar of events that rolls in the back of her head like a Rolodex twenty-four hours a day. And then she said maybe they'd have my party up at the farm, *ranch* she calls it, so her sister and mom could meet us halfway, just like that. Like I hadn't said I was moving up there. Then she was on when the boys were going to camp. By the time we went to bed, she was up to Christmas holidays."

"She's trying to see if you mean it, maybe."

"But the big preacher just said, 'Fine'?"

"He pretended it was old news, you know how Eben is. Ho-hum. To tell the truth, I think he's more worried about what your mother is going to do than anything else."

"I can relate to that."

"If she doesn't leave the church, he probably won't care I'm gone."

"Well, I didn't really think they'd congratulate us and

throw rice, I guess. Ask us if we'd set the date yet." He made a sort of growling noise.

I heard a car door slam. "I need to go."

"Come up right after you get the kids off."

"I'll be there."

"I love you."

"I get the Western Flyer," I told him.

THE CAR RADIO said hail the size of golf balls was falling in Dallas County, the storm heading south toward Waxahachie, due down our way by midday. I encouraged the accelerator.

It had hailed Ping-Pong balls the first March Drew and I met at the farm. In bed, hearing the pounding ice hit the roof, we'd been wild, frantic that my old vehicle would return home with unexplained dents on hood and fenders. Holding layers of newspaper over our heads, hastily back in jeans and tennis shoes, we'd run out to move Drew's pickup from the shed and pull my Pontiac in its place under cover. Drenched, back inside, we'd clung together under a pile of faded quilts, listening to the globes of ice strike the sloping sheets of tin above our heads.

Our first April there'd been a tornado watch, and I'd driven through that flat yellow light that goes with twisters, air as still as the inside of a closet, watching to the west for the sighted black funnel. Imagining my car picked up and thrown through the side of a cake-shaped milo silo, much as straws are pushed through trees. My family left to wonder what I'd been doing out on the interstate with warning sirens shrill in the air.

I'd had a flat on the way home, as if nature had refused to let me off without some sort of retribution. While the motionless air began to turn almost gold and a faint whining rolled across the prairies like a giant airborne tumbleweed, I struggled with the nearly rusted-on lug nuts, standing on the lug wrench and jumping up and down, hoping my physics was sound and that one hundred and three pounds in motion could loosen what my extended arms could not. The spare hadn't been much better than the flat, which had picked up a nail, but it had got me into town and to a service station.

Drew, when I told him about it, was mad at himself because in his affection for my car he'd been so busy imagining it reminted to its original flashy glory that he hadn't paid enough attention to its present state of decline. Over my protest, he set about to get me four new tires. I said he couldn't buy stuff for me: it was like accepting silk stockings from a traveling salesman. He said that I was taking all the risks coming up to the farm; that if I could take the risks, he could at least minimize them. He'd got the tires one at a time, slightly used, then knocked them around, rolled them along the gravel and dirt roads at the farm, to give them an old look. A distressed finish, he said, the way furniture dealers worked over dining tables and washstands to pass them off as antiques.

I hated most to drive up the highway when there was a hurricane watch; it had a creepy echo of my mother's heading south into a sudden flash flood. Although these cyclones were usually confined to the coast, once in a while one would streak up the fault, like electricity along a wire, wind blowing to sixty miles an hour, uprooting trees, plastering trailers against tractors, lifting roofs from farmhouses, floating stores down rising rivers. But I had done that, too, in our three years of meeting at the farm.

Today, the storm was holding to the north, the line of clouds piling higher and higher above the horizon, occasional streaks of gray straying to the ground. From time to time I could hear a clap of thunder, but mostly there was only sheet lightning to the west. Dairy cows crowded in black and white clumps under the oaks, waiting for it to pass. Their picnic lunch—bluebonnets, paintbrushes, buttercups, daisies in a field of grass and clover—left until later.

Drew loved to talk about how animals, insects, birds, even plants, knew what was in the air. If the first thing he was going to do when we were up here was fix up my Firebird, the first thing I was going to do was repair the white slatted box on stilts that had been his grandfather's weather station.

His granddad had been an official volunteer weather observer for McLennan County all his adult life, a job he'd inherited from his dad. Twice each day, in his big script, he had recorded the high and low temperature and the amount of precipitation—droughts and heat waves calculated in their smallest increments.

Drew still had the notebooks of these grandfathers, with data going back to 1870, one hundred years of records without a day missed. But when his granddad died in '70, two years after Drew's family moved back to Waco, no one assumed the task. Drew's dad had a new medical practice to set up; besides, he claimed, the National Weather Service had taken over the function of the old-time weather stations. Drew had thought he might start it up again after he graduated from Baylor, but he never did. Then, when his dad died in the awful ice storm of '78, the worst in recorded history, Drew lost his interest in meteorology. A case of kill the messenger, he said. Instead, he'd thrown all his energies into the business of managing the family land—vast holdings that ran north to the government's current claims, west to the grain sorghum fields and the tall grasses, east to stock pastures and the bobbing metal grasshoppers pumping residual oil.

I wanted Drew to clean up the white slatted box, which resembled a beekeeper's hive, install a new thermometer and rain gauge, and resume the old record keeping. Maybe he would, when we were living at his granddaddy's farm, east of West.

THE FIRST TIME we got together, in high school, it was through *my* mother, not Drew's.

She, Celia, was the woman at the Planned Parenthood Clinic whom the patients called the nurse, the board called the director, and she called a glutton for punishment. The first years on the job, the clinicians (doctors who took turns at the clinic, pro bono work) drove her crazy, being, in her words, "country clubbers with tunnel vision." She'd be dealing with the usual crises: an unmarried twenty-eight-year-old with fourteen living children and no man to fill out the common-law husband blank; a married woman who'd hemorrhaged during her last childbirth but whose

husband refused to sign a permit for her to get a diaphragm because she might "lose her nature." The doctors
would turn a deaf ear. The rules were the rules: no advice,
counsel, or contraception to unmarried women; no pre-
scriptions without the husband's written consent.

Then Andy's (Drew's) dad took over as head clinician,
and turned everything around. Mother said he hadn't much
of a bedside manner, that he was quiet the way a rancher
is quiet, but that he dug his heels in and brought them into
the second half of the twentieth century. He told her there
were enough ill-treated kids in the world already: heart-
break cases you couldn't drink your morning coffee if you
let yourself think about. He said he'd delivered his share
of unwanted kids and that he wasn't interested in provid-
ing the world with any more. With his arrival, they made
immediate progress: the pill was permitted; men did not
have to give permission for women to obtain birth control;
and my mother, Celia, was given time off to travel around
the state to set up other clinics, like a circuit-riding
preacher, she used to say.

Andy (Drew) and I had had classes together, Texas History, Physics, Trig. I knew him as a skinny long-legged guy
who always wore boots; a smart kid who was always trying
to look like a kicker and not quite succeeding. But he was
the only other person who knew what my mother did,
sticking her nose into the sexual business of half of east
Austin (because in those days they were working only with
some nebulous group called the Poor). I figured he must
feel the same way, only more so. Who would want an OB
for a dad? Who would want even to think about what your
dad did all day, where he put his hands and what he got
out of it? So we stood around and talked, because he knew
what my mom did, and I knew what his dad did. It wasn't
that we talked about it; we didn't. Any more, say, than
two black kids in those days stood around talking about

the fact of being black. They'd just be looking around, making sounds at one another, being a unit. That's what Andy and I did. I can't remember anything we said.

Then one Friday, in March of our senior year, at the start of the spring, he asked me, "You want to go hear some country?" He named a nothing band I'd never heard. Friday nights at my house no one was ever home; I assumed the same was true at his. My mother was driving south and west, getting a start on the weekend clinics; my father was already up at Lake Travis, getting a start on a weekend of bait fishing.

I said, "Sure." I asked him, "Can I go like a normal person or do I have to wear those shirts with pearl snaps and Tony Lama specials?"

"Just jeans," he said. "I'll pick you up. You want to get a hamburger first?"

We drove up to Round Rock, which was then a smaller town, not the huge bulge on the north end of Austin it is today. Round Rock: out of town but near at hand. There were a couple of country music dives, square windowless buildings with big wooden tables and chairs along one side, a beer bar at one end, bandstand at the other, the rest a vast waxed dance floor. These were not Austin's famed country music night spots, where Waylon and Willie, Delbert and the rest played with a packed house swaying and screaming. These were where pickup bands were glad to have a place to make music; where the smell of beer and sawdust spread to slick the floor got all mingled together. We weren't yet eighteen, not quite, my birthday in a week, Drew's in two months, so we each got one beer. Most of which sat that first night on the table in big draft mugs growing warm and flat. We had to show we could order them, underage; we didn't sit still long enough to drink them.

(I remember that the band played the best country gold

sounds—"Slide Off Your Satin Sheets," "You Picked a Fine
Time to Leave Me, Lucille"—but these must have been
later, songs I heard on the radio when I had the babies,
when I was single dancing around the parsonage while they
napped.)

We'd got our token beers, set them down, put our wal-
lets in our back pockets, and gone out on the floor. He was
a mile taller, but that didn't matter a bit. He held out his
arms, not even really looking at me; the light was dim, the
noise of people laughing, pouring out their first pitchers,
drowned out any words. He hooked two fingers of his right
hand in my waistband, then held my right arm way out
with his left arm, up for me, down for him, almost rigid
so we could steer, and then we looped our way around the
dance floor until the band took its first break. They ended
each set with a waltz—if not "Lucille" then one as fine—
and we collapsed panting in our straight chairs.

"How'd you know I liked to dance?" I asked him, when
I had my breath back. My face was beet red, as his was,
from the exertion, the way it gets when you get a stitch in
your side and a rattle in your throat.

Andy had leaned closer so I could hear him. He was
trying to drink a gulp of his warm beer. "You never sit still
in class."

"What do you mean?"

"You're all the time getting up and down or turning
around or sticking your feet out."

"What class?"

"You always do that."

"But I like school. I'm going to be a teacher."

"The teacher gets to move all the time. Haven't you
noticed? Going out in the hall, going to the back of the
room. Did you ever see a teacher sit still for fifty minutes?"

"Miss Moore." Theodora Moore, our English teacher,

was my role model for everything I meant not to be. Stout,
brisk and, worst of all, convinced she had a "young person's" sense of humor.

"She digs that pencil in her ear," he said. "That's
moving."

The band filed back in.

"I didn't know you'd be any good." He held out his
hand.

I hooked two fingers in his belt and thrust my right
arm up in the air. "You didn't know you'd be this good,
did you?"

He twirled me around a couple of times so we could
warm up with the musicians. "Naw," he said, "I didn't
even know I could dance."

Afterward we leaned against his pickup—the same '58
rebuilt Chevy he had now—him with his feet spread way
out so he wouldn't be too tall, me leaning into the space,
leaning up to kiss him whenever he quit talking about the
truck. That's all we did; but then that's all we ever did. A
lot of kissing afterward. Sometimes, later that spring, we'd
have a beer in the cab, talking about nothing while he
warmed up the motor and we cooled down. I don't know
why we didn't do more, why we didn't have sex. Wasn't
everyone else then, in those days? Twenty-two years ago,
wasn't sex all over the air, everybody free and consenting?
Or was that just a glazed memory of the times, a yellow
hazy backdrop of the way we thought it was going to be?
Nobody saying no, least of all females who had nothing to
worry about anymore, not guilt or reputation or accidental
pregnancies.

That was why, of course. We couldn't bear to get ourselves in the position where one of us would have to ask
what we were doing about staying safe. One of us was
going to have to mention that which we spent most of our

time not wanting to deal with. I believe we'd have lasted one minute once we'd started in on the relative merits of rubbers, diaphragm, pill. Because I'd have imagined my mother, the missionary, looking over my shoulder, and he would have seen his father, the deliverer—and then we'd have stopped cold on the spot, been dating someone else within the week. What we had on the dance floor was more than anything we'd ever had before. That was enough.

That first night, after we'd put the band to bed and were out there in the dirt parking lot, and he'd got his tongue out of my mouth and quit sliding his hands around on the back of my T-shirt, and was just rocking back and forth, his arms all the way around me, nice and easy, he asked, "You got somebody?"

"Couple of guys on the honor roll."

He tightened his hold. "This going to be all right with your folks?"

"Us waxing the side of the pickup with your jeans?"

"Yeah."

"Sure. My dad still thinks I'm going to birthday parties at the roller rink; my mother thinks I spend all my spare time making out."

"At my house it's sort of like that in reverse." He seemed to go away.

"This going to be all right with yours?"

"I guess. My mom has a lot of plans for me; she doesn't much like to go along with mine."

I should have figured out later that he'd moved to Waco; I remembered his saying his mom had picked out Baylor for him. But by the time I got around to looking for him—after Mother had died and the schoolteacher was spending all her waking hours at our house, talking fishing tackle with my father—Andy was gone.

I asked around, later. By then I was tutoring kids for their SATs, guaranteeing a one-hundred-point rise in scores, and not one kid let me down. Mostly I dealt with doctors' young who had done all the right things—run track and dissected frogs, played the cello and got Westinghouse Awards, been the class favorites and debated Vietnam—but who couldn't manage to get their scores above 1100. Doctors' young who with my help entered Stanford, Duke, Rice, and who made my name a good word in certain households. Lord, how I'd loved that no-failure job.

"You wouldn't happen to know where a doctor named Williams moved, would you?" I'd asked the younger Mrs. Dr. Croft, who was friendly, one of the nicer mothers, and who had taken me under her wing.

"What kind of physician?"

"Obstetrician."

"OB? Dear, no." She didn't even think it over. How, her voice implied in a very nice way, did I think someone married to a thoracic surgeon would have any idea about the whereabouts of a baby doctor?

"It's been three or four years."

"Do you know his wife's name?"

"I knew their son," I told her. "We went out in high school."

She took off her glasses and looked at me kindly. "You're better off without the ones you knew in those days, Cile. Let me tell you. The near misses I had must have turned my mother's hair white."

"He was the one for me."

DREW WAS STANDING under the pecan tree when I pulled off the farm-to-market road, watching me race the storm. We got my car into the shed just as the sky darkened and began to hail icy pellets the size of mothballs.

"When we live here—" Drew said, wrapping an arm around me as we fled toward the snug weatherbeaten house.

"You'll still put the Firebird under cover; by then you'll have it gilded like a baby shoe."

"We'll have a real garage. I'll have got my '57 Chevy Bel Air, bored-out, fuel-injected, two-eighty-three cubic inch V-8."

"We can put them on blocks in the yard, all the old cars."

"And keep turkeys."

"And raise hogs."

"Put up a sign in the yard saying BEWARE THE COW. And on the door: NO SOLICITORS OR PHYSICISTS."

We pulled shut the heavy door and leaned against it kissing, the way we always did. As if we couldn't make it across the hall to the bedroom.

The frame house had basically two large rooms down and two up, divided by wide halls. A later room had been added across the length of the back, for a kitchen and bath downstairs, and a sleeping porch upstairs. If we ended up with the four children here, at least for the summers, we'd put them upstairs and us down in the bedroom that had been made from the original parlor, across the hall from the dining-sitting room that opened into the kitchen. The old house would be crowded—the idea of our kids all sharing one bath blew the mind. But his mannerly boys wouldn't have a lot of time for us, what with prep school and summer camp, at which Trey would this year be a counselor-in-training and next year a counselor, with Jock not far behind. How mine would deal with it here, I could guess. Cow wrangles would be a daily matter. But sticking it out here a few summers eating creamery butter, and homemade hand-churned ice cream with local peaches, and pecan-fed ham for breakfast would certainly toughen them up for the real world: a crowded planet wanting to raise grains and livestock, grasses and atom smashers, all on the same rolling land.

Drew pulled down my jeans and pulled off my T-shirt, which today was slightly damp even though I'd worn a windbreaker over it. This was a ritual, me standing there with jeans around my ankles while he undid his heavy longhorn belt buckle (once his dad's) and let his own jeans fall with a clang to the wood floor. It felt every time I came up here as if we'd just slipped off into some empty house to which parents were due to return any minute. And even as we kissed our way into bed, piling feather pillows behind us against the massive carved headboard, crazy with being back together again, touching each other all over, we were always listening. For the grown-ups, parents we'd once had.

We did it the first time missionary, not able to get to each other fast enough, and then rolled over, still connected, and did it again, slower, with me on top. Drew put a George Strait tape on, and "Heaven Must Be Won-dering Where You Are" drifted around the room, filling our ears. I lay there thinking how unbelievable it was to be together, amazed and happy that we were really going to have it like this forever and forever. Until we were old decrepit folks with wooden walking sticks and hearing aids and watery eyes, loving each other out of our nightshirts, saying, Oh, Lord, God, did you ever think we'd be so lucky?

By the time we were back in our jeans in the kitchen, the hail had stopped. While Drew made us breakfast, I opened the back door. The air was fresh and clean; past the old slatted white weather station, across the grassy field, a line of dairy cows moved slowly into the open.

I'd brought a bowl of cooked potatoes, which Drew made into hash browns, and a stick of butter that he used to stir them with and to brown the thick slices of fresh bread I'd got at the Czech bakery on the way. He fried eggs in the fat from slices of slab bacon he'd cooked in a big iron skillet which looked as old as the house, and most likely was—someone had loved to cook here once. He put coffee on to boil in a blue marbled tin pot, blackened through the years, tossing in an eggshell to settle the grounds. The electric twelve-cup perc pot on the tile counter worked fine, but he liked to fix a greasy, old-time, wood-stove type of breakfast. Which meant boiled coffee so strong it socked a fist into your stomach, in blue tin cups that conducted all the heat, so that you had to hold the handles with napkins until they cooled down.

The big kitchen, with its old table, was the kind with pans hanging from nails, and mason jars holding whisks, wooden spoons, spatulas. The white-painted boards of the walls were hung with signs from his granddad's time: WE SELL SHELL, BUY FROM THE PUMP, DRINK DR. PEPPER. And,

over the stove, STRIKE MATCHES HERE. Two posters behind
dusty glass indicated even older times. One, showing a very
young man in uniform, warned HALT THE HUN. The other
was a framed page of a story from *The Boy's Own Paper*,
dated January 5, 1901, the year his granddad was born.

While Drew served our plates, I read aloud from it:

"There was sorrow in their hearts and tears in their
eyes as they stood for a few minutes and gazed back
at the grand old building where they had studied
so long and had so many escapades and so much
jollity and fun."

When we were mopping up our egg yolks with the tail
end of the bread, the hash browns and bacon long gone,
Drew poured us a final enamel-chipping cup of the boiled
coffee. Behind him on the counter, lunch waited its turn:
two T-bones as thick as his thumb, and a sack of peach
kolaches from the Czech bakery.

Grinning at me like a kid at Christmastime, he said,
"Honey, what took us so long?"

"We should have run away the day we graduated high
school."

"You could be waiting tables and I could be pumping
gas."

"You could be running a weather station and I could
be teaching school," I said.

"Yeah." He nudged my foot with his under the table.
"This is great, isn't it?"

"We can do this all the time, can't we, when we're
actually here?"

"If I'd known it was going to be this easy, shit—"

"I know. I expected to be put in the stockade in front
of the church."

"I guess we're kidding ourselves a little. It isn't over

yet. I mean, Mary Virginia has not mentioned word one about bullion, ingots, gold, lucre, community property accounts, settlements—in other words, she hasn't started thinking about it yet. Her last handful of new jackets—fruit colors, that's what's new, lemon, orange, lime—and those tiny skirts that are here today and going to be gone yesterday, came to, are you ready for this, five gee, I mean three of each, and she's telling me what an unbelievable bargain, how her mom and sister know this little place. I'm thinking that was the down payment on a house when we got married. When I was a kid, it was the price of a good car. That was last week, the fruit suits."

I didn't comment. I'd never talked about money with Drew or his wife; it was like a butcher talking to somebody in pork futures. We weren't in the same frame of reference. My idea of fluctuating income had mostly to do with whether the potato bake was going to have heavy cream or canned milk. But they had seemed to me mismatched from the start: her always wanting what was new, him hanging on to anything that was old.

"Eben said you were getting out because the price of land up north has gone from five hundred to seven thousand an acre. He must have got that from Lila Beth. Maybe Mary Virginia wants to see how high it goes?"

"I heard. I heard the same thing." He groaned. "It's a big power competition. Our collider has to be more super than Europe's collider; our fifty-three miles of tunnel, compared to which Europe's is just an underground Hula Hoop, a better conductor. It's the new space wars, subsoil space. What they don't know is that when they get through spending all that money and time smashing atoms to find the alpha particle that started it all, the earth isn't going to work anymore. It's going to be like the kid who tears apart a clock to see what makes it tick."

He poured us two glasses of milk from a pitcher on the counter, cool country milk to line our stomachs against the coffee. "What they don't know, Cile, is that the soil around here has taken ten thousand years to form, that's how long it takes to make a hundred inches of blacklands out of mud and chalk and decaying plants. We've only had a plow in the ground here for a hundred and fifty. They don't compute that if the U.S. loses even two of its crop-producing states, it'll lose its surplus and be starting down the road to starvation. But you know the federals: they think *farm* is a hyphenated word with *subsidy*." He stopped. "You want to hear this?"

"I want to hear it."

"They gave us, everybody holding land up there, a twenty-five-pound, ten-thousand-page environmental impact study. It's phone book size and then some. I've got it at the office, using it as a doorstop."

His face was red thinking about his least favorite topic. He poured the last of his milk into his coffee cup. "First my great-granddad gave up the right-of-way, that's when fences came in, then my granddad leased out the mineral rights, then in Dad's day he had to give up riparian rights, that's navigable streams, or hell, I don't know, maybe it's just running water. So now you own your land, see, but not the roads crossing it or the oil and gas under it or the creek running through it. Next thing, they'll sublet the air, sky rights, so you'll own, say, from the surface of your pasture up maybe twenty-five feet, free and clear except for vertical easements. Just like offshore drilling. Off-ground probes."

I ran my foot up his leg under the table, wanting him to know I sympathized.

He fiddled with the cassette player until he got us "Second Chances," a nice country waltz we liked, and that calmed him down. "I bought this extra tape," he said, "duplicate, so I could leave the other in the pickup, see. I went in this record store that doesn't sell records anymore, and asked this girl, 'Where's your George Strait?' She said, 'Is that easy listening?' I said 'Country,' but I must have looked at her like she was crazy, because she said, real defensive, 'I only know the music of my generation.' Can you believe it? I had to spell Strait. S-T-R-A-I-T. Then when she saw me squinting at the little tapes, she said, 'You want me to read the titles for you?' I looked at her, this seventeen-year-old punk, and I got to thinking, if her pa was eighteen when he had her, her dad could be five years younger than me! Her generation. What's that if it's not what's on the radio? What does she know? Crudescence and the Maggots? Gag Reflex? Even my boys know who George Strait is. Don't they? How do I know what they know? What do preppies listen to?"

"She was just nervous," I said. "It was her first sale. Her folks don't think she can hold a job."

"Yeah, I know." He caught my foot with his hand. "I just want this to be over, this part, don't you?"

"Show me the bikes," I said.

At the back door he grabbed a hat from the hat rack and hooked a finger in the waist of my jeans. "God, won't it be great when we're here all the time?"

DREW LIKED POKING around in the shed, which was a single car garage with barn doors, freestanding from the house and filled with treasures.

"We'll extend it here," he said, gesturing with his right hand. "Then I'll find that old '57 Chevy stuck in somebody's garage, they don't know it's worth sixty gee, they let me have it cheap, what they paid for it. One of those cars that somebody had and only drove it to church."

"What did your dad do with his cars?"

"Traded them in every other year. He thought a doctor should have a new car; or maybe my mother thought that. How do I know? I know the reason all the stuff out here is in such good condition is because Dad's folks lived here and used the place, took care of it. They didn't care that the chairs were Stickley chairs, big antiques, they kept them fixed because kitchen chairs were for sitting on in the kitchen. I don't know how my mother kept her hands off the stuff up here. You know those things on the wall in the bedroom, used to be the parlor, one shows a bear hunt and one a buffalo hunt? They happen to be Pratt pot lids worth about a grand each. Granddad and his wife just liked how they looked."

"I'm going to miss the parsonage," I said. "Your grandparents had nice houses."

"Yeah, I wish you could keep it. We could use it in

town. I'm going to have to keep the office there, for the paperwork."

"Just think," I said, leaning against him while we talked, "we can go anywhere together in the city we want to. We can eat in Circleburgers, we can eat barbeque at Eva Lee's, we can toss a few at the Greatest Little Horseshoe Pits in Texas. We can—"

"Don't remind me of back home. I can feel panic sneaking up on me when you do. It's been two days and she hasn't said one single let's-talk-about-who's-paying-who-how-much word. You know how the hair on the back of your neck rises up? I bet right this minute she's talking to some Dallas lawyer on the phone. Make that plural. Getting all her ammunition loaded in the cannon."

"How'd you ever find the bikes in here?" I was looking at farm equipment and tools six feet deep along the back of the shed.

He gestured behind the implements. "We're going to fix them up. We're going to rebuild them and then rebuild the Pontiac—" he patted my car, which was taking up most of the front of the shed—"so we can toodle all around the blacklands like vigilantes, checking up on what the federals are doing. Pa and Ma Williams." He pulled me against the side of the Firebird, kissing me the way he used to against his old fixed-up pickup.

The bikes were great; he was right. I could see, when he uncovered them, that they were in amazing shape, with fitted "slipcovers" over each. Plus locks on the wheels, as if thieves were going to drive by and know to root around behind every neat stack of two-by-fours and four-by-eights in order to lift a couple of bicycles that looked like props from a late fifties movie. The Western Flyer—my bike— was just a basic boy's red and white, with fat whitewalls, if that's what you called the tires, and fat pedals and those things like streamers coming out of the handlebars. Drew's was a Schwinn Black Phantom, totally deluxe, weighing in, he said, at sixty-five pounds. It was green and had enough chrome on it that you almost needed shades to look at it. Might they have been bought for him?

I could remember how gross these things had seemed when we were in high school; then everybody wanted lightweight imported bikes. I reminded Drew of that.

He shook his head. "The LeMond carbon-fiber racer I wanted to buy then? You couldn't touch it now for under twelve gee. Minimum. Anyway, that's not what you need on the farm-to-markets. What you need is what we got."

I couldn't argue with that.

For lunch, we ate our steaks, almost black on the outside, almost raw on the inside, and then had two peach kolaches from the Czech bakery, all of it washed down with a fresh cup of boiled coffee. We'd worked off breakfast messing with the bikes, getting them out. And then making love once more, feather pillows at our backs on the old four-poster.

Drew propped his 1927 Rolex Oyster on the table so we could watch the time. Usually after lunch we made a pallet on the floor and stretched out to talk, mostly about how someday we were going to tell them. Today we stayed at the table, to celebrate that we really had done it.

"I'm thinking of our wedding," Drew said.

"Wedding? Bridesmaids, flower girls, ring bearers, rice, that kind of wedding? Maybe they'll throw potatoes at ours."

I could see him squirm around like a kid with a plan. "Not that kind."

"A simple church wedding, with Eben officiating?"

"Not that kind. Anyway, you're about to become an Episcopalian."

"Not me."

"What do you care? You don't believe all that."

"Maybe not, but the Presbyterian church is the place in which I'm not going to believe it."

"I'm thinking of a dance." He looked happy with himself.

"A dance? A real honest dance? Somebody playing guitar and bass and piano? A big slick floor with sawdust on it?"

"Yeah." He laughed. "Maybe we can do it at the Czech Fest. An anniversary, sort of, right?" He counted on his fingers. "A month, three weeks really, till Easter, call that a month. Another month, then we move out. Two more for the divorces. One more for all the snags. One more to pay off the Dallas lawyer, make that plural. That's September. We can bring the kids all up to West for the Fest, then drive on over here for a big barbeque. I mean the real stuff, hill country best. The kind where the brisket's been in that closed pit for thirty-six hours, with that burnt crust and the juice dripping out. We can have a band here, too. Hang lights from the trees."

"How can you be thinking about food again?"

"I don't have any trouble." He rubbed his foot up the side of my leg. "A person eats when they get hungry in the country."

"Is that right?"

He looked sly. "When are you going to tell your folks?"

"They can read about it in the papers."

That's more or less how I heard about them. Actually I heard it from Theo, back when she was Miss Moore and still my unfavorite teacher out of a crowd of contenders. *Your daddy and I are going to tie the knot*, those were her words. Maybe I'd drop by their house, over in the part of town where all the streets were named for birds, and tell her my news. The preacher and I are going to split; my boyfriend and I plan to tie the knot.

"Shorty'll hear it from some fishing buddy, one of the retired coaches, and say, 'Who? Cile? You mean my girl?' "

I laughed, because Drew did try to get under my skin talking about my daddy, and I didn't mind letting him see that he had. Usually that meant his mind was on his mother. Anyway, mine was. "Do you think it'll be all right at Lila Beth's on Easter? I want it not to be awkward."

"Don't sweat it. Nothing fazes Mother. She's got a set of manners that covers everything. When Dad died in the ice storm, she read up on Thank You Notes in Reply to Letters of Condolence."

"You're making that up."

"She'll look over the chapter on Divorce in Close Family Members, Such as a Daughter or Son."

"I owe her a lot."

"Me."

"Besides that." I looked at him, at the way the freckles had faded together into what looked now like a deep windburn. How the brick red hair had faded to a dark rosy brown. To me he was always Andy and Drew, rolled into one.

"She thinks you're great," he said. "There's never been any love lost between her and Mary Virginia. You know that. She never warmed to that Dallas routine." He picked up the '27 Oyster and waved it in front of my eyes. It was countdown time.

I nodded and leaned over to kiss him on the nose. Then the mouth. Then we washed up the kitchen. We threw out the rims of fat from the steak and the rest of the loaf of bread, putting them out back for whatever might come along: raccoons, black bears, bobcats. Probably nothing that wild anymore; these days more likely bluetick hounds from one of the nearby farms.

Together we closed up the house, got my car out, and padlocked the shed. Turned his truck around. Then we stood a minute. It was good when we weren't in such an awful hurry, when we didn't just wave and rush off, looking at the sky over our shoulders, hoping nothing would drop out of it on the way back.

"We never talk about the kids," I said.

"Sure we do. What do you mean? We did. We're going to invite them to the wedding, remember?"

"What if the girls want to stay in town? I mean even in the summer?"

"Then they can stay in town. Come out weekends."

"I don't know. I don't know what I think about that. They're such jocks, their lives totally revolve around the teams they're playing on. They talk about this ecology; argue it all the time. Cows. But the truth is, their eyes light up most when they're competing. Even Earth Day, which they're already working on like crazy, the main event for them is the marathon run along Lake Brazos. Lord, of all the people in the world to end up with these giant jocks for children, I'm the last one you'd imagine. I thought, if I thought at all, that I'd have a couple of little sweet-faced soft-voiced wallflowers. The kind I was always going to have to be nagging to get out there and make friends or get interested in something. You know?"

"Instead," Drew said, helping me into the car and leaning in the window to finish talking, "I'm the one expected to have the giant jocks and ended up with the sweet-faced wallflowers. You never can tell."

"Drew, don't. Don't ever say that. What a thing to say. Trey and Jock are the"—I bit my tongue not to say *sweetest*, which was the first word that came to mind—

"neatest, brightest boys in the world. And the most athletic. Come on. What's got into you? They're great tennis
players, good students, and . . . great guys."

"Yeah, forget it. Hell, Cile, we never have time to even
have half a conversation about anything. I'm not dumping
on the boys. You know that. It was a joke. We need to get
this done and get ourselves out here where we can have
time to start something and finish it. I was thinking again
about what's going on up the road. How they don't get the
picture that when you lose the grasslands you lose the
country. Thinking that with my luck, the boys would both
end up being Dallas lawyers, representing the government
in its fight between the superfluous supercollider and the
nesters down here south of Waxahachie making all the
trouble."

"I know. I just had an attack of the nerves."

"I'll call tomorrow."

"Okay."

"I love you, honey."

"You're right, the bikes are swell."

While I warmed up the Pontiac, Drew headed back
toward his pickup, singing off key, "All My Exes Live in
Texas."

THE HAIL HAD moved on, south and west, the line of clouds now a distant stacked wall on the horizon where the land shifted from cane to grain. As the sun showed through, I passed a roadside litter sign saying DON'T MESS WITH TEXAS and a pasture filled with black and white Maine d'Anjous chewing their way through Monday afternoon. A car passed me on the narrow two-lane farm-to-market, slowing to check for tractors around the curb. The bumper sticker on her back fender read MY DAUGHTER AND MY MONEY BOTH GO TO A & M. And, on radio's Best Country in the City station, someone started singing, "I'm just catching up with yesterday, by tomorrow I should be ready for today."

Lord, how fine it all was. How long I'd waited for today.

But, to be honest, if dancing in Waco hadn't been all but banned, we'd never have got our children as grown as we did. If we'd found ourselves moving around the dance floor once more any sooner, likely we'd have made an awful mess, had a wild affair breaking hearts right and left, our own included. How could we have ever got together with four babies? How could we have pulled apart those Baby Days' homes?

From the minute he'd shown back up in my life, at Lila Beth's that first Easter, I'd had dancing with him on my mind. I'd waltzed around the smooth floors of the parsonage all that next week—remembering the dances we'd had, back when everything had been all right, our parents all in place, us thinking of nothing but holding on and moving our feet.

And soon, like an answer to a prayer, Eben and I had got a thick vellum invitation to the Cotton Ball Pageant, with its small enclosure card, its tiny envelope for our reply, "Complimentary" written across the price, Lila Beth's name listed as sponsor. A gesture she'd clearly set in motion before I'd turned out to be that suspect girl from Andy/ Drew's past; too late to change her mind, if she'd wanted to.

I was delirious with excitement. The younger Mrs. Dr. Croft, whose son and daughter I'd tutored into Stanford and Duke, had been to all the socials in the state. She and her husband (and the older Dr. and Mrs. Croft as well) were part of the circuit. They did Idlewild in Dallas, Fiesta in San Antonio, the Rose Festival in Tyler, a dozen others. But her favorite, the one she used to talk about the most, was the Cotton Ball in Waco. "I think the reason that one's so special," she'd said, "is that dancing is still so spicy up there. It's like drinking during Prohibition must have been. You can actually feel the excitement like fireworks when everybody gets out on the floor and actually hug dances, as they call it. Isn't that rich? It's forbidden at Baylor, you know. So the old folks have formal promenades with the men and women in facing rows, and the younger set has functions, as they call them, meaning nighttime garden parties with a band, where everyone takes off their shoes and splashes their feet to four-four time in the swimming pool. It's that literal way Wacoans all talk. Saying 'lap baby,' when they mean a nursing infant, and 'knee baby' when they mean one who's weaned. No telling what they call sex. 'Hip coupling'?"

I'd been a voyeur of such dances for years, reading

about them in the Sunday paper back in the university even when I was doing nothing much but studying, deciding what to do with my life other than not become a teacher like the woman who'd married my dad. I'd see pictures of the guests—sometimes the older or the younger Mrs. Dr. Croft, whose ambitious children were still in my future—in their long (and then short and then long again) gowns, of satin, chiffon, crepe, peau de soie, georgette, names from novels, captured in the orangy colors of the Living Section. Sometimes the dances were called charity balls and held in the ballrooms of downtown hotels; sometimes they were galas that took place in almost-finished skyscrapers or automobile showrooms before the cars were delivered; sometimes benefits, black-tie events out-of-doors, in city parks, on riverboats, on docks by the lake hung with lights, orchestras playing to the stars.

As soon as the invitation came, I'd spread my treasure trove of gowns on the bed—my secret dowry, which I'd kept stored in the back of the large linen closet in the hall of the parsonage. (It had always seemed strange to me how the families who'd first lived in the seventy-year-old house had had enough linens—monogrammed towels, hemmed sheets, appliquéd runners—to fill two deep closets, yet so few clothes that the parents shared a single shallow one.) The legacy of dresses had, of course, come to me from the younger Mrs. Dr. Croft. So pleased had she been at my results with her children that she'd insisted on some extra gift above my fee, some special present just for me. A week at a health spa? An airline ticket? I hadn't even had the manners to hesitate. I knew she never wore the same formal twice; I'd seen that from the papers. They had to be somewhere, I'd reasoned. Packed off to the Next to New Shop, or at that very moment languishing in the back of one of her walk-in closets.

My request seemed to please her. "Get your mind off that high school beau of yours," she'd said. "Get you out there with better options." Then, locating the gowns, packing them lovingly in tissue paper and garment bags, she'd hesitated. "They look so dated, dear. Honestly. Clothes you think are the latest thing look worse than old hairstyles. You wonder what on earth you could have been thinking of."

Spread out on my bed in Waco, they looked as if some magic trunk from the past had produced them. What wonders, the yards of fine fabrics, with tiny hooks or invisible zippers, tucks and linings and finishing seams a work of art. Some with lace across the strapless bodices, some with petticoats under layered taffeta, some with brilliants in a band around the chiffon neckline. My favorite: a floating white gown with a halter neck, narrow waist, and skirt a full circle at the ankles. It had been worn to a Fred Astaire–Ginger Rogers Gala. And the photos in the paper had lines of lyrics under the beaming guests: *Shall we still be together with our arms around each other, shall we dance? On the clear understanding that this sort of thing can happen, shall we dance?*

Eben had scratched around in the deep loam of his conscience trying to decide if we should accept. It wasn't, after all, he reasoned, as if he was a Baptist preacher, although there was the general community at large to consider. And the invitation had been proffered by Mrs. Williams, the mainstay, in fact one of the elders, of his church. That must indicate that it was acceptable for us to go; especially since the tickets were complimentary.

Seeing the wealth of gowns I'd spread out on the bed, he was angry. He'd only hesitated, he explained, fearing I might not have a dress to wear; that our budget would not stretch for something new. I'd said I didn't realize he'd never seen them, not able to admit how much I'd liked keeping them secret, how much I'd liked having something of my own he didn't share.

As it turned out, the formals were inappropriate, the ball was actually only a pageant, and we didn't get to dance.

I'd asked Mary Virginia to stop by, to help me choose one to wear. She had been kind, somewhat embarrassed, explaining that the Cotton Ball Pageant was an umbrella term for what was really a dozen events. Suppers for the princesses and their escorts, parties for the queen and the entire court, a sponsor's evening for the parents and out-of-town friends (this did have dancing, and perhaps my doctor's wife had come to that?), a garden brunch on Sunday for all the people who put the week together. That, actually, we were invited only to the nighttime pageant, to which people dressed up, but in cocktail clothes, no black tie, so they could sell more seats.

"You could describe the scenes yourself, Cile, even though you just moved here. It's all the same old stories, each with about a zillion people participating, all of whose kinfolks pay to come. The tepees on the west bank of the Brazos; hauling the first load of cotton across the suspension bridge; the first skyscraper west of the Mississippi, south of Kansas City; the invention of Dr. Pepper. Same old stuff." She'd laughed, sitting on my bed, holding up first one dress and then another as she pretended to act out the scenes.

"But so much money for that—" I was crushed.

"Oh, well, those tickets aren't general admission. We get a buffet first, and special seats, and the big reception afterward, you know, the perks. That's for being part of the crowd who gets to arrive from somewhere else and adjourn somewhere else while all the mob are trying to find their cars and their kids."

Possibly I looked close to tears.

"I can lend you something," she said, "if this is all you've got. Don't go buy anything."

But I shook my head. I was going to wear one of those anyway, in case this was the nearest I ever got to a ball in this life. The white Ginger Rogers chiffon with the halter neck would do just fine. I didn't care if I looked out of place; I had my own agenda. I could write the younger Mrs. Dr. Croft that I had been to the Cotton Ball Pageant in her Buick Showroom Gala gown.

T HE CITY LIMITS sign said: WEST, CZECH POINT OF CENTRAL TEXAS. West stood in relation to Waco as Round Rock had to Austin when Drew and I were dating: out of town but near at hand. And with the same mix of county marketplace and elegant little city that Round Rock had had twenty-plus years ago. I felt at home here, and it made me happy to know that soon I would be. I liked to drive along the clean, paved streets, around the square, because there were always old cars pulled up like horses to the posts in front of the Victorian stores.

Today, there was a dull green Chevy pickup that Drew would have loved; older than his shiny red rebuilt '58. I'd learned to tell that, because it had single headlights and rounded back fenders, not double heads and flaring fenders. Beside it, a Model A was parked, black and shiny as a mirror, but something about it wasn't authentic. It had been messed with by a street rodder; the windows had been lowered. Still, the two of them made a good pair, echoes of the past sitting side by side, somewhat like a grandfather and father come to town for the day, the older man dressed spit clean as if for church, the younger still in faded work pants and boots.

If we lived at the farm together, I could turn back and get Drew. We could walk around the vehicles, have a Dr. Pepper in the drugstore, and watch for the owners out the window. The farmer, maybe, coming out of the feed and seed store, the banker, probably, bringing a customer out to admire his antique toy. Drew could talk motors to them and introduce his new wife.

Turning from the square into the residential area, moving at a crawl, I could see that almost every front yard had a staked campaign sign reading CZECH YOUR BALLOT. A reminder that even here in what seemed like day before yesterday, a woman was running a strong race for governor of the state.

It wasn't much out of the way to swing by the rodeo grounds, and I did; the weather was holding, my tires were in good shape, and it seemed a fine idea to return to the site of the Czech Fest, where it had all started up again between me and Drew. There was nothing much out there now, midafternoon on a weekday. A tent where maybe there'd recently been a livestock sale, a couple of pickups. Evidence showing where the recent hail had bit the dust. A power line eaten through by fire ants.

We'd most likely both gone to every dance festival in the area for years, missing each other in the crowds of thousands. I'd taken the girls to the Mexican Cinco de Mayo, the German Oktoberfest, the Czech Fest at West, all with their own sausage, beer and polkas, all with that wonderful fairground atmosphere.

Three years ago this coming September, I'd gathered the girls, then nine and ten, and driven them up the interstate north toward West. It was hot as midsummer, baking hot, and I was in a thin cotton skirt and T-shirt, my hair pulled back with barrettes, sandals on my feet. We'd worked out the rules about spending money and not getting lost and our point of rendezvous, and I was heading through a crowd the size of a small city toward the sound of the loudest band.

Then, right in my path, walking single file in total concentration, like scouts in the wilderness, appeared Trey and Jock. My heart went smashing against the walls of my chest, and I looked in front of them and behind. No parent.

"Look who's here," I said. "Where are the big people?"

They laughed, little neat country-club gentlemen of nine and ten in tennis whites, socks and sneakers that looked fresh from the sporting goods store, shiny clean cheeks. Both had trim haircuts, a bit of Trey's red-gold cowlick shooting skyward at the crown, a tuft of Jock's dark locks falling across his forehead.

"Mom's in Dallas," Jock said, looking up at me, for they had not yet got their growth and were still skinny little baby-faced boys.

"I think we're supposed to call her Mary Virginia to her friends." Trey, his freckles still thick as measles, asked with total seriousness, "What should we say?"

I tried to match his tone. "I think you say 'our mother.' "

"Yes, ma'am."

"How about 'our father'?" I asked, giving them a grin.

"—is in Heaven." Jock doubled over with laughter.

Trey gave him a stern big-brother glare. "Our dad is dancing, Mrs. Tait." Then, hearing his words (how could their dad be dancing if their mom was in Dallas?), he made the sudden gulp that I remembered well, the one that went with watching his purple Popsicle slide off its stick onto the floor, and amended himself. "I mean he's watching the dancing in the tent." He pointed. "Over there."

"What's this 'Mrs. Tait'? You knew better than that at three."

Trey frowned. "Our mother has us call her friends 'aunt.' "

"*Cile* it is to you guys."

"Yes, ma'am."

Jock came close enough to touch me and sort of rocked up and down. "You ever think about opening a camp?" he asked.

"Not once, not one time. You go to camp, now, don't you?"

"Last year was our first," Trey answered for them. "We're probably going to be counselors." He gazed off at his future.

"I sure wish you had a camp," Jock said, still rocking.

"She doesn't *do* that," Trey whispered angrily.

"I mean, we'd have a lot more fun." Jock butted his head against my arm at that.

"I guess they don't sing 'Ring Around the Rosy Rag' at camp, do they?"

"No, ma'am," Trey said. "We do archery and canoeing and tennis and overnight horseback trips and—" He faltered, searching for what else there was.

Mine were already doing team sports even then, even in the young grades, even if it was only kickball. I wondered whether that was the difference between boys and girls, or something more subtle, a class distinction. Boys debating Princeton and Baylor at their age were learning individual sports. "Swimming," I supplied. "Diving."

"Sure, we do those. I can do a half-gainer."

"Have you seen Ruth and Martha?"

"At the corn-on-the-cob booth—" Jock said.

"The one where the corn comes on sticks," Trey explained.

"—they were with a bunch of big kids."

"They *are* a bunch of big kids," I told them.

They looked embarrassed that I'd said it, but laughed.

"I'll try to find your dad. Do you have watches?" Silly question, Drew's children. They showed me their fat black waterproof campers' watches. "I told the girls I'd meet them at four on the dot at the Vlasek Kolache stand. That's the big one right in the middle, with a sausage booth on each side of it. Can you remember that?"

"Our dad said to come back to the tent in an hour." Trey hated a change in plans.

"Look for us at the Vlasek Kolache stand first. I'll get you both a couple of apricot jumbos."

"If you ever do open a camp—" Jock said, looking back as he was dragged away by his older brother.

Drew wasn't hard to find. First, he was tall, but mostly it was because he wasn't one of a thousand Czech men in costume, and because he sent off vibrations that waved at me like flowers hollering for bees in the sunshine.

I walked up behind him, pushing my way through a double ring of watchers, and hooked two fingers in his belt.

Without turning, he said, "Where you been?"

"Powdering my nose."

"You missed a waltz."

Then he turned and we just put our arms around each other right there and moved out on the dance floor without missing a beat. The exhibition polkas weren't until sundown, and it was country music for everybody with a general admission ticket until then.

It was like no time at all had gone by. Nothing was different. Maybe we got a little more winded sooner, but it didn't seem that way.

"God," Drew said.

"Lord." I tucked my head under his chin.

"What've we been doing all these years?"

"I don't remember."

"I love you to pieces."

"I miss the sawdust on the floors."

"We were crazy to let it go. Crazy to wax that car with my backside when we could have been doing what we ought to have been doing."

"I know."

"I want it now."

"Me, too."

"Right here, at the fair, in the parking lot. In my pickup."

"Don't be nuts. The kids are going to be waiting for us in"—I checked my watch—"thirty minutes."

"I told mine to come back here." He looked at his Oyster.

"I saw the boys. Change of plans."

"In thirty minutes I could come six times."

"Aren't you the braggart?"

"How about you?"

"I don't even have to leave the dance floor."

He pulled me so tight I thought his belt buckle would crack a rib, and we danced like that until the band shook loose with "You Picked a Fine Time to Leave Me, Lucille," and then we waltzed around the edge of the crowd, around and around the tent, cooling down, looking at each other.

When we went to get the kids, we didn't even make any plans. He didn't say, I'll call. I didn't say, We can't do this. We didn't go through any of that. We were just trying to stay upright and not go nuts with four youngsters following us around, hitting us up for more corn, more potato pancakes, more sweet pastries, more cider. We loaded them up, drugging them on food, trying not to touch each other.

"The last dance," Drew said, as it finally got dusk and began to cool off. The kids had each had two ciders and two lemonades, been to the mob-filled bathrooms overflowing with sweaty beer drinkers, and were dragging behind us. Even my two, who'd started out with half a dozen friends, were running down, steaming in their bandanna halters and cutoffs, their damp hair tied up with yarn to give their necks a breeze.

"The last," I said.

We settled the children at the edge of the tent, outside, with one last round of sticky peach kolaches. The band was about to call it an afternoon; the polka crew was already getting set up for the evening's exhibition. The final number was a Willie Nelson, and their hearts weren't in it. It didn't matter; ours were.

"We're going to do it, aren't we?" Drew asked.

"We are. I hope we are. Don't glue yourself to me like that; we've got four sets of eyes on us."

"They can't see in."

"Because I'm going to come right here if you don't stop."

"Give me some tongue."

"You're crazy."

"Come on."

We deep kissed once and then pulled back and finished the number eighteen inches apart.

Gathering myself back under control, getting ready to herd the girls into the car, I remember thinking that the Baptists sure knew what they were talking about, banning hug dancing.

I'D GROWN UP with opposition of a different sort to dancing, from a different source: my mother. (Recalling her now, tall, full-bosomed, with the thick brows and full lips of my daughters, I realized that in a few weeks I'd be replaying arguments with a parent younger than I.)

She'd refused me dance classes when I was small; later, had turned a deaf ear to my happy accounts of spending the evening waltzing my feet off in a Round Rock dance hall. If it's the *arts* you want, she'd said more than once—pained, disappointed, her mind obsessed with the welfare of the world—there are other fields. A book has a text to show for itself, a play a script, a movie a film, a painting a canvas. But dance? She shook her head, not comprehending. What wasted motion.

Her attitude was not uncommon: Once danced the dance is gone. The dancer turns, the swan dies and it is over. The houselights rise, the audience leaves and the moment is forever lost. But this is the spectator's view. I knew even at seventeen that for the dying ballerina, making one last time the grand moves of a lifetime (seen by the watching nurse and kin as a few distracted departing twitches), all was still present in bone and sinew.

Knew that for the dancer, the dance once danced remains as long as breath.

PALM SUNDAY rose bright and blue, a stunning sunny April day. On the steps of the church, the children, mine included, made double rows, waving palm fronds for the congregation to walk beneath. "Hosanna," I said to them. Hosanna to everyone, the word rising from my lips, borne by happiness. I knew the word had originally meant *save us now*, but that was not out of order, either, as we climbed together toward the message of the morning.

I always liked to listen to the crowd murmuring in the pews before the service started. They, the parishioners, and Eben were like two variations on a single theme: the paradox of free will and determinism.

Behind me, where I sat on the front row, a group of elderly ladies and old thin-chested men began the refrain, women with lace at their collars and heavy dark slips under their silk dresses, men with handkerchiefs in their breast pockets and parts in their slicked dark hair.

"I say when a cold's got your name on it, there's nothing you can do to ward it off. Dristan, Novahistine, Nyquil, Robitussin, it doesn't matter."

"That's not a bit true. If you see one coming you can double your vitamin C and drink fresh-squeezed juice."

"When a cough's going to cough, it coughs. There's no stopping it. When trouble's got your number, the phone's going to ring."

"It's the truth, some people can stand out in the rain, never wear anything on their heads, never get sick a day in their lives. This woman I know, people can sneeze right in her face, she never gets a germ."

"Young people know about nutrition."

"It's like a tornado is heading for your house. You think eating an orange crate of oranges is going to make it change its course?"

"You can open the windows; you can get under the table."

"You can say your prayers."

"Hush, here comes the choir."

It pleased me to listen to them, setting forth the strains that would soon come from the pulpit. The king of another world arriving on the donkey's colt; the congregation riding mortality in an earthly city.

It didn't matter the title of Eben's sermon of the week ("The Archaic King at the Crossroads," "The Freedom to Disobey," "Lead Us Not into Temptation"), the matter he explored never varied. What does it mean to act if God has foreknowledge of our actions? Today, the lesson of Palm Sunday turned not on whether the crowd on the road to Jerusalem was wrong in wanting a different kind of king, for being fickle in their reception of Jesus, but rather whether either the crowd or the Son of God had any choice in the matter. Could He *not* have come into the city as had been prophesied? Could they *not* have waved their branches and lifted their voices in praise? Were both reading scripts in a Passion play that neither had written? And then, of course, the foreshadowing of Easter and the larger question of the crucifixion. Did Jesus have a choice? Did that matter? Today, in choosing Matthew 21 for his reading, I knew Eben would end his sermon, as he did, with the passage in which Jesus says that if you have faith you can move mountains. What, the pastor asked us, did this mean? If the mountain truly moves, does it matter that the moving was foreordained?

After the sermon had been considered and received by all of us, we stood to sing: "All glory, laud and honor, To Thee, Redeemer, King! To whom the lips of children, Made sweet hosannas ring." Then the old woman who had to blow her nose did, and the ones who didn't sang loud and clear, full-throated and rejoicing in their immunity.

Seated again, for the prayers of intercession—the pause in the service when anyone may mention a loved one in the hospital or nursing home, grieve aloud over the loss of someone dear, or request help for a troubled friend—I was thinking that I was going to miss this church a lot when it was no longer possible for me to be here. Thinking back to the days when the girls were little and sat up front with me, rather than in the rear with their Sunday School friends. Back to when they had to be poked to keep from squirming. Then, older, when they'd wanted to know why it had to be their daddy every week up there and not some-one else's. Their amazement and interest when they learned it could even be someone's mother up there. It pleased me how they had grown to be a part of the church through the years. Preachers' kids were known for acting out, for rebelling, making waves, but mine, natural competitors, had become team players even here: partisan Presbyterians against the Baptists in a Baptist town. At least I had not failed in my duty in this regard; my children were firmly in the fold.

Then, all at once, I became aware of Eben speaking from the pulpit.

"This is the last Sunday," he said in an even tone to the sea of bowed heads, "that my wife, Cile, and I will be here with you as a couple. Please know that there will be no loss of love within our community because we have reached this mutual decision to go our separate ways." He paused, then, after a moment of silence, raised his voice in the benediction: "And now may the grace of our Lord Jesus Christ, and the love of God, and the fellowship of the Holy Ghost, be with us all evermore. Amen."

Shaking with anger at his making our news public without forewarning me, without a word to me, I kept my eyes straight ahead as Eben in his robes strode rapidly past me up the aisle. "You always like Palm Sunday," he'd said slyly the night I told him I was leaving. Making plans no doubt even then to spring this surprise on me; to scoop me in my own infidelity. To orchestrate my faithlessness as if it was merely a part of his own composition.

I debated slipping out through the choir room, but that would only take me into the Fellowship Hall, from the frying pan to the covered dishes. Still, I couldn't bear the thought of heading out the front door where Eben, standing by his daughters, would be greeting his flock as if nothing had happened, shaking each firm hand, bending over each tanned face, accepting their praise for his sermon as his due.

I scanned the sanctuary for signs that anyone at all was shocked, astonished, dismayed by the news. But no. The usual steady hum of good wishes and family gossip fell like a blow on my shoulders. Eben had already told them all.

A polite crowd of the faithful moved around me in a cluster, saying in kindly tones that they would certainly miss me, what a dear thing I'd been, such a good cook, too, they hoped I'd be fine, it had been nice to know me. Bustling around me and then past me, on about their business, having paid their respects as if to a visitor.

No stone thrown; not even a pebble skipped. No curses placed on my head, no muttering among themselves, no sending me to Satan. Rather, it seemed a minor matter: the parson and his wife splitting. As if they'd learned I'd decided to bring potato puffs this week instead of my usual potato bake.

I felt cheated. A heathen, I had assumed that true believers would want to cast me out, to tear, symbolically at least, my garments, to cover my face with ashes. Not merely pat me good-bye, as if I were a college freshman moving her letter to another congregation.

Only Lila Beth, whom I glimpsed through a circle of elders, turned her back on me.

Eben's three new parishioners, perhaps not knowing any better, took the news seriously. Boyd, the skinny math teacher who'd bought a ring in order to marry himself, put a thin arm around my shoulder and said that being alone didn't have to mean being lonely. Blanche, the plump widow who'd had the stress reaction to her husband's death and lost her hair, took off her hat to show me the beginning of beige waves, and offered me the name of her hairdresser. Jae-Moon, the Korean woman who'd fussed at Eben for his sexist sermons, seized my palms in hers and squeezed them fervently. Her tone joyous, she said, "This is good, what you have done."

I thanked the trio, then stood at the front of the church until the crowd thinned out and the last few slow-moving, hard-of-hearing members began to make their way with canes and walkers up the aisle. One of the women who'd sat behind me caught my arm for support and we brought up the rear.

"I still say," she croaked hoarsely, "when trouble's got your number, you can't hang up the phone."

"Hosanna," I said.

DID YOU HAVE to do that?" Eben and I sat at the table over coffee. The girls had fled with the Bledsoes for the afternoon.

"I did. I could not pretend any longer to something that wasn't true. The congregation is entitled, as long as I am in this job, to full disclosure about any matter that they will hear gossip concerning."

"I wanted to tell the girls."

"Have I restrained you?"

"In my own way, at my own time." I was so angry I could hardly get my breath. "You anticipated me. You jumped the gun. You promised to wait until after Easter."

"You bargained for that delay; I did not agree to it." He rose to refill our cups.

"You told Lila Beth, didn't you? Didn't you? You sprang it early so you could be the one to tell her."

"It was your choice to cling to your secret."

"You went public today so that we couldn't have Easter Sunday at her house." I didn't trust myself to lift the hot cup without hurling it.

"Is that worse than your intention to prolong the deception at the expense of her family and yours?"

"Yes." I clenched my hands in my lap. "It is."

He put his gray suit coat on, pulled tight the knot in his navy tie, lifted his thin hair with his fingers. "I have to check on the shut-ins and the hospital."

"Eben?"

He waited.

"What else?" I asked.

"I have seen a lawyer." In a level tone he mentioned a man in the congregation, one of the thin-chested faithful with a ruler-straight part in his dark, sparse hair. "It will be less awkward, there will be less talk, if I file."

"Had you planned to serve me papers with no notice?"

"You stay here tonight," he said evenly. "We'll talk when the girls are asleep about the logistics of your moving out. Does that suit you?"

For him to pick the time and place for us to talk? The time for me to move? For me to talk to my own children? "What do you think?"

"I suppose it's to be expected that we are having this same fight at this especially painful time. It has always been a problem between us."

I breathed in and out. Took a large gulp of coffee. Shut my eyes, opened them. He was right: the battleground was studded with losses. The troops were barefoot and ragged. I raised a white flag. "It was a good sermon," I told him. "One of your best."

"You always liked Palm Sunday," he said.

Y OU BY YOURSELF?''
"I'm so glad it's you."
"I figured the parson'd be visiting the afflicted."

"He just left. I was wild to talk to you, but I didn't dare call—"

"I'm not there. I'm not anywhere. I'm at a pay phone, actually." I could hear him suck in his breath. "She told everybody, I mean everybody. Mary Virginia. Her mom and sister, the boys, Mother. I expect to find my stuff in the driveway already boxed when I come home. I got back yesterday from the meeting in Waxahachie, listening to them raise the price and butter up the deal on the land they're wanting to tunnel under, and the news was out."

"Eben told everyone, too."

"You mean the girls?"

"I mean—everyone. He stood up in the pulpit and told the congregation."

"You're kidding."

"I wish."

"How'd they take it?"

"Nobody seemed surprised. That was the worst. I think Eben's who told Lila Beth. She was in a crowd and wouldn't look at me. They all hurried out front to shake hands and then went off to Fellowship Hall to eat. I hope they said good things about my potato bake; this was their last batch of it."

"How'd the girls take it?"

"He must have told them, too. 'See you, Momma.' "

"God."

"I know."

"Maybe we should have waited until summer. But I couldn't stand the idea of Mary Virginia doing the whole surprise Four-Oh birthday party number on me."

"They would have done the same thing whenever we told them." I could hear over the line the sound of traffic in the background, and that pay-phone hum. "I may arrive at the farm with a moving van. Eben is kicking me out."

"Wait till we see if I've *got* a farm." Drew made a swallowing noise. "I'm supposed to see Mother tomorrow."

"Lord."

"Yeah."

"What's she going to say?"

"I don't know. Bad boy."

"Eben's seen a lawyer."

"A lawyer? I didn't know he knew about that stuff."

"He's filing."

"Shit. Mary Virginia's probably already got a lien against my collar stays and shoehorns."

I laughed. "You've still got your pickup."

"I'm steaming up the phone booth, talking to you."

"I'm steaming up the study on this end."

"I've got to see you."

"What time is Lila Beth's?"

"Noon. She said, 'We'll have a salad.' " He groaned.

"You want red beans and rice for dessert?" I was suggesting Eva Lee's, a barbeque café across the Brazos.

"Too many business types go there. Homestyle gives them nostalgia."

"We're not hiding."

"We're not hiding but we're not advertising. Mother doesn't need to get a report from some banker just now."

"Circleburgers?" This was a place we'd never been together, a landmark diner south of town, where a cluster of highways came together like the spokes of a wheel.

"Best hamburgers in the county; second best jukebox. Great. Nobody but truck farmers uses those old roads anymore."

"What time?"

"Two? Two." He sounded scared to death.

"It'll be okay," I said.

"Sure it will, honey, it'll be fine." He laughed. "Are we lying to ourselves or each other?"

"Hold out for the shed and bikes."

"That's the bottom line."

I listened to the hum for a minute before breaking the connection.

THE GIRLS CAME right to the table and sat down for a bowl of soup and some corn bread. They didn't seem to be avoiding me; they'd waved the Bledsoes goodbye, not asking them in.

I sat across from them, feeling a familiar ache, a dull

sense of repetition. Of their being pulled away from the dailiness of me, of a looming absence where once presence had been. An echo of the years in my life when people were always leaving and being left. I'd washed my hair and put on jeans. Already I had the sense that I didn't quite live here anymore, although I tried to shake that off, tried not to be defensive. "I gathered that wasn't news to you," I said, "this morning in church. About your dad and me."

"He said not to tell you till you brought it up." Ruth dipped her spoon in the thick soup. She had on a T-shirt that said BE GREEN-SPIRITED: STOP DEFORESTATION, and striped shorts with a fly front which looked like men's boxer shorts. Maybe they were. (Where did my kids get clothes that I'd never seen before? Where did they appear from? Where did they live? Was there a garment clearinghouse, something like a lending library, proceeds going to Clean Air Fund?)

Martha had on the same sort of shorts and a T reading SAVE THE DOLPHINS. She took a big swallow of milk, getting herself a white mustache which she quickly wiped away. She made a wavering dimpled smile in my direction.

Maybe they were as nervous as I was.

"You and Drew going to live on his farm?" Martha asked me.

"I think so."

"Does he have a lot of cows?"

Ruth snapped to attention. "I hope he's not part of that genetic engineering project they're running up there. You know they produced four calves that have genes from three other species, including *humans*. That is obscene; that is direct chromosome manipulation. It's Frankenstein."

Martha came to my defense, to the defense of cows everywhere. "For your information, those are dairy cows on those farms, Ruth. They're vegetarians just like you are. You can sit out in the pasture and eat clover with them. They're milk cows. And the farmers sell this absolutely pure milk, completely free from growth hormones or sulfa drugs or anything else like that. *Milk* doesn't happen to be a *crime.*"

She took another gulp from her glass, this time leaving the mustache on.

The matter of my exodus had been derailed by a familiar argument. What had I wanted? For these fair daughters, whose existence still filled my heart, to fling themselves on me and beg me not to go? Beg to go with me? Your people are my people and your farmhouse is my farmhouse? Probably I had. I didn't know what to say. I wanted to be eating soup with them this same way until they put on their backpacks and went off to seek the world's fortune; I wanted their blessing on me and Drew. I said, "You can stay here during the week, so you can walk to your schools."

"Dad told us that." Ruth looked as if this was old news. "He said we'd work out summers and stuff like that."

Martha reached across and patted my hand. I must have looked the way I felt: at a loss. At a lot of loss.

"You know what, Momma?" Beautiful deep-eyed Ruth made her own sort of rescue effort.

"What?"

"Dr. Song is going to install a computer here for us, in the study. She doesn't need it anymore. She's on a mainframe in Austin and she's going to be part of the information highway, you know, the gigabit network that does billions of bits of data per second. She says we'll be *know-bots* by next year." She tugged on her clumps of hair, as if sending signals. "It'll do graphs and everything, ours will. You can show that two hundred sixty thousand acres of forest have already been cut to support a meat-eating society, and show that every single individual who switches to a vegetarian diet saves an acre of trees. You can *show* that. It's fantastic. I'm going to do some charts for Earth Day. For school."

Dr. Song? Could that be the chiding Jae-Moon? Or someone else from Eben's new Korean sister church, perhaps the reason for the sister church? He had been busy indeed, the pastor, making sure my leaving was definitely minor news on the home front.

Angry, I spoke before I could stop myself. "How does that compare ecologically? Trading a mother for a computer?"

Ruth leaned her curving GREEN-SPIRITED self toward me. "Gee, Momma, you don't have to take it like that."

Martha came around the table and gave me a squeeze, burying her soft face in my hair. "We didn't want to make you feel bad, talking about the divorce. You know, acting like we were upset."

I shook my head, apologetic. "I was out of order. Sorry. I just wanted—" If they argued cows and forests, who was to say that was not the constancy in their lives they required now. And if they had technology to help them along, so much the better. I needed to recycle my response. "I only wanted you to know that my leaving your daddy doesn't mean my leaving you."

"Sure, Momma." Ruth seemed impatient with my speeches. Maybe Eben had said the same things; maybe she had a harder time hearing them a second time, having to put up her defenses twice.

She carried our bowls to the kitchen. When she came back, still standing, she said, as if it wasn't important, "That's what Dad said. He said that you all splitting and them getting together didn't have anything to do with us.

We know that." She crossed her arms over her chest, looking at the two of us. "How about if we go get some Bluebell ice cream?" She stared at her younger sister, her face sending the message that this was the concession of a lifetime. *"Ice cream*, Mart."

"Can we?" Martha jumped up, beaming. "Really? Can we, Momma? I want fresh peach."

MONDAY MORNING I decided I'd better bite the bullet. It was clear that I was going to need my next of kin.

Before I could dial, though, while I was having one cup of coffee too many and trying to psych myself up, she beat me to it. My unfavorite teacher, also known as my daddy's wife.

"I hear you've got yourself in a big mess," she said.

"Hello, Theo."

"I've come up in the world. Last time it was 'Miss Moore.' "

"Come on."

"It wasn't? Worse than that?"

"How'd you hear?"

"Little birdie."

"Teachers always have their spies."

"Come for lunch."

"Why don't I?"

"Shorty'll be pleased."

"How come he's not fishing?"

"Folklore. Fish don't bite on Monday. Besides, you must not have been out. There's a tornado watch."

"Watch? I don't have the radio on."

"Watch, not warning. That just means it's officially April."

"Give me half an hour."

"Don't get lost this time, girl. Remember R-O-B-I-N."

"Right."

Theodora Moore and Shorty Guest had lived in Waco now for three years come summer, their arrival preceding me and Drew at the Czech Fest by a couple of months. I hadn't been a bit glad at the time to hear that she'd got Daddy to retire and was moving him back to her old home grounds. I hadn't wanted to claim kin to them, for one thing; for another, I couldn't bear for Lila Beth to have any inkling that I could be related to a couple whose house with filled with *objet knickknacks* and whose car had a bumper sticker saying DOO-DOO HAPPENS.

Once a month maximum I dropped by for coffee. Theo taught at Waco High, English same as always, and sooner or later Ruth and then Martha were going to have her, and then she could announce that these girls were her secondhand grandbabies, but they could deal with that. They went over with me once or twice a year, for birthdays, somebody's, just often enough that I didn't have to feel guilty for keeping my only kin in a closet. Eben had come along at a time when I was scarcely speaking to them, had actually not met them until two weeks before our wedding. They weren't churchgoers, and one reason I had them on my mind now was that they might be the only people in town that Eben hadn't got to first.

R-O-B-I-N was an acronym designed to help me find

their house. It was clear I had a block of some sort, because I never headed over there that I didn't get hopelessly lost. I could find any street at all in our area; weaving around Lake View, Loch View, Lago Vista, Laguna Vista was no sweat, they presented themselves to me without a wrong turn. Or the woody section where Baby and Sugar Bledsoe lived—the Wood Oaks, Oak Wood, Forest Oaks, Oak Forest fell into formation for me. But let me turn into Shorty and Theo's part of town, an area reclaimed, like Holland from the sea, from the marshy shores of Lake Waco, and I was instantly lost.

The first time I went calling, map in hand, to welcome them to town, I never found their house. All the streets were named for birds (Whippoorwill, Thrush, Falcon, Wren, Finch), and each street curved in a circle or semi-circle or cul-de-sac, most of them winding back around on themselves, so that it was worse than a maze. They were junky, new, expensive places, freestanding condos close to all Shorty's favorite fishing spots, and near lots of his retired fishing buddies. R-O-B-I-N was the order of the streets I was to take off Lake Shore. The trouble was, no matter how good my intent, it was impossible to tell if I was on the right route until it was too late. Both Redwing and Redbird ran into Oriole, and Oriole opened out into both Bobolink and Bobwhite, so that if I got to that point and didn't find Ibis, then I knew I'd taken the wrong turn. Once I found Ibis, then it was a choice between Nighthawk and Nightingale, and if I took the wrong one I ended up back on Redbird, and had to start over.

"You made record time," Theo said at the door.

"I'm educable." I'd made it in fifteen minutes flat, no errors. It was a piece of cake. All I had to remember was -wing, -link, -gale. W-L-G. Where Lives Guest? Absolute cake. It just went to show how much resistance there'd been to ending up on this doorstep.

"That I know." Theo smiled a proud teacher's smile. She was a dumpling of a woman with chubby cheeks and curly hair and always some sort of flowery flour-sack kind of dress, over, I was sure, an underwired push-up bra.

"How come you're home at noon?" I asked her.

"I've got such seniority I have my two free periods back-to-back. Gives us time for a bite and a nap."

Shorty was in the carport on a stool, working on what looked like a funnel made of close-weave chicken wire. A bait trap. "I've got a wager going," he said, nodding to acknowledge me. "Buddy of mine runs a trotline, he uses bluegills. Me, I use goggle-eyed perch. I wouldn't bait out with anything else. For big yellow cat they're the best. They're soft; catfish like that. Little ones, two inches. Plus goggle-eyes stay alive on the line for the best part of a week. Bluegills, bream, they die whenever they feel like it. I got him beat last year, six yellows over forty-five pounds. One big yellow weighed seventy-six. But he caught an eighty-five pounder. So we've got a wager." He stood and gave me a kiss. Not smelling of beer the way he always used to. Smelling maybe of mouthwash. "Go on in. I'll be there."

"Campaign posters in the yard." I gestured as Theo and I headed for the flowered kitchen hung with wall sconces and potted ivy.

"Runoff's tomorrow. Our hometown girl better win."

"Will she?"

"Be nice to have governor number four from Waco. Be even nicer to have a woman in that mansion, somebody with a little backbone. I've been calling every name in the book, canvassing. I'm taking a day of sick leave to drive folks to the polls. But I don't know. It's pitiful, just pitiful how nasty the campaign got there at the end."

Shorty came in and pulled out a chair. "Sit," he said. "Let me look at you."

"We're having a sandwich," Theo said to me. "What'll you have?"

"What are my options?"

"I'm having a Cream Cheese and Olive on White. Your daddy is having a Garden of Eden on Wheat."

"What's that?"

"Peanut butter mixed with butter on both slices, a leaf of lettuce dipped in French dressing in between."

Shorty said, "I named it. They haven't let us eat like that since the Garden of Eden."

"Give me cream cheese," I said. "Cut the olives."

Looking at my daddy always gave me hives, right off. Because he resembled me a whole lot, but was double the size, and had an attitude of insubordination to the universe in general, which seemed a total mismatch to Theo's reverence for the system. What I did like about him, a lot, was that he never reproached me for the fact that we lived in the same town and didn't set eyes on each other for a couple of months of Sundays at a time. Mother was in the way between us, and I guess he knew that.

He was recounting now his latest trip to the doctor, for, he said, a little "pros*trate*" trouble." Wheezing laughter at his joke.

"Iced tea?" Theo said.

"Fine."

"Sweetened?"

"No." I looked at Shorty. His hair and eyebrows were a sort of tan-white and bushy. He had a million laugh or sun lines around his eyes and mouth. It felt somewhat like looking at myself down the road. I hoped I wasn't going to be rotund. "So how's it going?" I asked him. "Your plumbing and your gums?" He'd also been on the periodontist circuit.

"Ask the wife." He waved a hand at Theo. "No booze, no smokes. She's got me on a health regime."

"Obviously not a diet."

"Trade-off. All the food and nookie I want, no other vices." He lifted the top of his sandwich and took a peek at the oily ruffled lettuce leaf inside, then stirred a pudgy finger around in the creamy peanut butter. He took a bite. "You know how you can tell old folks in bed?" he asked with his mouth full.

"How?"

"He lifts her nightie, gets his hardware out, and after they're done, he says, 'Did you aerobic?' and she says, 'It was cardiovascular for me.' " Wheeze, wheeze.

Theo sat down, bringing my sandwich and hers.

"What did your little birdie tell you?" I asked her.

"That there was a particle physicist in the church-yard."

"The wife is the last to know," I said mildly. I was recalling Eben saying he'd asked Jae-Moon to help with Easter. Seeing the Korean woman with the high cheek-bones and glossy black hair seize my hands in obvious joy on Palm Sunday. Hearing the girls report that Dr. Song was moving in a computer. It was clear I'd handed the pastor a bow-tied gift.

"And that you've hooked up with your old school days' boyfriend."

"Drew. Drew Williams."

"He changed his name," Shorty said. "Used to be Andy."

"His wife did that."

"You going to change it back?"

"If we get around to it."

"His old man was a doctor, friendly with your mother."

"Yes, he was the head clinician—" I looked at Theo,

always making the mistake of thinking she was going to be jealous of somebody who'd been dead for twenty-plus years. When she actually owed my mother a lot, namely Shorty.

"Nice boy."

"His mother was a Jarvis." Theo said. She'd polished off her cream cheese and sliced olive sandwich with mayonnaise, and was looking at the remains of mine with hurt feelings. "I was in school with her. What a priss. Everything was monogrammed. Most likely even her heinie. Lila Beth Jarvis. LBJ this and LBJ that, on her notebooks and her hankies and her Ship 'n' Shore blouses. Most likely her boy's got that monogram somewhere. She going to let him go?"

"That's the question."

"But that's not what brought you here, is it, girl?"

"No."

"You want the guest room? The Guests' guest room. Be our Guest."

Oh, Lord, I'd forgotten that routine. Doo-doo happens, I reminded myself. "I might," I admitted. "Eben has given me two weeks to get out."

"Used to be," Theo said, "in Texas law you could kill your wife for messing around."

Shorty licked his fingers. "Only if you caught them flagrant."

"That means blazing or burning," I told him.

"That's what I said, caught 'em hot."

"That reminds me." Theo looked at her watch, looked sadly at my half of the cream cheese sandwich, and stood, her uplift shaking.

"What does?"

"You whipping out that definition. I've got something for you. I dug it out when I heard the news, brought it home. Let me go locate it. Sit tight; don't jump up and run off the way you usually do."

"I'm not budging."

Shorty gave me a fatherly look. "Nice boy. So what's going on?"

"He's the one for me."

"That's good. Old age isn't for sissies. Being happy helps the odds." He gazed off after Theo. "What's he up to these days?"

"He's worried about losing his land. The government's wanting to buy up the acres around Waxahachie for the atom smasher."

"Tell me about science. Worse than boll weevils. This used to be great country for hardware. Farmers buying out the stock faster than you could order it. Then we started hug dancing with the Japanese, and everything went soft. Now there's nothing but software from Austin to Dallas. No wonder I closed up my business and took early fishing."

"We're going to live on his farm."

"Any rivers?"

"Stock ponds."

Theo bounced back in, waving a sheet of paper. "Here we go. Remember this?"

It was Cile's Red Bird Quiz. Heaven help us. She must have squirreled this away nearly twenty years ago. I was touched, really touched. "Miss Moore," I said, "you old sneak."

She looked pleased with herself. "I still pass this out in my classes, to give the kids an idea what's coming down when they take the SAT." She pronounced it *sat*. "I figured you'd be needing it back yourself about now, for a little advance advertising. I priced around for you. The standard outfit that they all use, the cram course, costs seven hundred for seven four-hour sessions. That's twenty-five an hour. Seems to me you can charge twice that, charge fifty, for a one-on-one. Say you saw ten students a week, that would tide you over, wouldn't it? Now it's a seasonal market, like income tax and Christmas, but you'd have a spring crop and a fall crop. This is a good time to get your name out there, end of the term."

Cile's Red Bird Quiz. Lord. Did that take me back. To the younger Mrs. Dr. Croft and all her cronies who'd been so good to me when I'd been starting out. It had been my quick-check reading comprehension test to see where the student was. She took the test, he took it, while I watched, and at the point where they looked up, having trouble, I knew where to begin. The paragraphs and their multiple-choice questions in those days went through a consistent pattern: the word required was stated; it was in an earlier passage; its synonym or antonym was there; it was inferred.

Shorty motioned me to move over close and we read it together, him looking over my shoulder, moving his lips.

1. Out my window this morning I saw a red bird at the feeder. What color is the bird at the feeder?
   a. brown
   b. black
   c. red
   d. blue
2. A redbird swooped down into the pear tree. I watched as he took flight again, then landed at the feeder.
   What color is the bird at the feeder?
   a. brown
   b. black
   c. red
   d. blue

3. The crimson-breasted cardinal sang from the highest branch of the dogwood, a brilliant contrast to the brown-coated sparrows eating below. He landed in their midst, scattering them in the air.
What color is the bird at the feeder?
   a. brown
   b. black
   c. red
   d. blue

4. What a variety of birds at the sunflower seeds outside my window: a crow, a jay, a cardinal, a sparrow. Then they were joined by the tabby tomcat from next door, out for a morning stalk. Quickly the crow, cardinal and sparrow took flight. What color is the bird at the feeder?
   a. brown
   b. black
   c. red
   d. blue

It made me happy to remember how hard I'd worked to develop the stilted style of the prose, trying to match the stilted style of the paragraphs on the actual test. Reading it again brought back half a dozen faces, the quick grins and troubled frowns of my favorites. Great kids. I hoped they were all whatever they wanted to be. Imagining a coterie of thoracic surgeons and rat-lab researchers who owed it all to me.

"Hey, you pulled a fast one on that last one," Shorty said, reading it over again. "A switch."

"Harvard for you," I said.

"You want me to mention your name for a SAT coach?" Theo looked at her watch again and slipped into her tiny-heeled pumps, a bright blue the color of the garden on her dress.

"You kept this all these years?"

"All these years." She turned rosy. "You were my prize, girl. I followed everything you did. I wouldn't have set my cap for your daddy here if I hadn't wanted to have a shot at the source."

"Thanks."

"Clean sheets in the back bedroom."

"I might take you up on it, while I'm looking for a place."

"Tell your boy to come see us." Shorty was setting out bottles on the counter for his after-lunch fix. Geritol, Solotron, PABA, zinc, choline, folic acid, biotin. He washed down a handful of tablets with the last of his Dr. Pepper.

"When it's official." The idea of Drew over here in Birdville still gave me a slight skin itch, not quite hives but a kissing cousin.

"I won't hold his dad against him," Shorty said, shaking out a second batch of supplements in his hand.

"I won't hold his mom against him," Theo said, jiggling her car keys in the doorway.

"All I want to hold against him is me." I clowned, imitating a big squeeze.

Theo led me out the kitchen door—past bundles of newspapers waiting for pickup, and bags labeled PLASTIC, ALUMINUM and PAPER—and we got Shorty settled on his stool, working on his bait trap.

Exiting the area was as simple as pie. I did my trick backward, Guest Lives Where, taking Nightin-*gale* to Ibis to Bobo-*link* to Oriole to Red-*wing*, and there I was back on Lake Shore. I made the turn with a feeling of satisfaction. I, too, had spread the word: Theo would be sure to drop a little gossip in the teachers' lounge, and Shorty would break the news to his pals while they watched the big yellows choose between goggle-eyes and bluegills.

'D PAID NO attention to the sky in my anxiety about not getting lost on the way to the Guest house, but once safely back on familiar turf, I could see that the air indeed had that eerie yellow calm, that creepy stillness of tornado weather. I tuned the radio to the Best Country in the City, figuring the deejay would interrupt the Randy Travis vocal if there was any serious trouble.

When I was first learning my way around Waco, it had helped to see it as shaped like a kite, the top pointing northwest toward Ft. Worth, the upper right side being the Brazos River, the upper left the South Fork of the Bosque, the bottom right the Austin highway, and the bottom left the Old Mill Road, which I now turned onto from Lago Lake. Heading toward the kite's base, the circle where five highways intersected, where the kite tails were tied.

Drew pulled off the freeway just as I pulled up to the front of Circleburgers. It gave me a thrill to have him park his red Chevy pickup right beside my rattling, sagging old Firebird, bold as you please. For us to be having a date in a public place hadn't happened since high school. A couple of lifetimes ago.

He steered me through the door. "What do you want?"

"Chiliburger." Inhaling the great hickory smoke aroma I managed to forget that I'd already gummed up my stomach with cream cheese.

Drew ordered two chiliburgers, two flameburgers, one large vanilla shake, one large strawberry shake, one double order of French fries, one double order of onion rings and two peach fried pies with extra powdered sugar.

I dug out a fistful of quarters and headed for the jukebox. The green and purple Wurlitzer gave one selection for a quarter or three for fifty cents—so I played all our George Strait favorites: "Hot Burning Flames," "That's When the Cowboy Rides Away," "Second Chances," "All My Exes Live in Texas," "Heaven Must Be Wondering Where You Are." Then, just to be ecumenical, Hank Williams, Jr.'s "This Ain't Dallas" and Willie Nelson's "All of Me."

We sat side by side in the last booth, where we could look down the wall at a couple of dozen framed photos of the fifties high school scene: marching bands, drill teams, parades, football players, homecoming queens riding on the backs of convertibles, holding roses and waving at the crowd. Right at eye level at our booth was a fullback with gigantic shoulder pads and black smudges under his eyes, his arm around a girl in a suit and heels, who had a big mum corsage and smooth flipped hair. They were leaning against a Chevy Bel Air. I nudged Drew, who was staring at his stub, waiting for them to call our order.

"Look."

"Son-of-a-gun." He peered around me. "A '57. Green and cream, I bet." He looked closer at the black and white photo, sounding about as excited as if I'd showed him a sack of potatoes. Obviously things hadn't gone all that great with his mother.

When he brought the tray of food, we just sat there looking at the best hamburgers in Texas, the thickest shakes, onion rings crisp and juicy at the same time, fried pies still steaming, the powdered sugar melting.

"Bad?" I asked.

"Bad."

"Real bad?"

"Worse."

George Strait was singing about Heaven at top volume. We could have shouted and not been heard by the staff in the back. There was nobody else there; it was too early for school kids, too late for the lunch crowd. Probably we could have been meeting here for years, but we'd been too scared to try it.

He took a swallow of the strawberry shake so I sipped the vanilla, wondering if I'd got a milk mustache like Martha.

"Tell me," I said.

"You want to hear about it?"

"I asked."

"She's trying to box me in the canyon. They are."

Out the window, right past the highway intersection, we could see little whirls of wind pick up and drop bits of paper, and hear a slight whine in the air that hadn't been there before. Off in the distance, we could make out a couple of dark cones that might be little twisters touching down in cornfields.

"Great—" Drew interrupted himself. "We'll get a tornado warning and have to sit here until supper, or the whole place will be lifted up into the sky and they'll find us twelve blocks north on Baylor campus."

"How bad?"

"Bad." He ate half a flameburger, getting sauce on his white shirt. "See, we own the land jointly, Mother and I. Undivided halves. That's so one of us doesn't have the oil and one of us the milo blight. We split the proceeds and losses. Undivided half means survivor gets all. Dad went over it with me a couple of years before he died, the will. It was holographic, just a few lines on a piece of his office paper. I didn't really think about it; it seemed a couple of decades too soon, you know? I mean he'd just turned sixty but he looked the same to me as he always had. You remember him from when he used to hang around the clinic with your mom. He always looked like he just rode into town on a horse; that weathered skin and shoulders wider than mine even at his age. He'd grown a mustache right before we left Austin, but he shaved that off, and his hair had got salt-and-pepper, or whatever we redheads get: salt-and-cayenne."

"I know you miss him."

"He was a white hat." He stared at his burger. "You want to hear about it?"

"I want to hear about it."

"What Dad had in mind, undivided halves, was that Mother couldn't sell without me and I couldn't sell without her, so nobody could sell off the land. That's what he figured. But it doesn't work that way because of Mary Virginia. Half of my half is hers, community property, acquired after marriage, commingled. Mother says that makes Mary Virginia a swing vote, and that I might as well get it through my head that I'm not going to be able to get a divorce without selling off a lot of land. Mary Virginia and Mother own three-fourths between them, I guess that's what she means. I guess she was trying to say that they can vote to sell seventy-five percent of the whole spread if they want to. Good-bye grasslands, I think was the message over garden greens at lunch."

That sounded like a threat, and a threat didn't sound like Lila Beth. "What bothers her the most?" I asked. "The divorce? Us? The church?"

Drew put an arm around me, eating the French fries with his left hand. "Beats me."

We could hear the high wail that meant a tornado warning.

"Shit. It's going to hit."

"We have these six times a week in the spring; you're just spooked."

"I guess." He looked at me. "I don't know what Mother wants. What she said was—" He had trouble getting the words out. "—that I'd get over you. That I got over you once and I could do it again."

"What happens now?" I wanted to know where he was, if she'd talked him out of us.

Willie Nelson was urging us to take all of him, while outside the whine had got louder and the wind buffeted the sides of the diner. The sky had got dark, so it was passing through. The staff from the kitchen leaned on the counter, looking out the windows, watching also. They had cups of coffee and one of them was smoking under the THANK YOU FOR NOT SMOKING sign. They didn't seem bothered.

"I don't know, honey. I can't think straight. It's easy to say that we'll go ahead and move in together at the farm and I'll get a job pumping gas and we can tell them to go to hell. But all I know is that land; all I have is that land—"

"What does Mary Virginia say about it?"

"Same as always, zip. A closed subject. Goes on about my birthday, the boys' camp. Her schedule."

"Can't you talk to her?"

"Not a chance. Tomorrow, Tuesday, is her day in Dallas. Since it's the runoff election, though, she's decided the highways won't be safe in the morning or at night, country people going to the polls in their horse and buggies, to hear her tell it, so she's going up this afternoon, coming back on Wednesday. She does that now about twice a month. Her mother's under the weather, or her sister's having trouble with her husband, who's losing about a billion dollars on ParkGate, that planned community they sunk their shirts in. Two golf courses, beach and tennis clubs, stables, thirteen lakes. They thought they'd be getting thirty gee an acre for it; now it's on the market."

While Hank Williams, Jr., reminded us that this wasn't Dallas, I tried to read between the lines, to figure out what was really going on. "How about the boys?" I asked him.

"Come in wearing their tennis whites, go back to their wing and do whatever preppy types do. What do they do? File their compact discs? Buzz their computers? Amortize their tennis rackets? One thing they don't do is talk to their old man. They've been momma-pecked since the crib. Dallas boys. I've got a couple of sweetheart Dallas boys."

"Drew, don't. Don't say that. They're two of the— greatest kids in the world."

"You always could get along with them." He looked dejectedly at his strawberry shake, finished it off.

I was trying not to feel hurt, way down deep hurt, that Lila Beth could have such strong objections to Drew and me. I'd thought that she would be pleased; she'd never got on with Mary Virginia, not from the start, not really. It must be the church. Her loyalties were divided; she'd be bothered to think we were responsible for breaking up her pastor's home. "When Eben marries again," I said, "your mother will feel differently. Maybe we'll just have to wait."

"Him, remarry? I never figured out how he located some in the first place; he'll never get his hands on some a second time."

That gave me a couple of mixed feelings, none of them kindly. I told him about Jae-Moon, also known as Dr. Song, who apparently was already the successor designate.

"No kidding," he said, requiring the rest of his burger. "Him? With a Korean? A physicist? Tell me he walks on the Bosque or he's parting the Brazos, I'd believe that sooner."

"He wants me out in two weeks. I'm going to stay at Shorty and Theo's unless I can find a place." I was trying to spell out for him that I was putting no pressure on to move up to the farm.

"At your dad's?" He looked amazed.

"I had lunch with them today."

He laughed. "Any birdhouse in the storm?" I'd told him about getting lost in the bird streets every time I went to see them.

"Something like that."

Out the window we could see a funnel drop down and lift a billboard in the air like a paper cup and then dump it in a field a few feet away. Cars on the freeway didn't take notice. The siren went off once more, a sighting, and then the sky began to take on a dusty look, rosy and windy.

"The trouble with the spotters," Drew said, "is that they only spot it after it's happened. The Severe Storms Center issues *watches*, but it's the local weather stations give *warnings*. By the time they do, the tornado's history. They had a three-hundred-mile-an-hour wind in Kansas. Too late is long gone. Oklahoma's got Nexrad, a fancy Doppler radar system. They can tell, by winds going both ways at once, what's going to happen. We could get one of those here if anybody cared; we've got half of all the weather in the United States."

He studied the view of cars going on about their driving, started on the second flameburger. "What're you gonna do?"

"Eben is giving me five thousand. I can use it for a year's rent, or a down payment on a house. With the market depressed like it is, that should cover either."

"Five thousand? That's *it*? Fifteen years of working for the church and him and he's giving you five thousand? That's less severance pay than our maids get." He looked outraged, unbelieving.

"Pastors don't have money, you know that. That's half

of what he's got left from his father. I have a little bit from my mother. That's fair. He's going to be supporting the girls." I pressed my fingers to my eyes to stop them from getting the idea that they could cry. Smearing both milk shake and chili on my face: not a help.

I had no idea what I'd tell my girls. Their fighting about cows suddenly seemed the warmest of responses. The kindest of acknowledgments that I was free to go off with someone special, to a farm we both loved. It was permission for me to have a future. The idea of having to tell them there'd been a change in plans, that I was leaving them so I could crash at my old teacher's house and help her recycle Dr. Pepper cans and plastic detergent bottles made my heart sink. "I need to go," I said. "I have to get back."

The twister had moved on, out to pasture or up the road. They always came from the west, dying when they met civilization; they were like wild animals in that regard.

Drew wiped my eyes with a hickory-smoked paper napkin. "I didn't want to tell you," he said. "She dropped that on me, that Mary Virginia could probably force me to sell, and then, when I tried to talk about it, she closed up. We had our salads, and I couldn't tell you if you asked me what was on that plate." He kissed my eyes dry. Then pulled my hand down under the table so I could feel he was hard. The staff was busy in the kitchen. The football player and his girl were still leaning on their Bel Air. "We'll work it out," Drew said. "I love you."

"I think that's a '55," I said.

Getting out of the booth, leaving him with the peach fried pies, I located my car keys and waved good-bye. I could hardly see to walk across the floor; it didn't help that George Strait, out of all the songs he knew, picked just then to sing "This Is Where the Cowboy Rides Away."

COW'S PARTY AT the farm seemed to be disappearing down a distant farm-to-market, the way an apparent puddle glints always just ahead on the interstate, a mirage dwindling just out of reach. Such was my vision of Martha, dimpling her cheeks against the soft hides of Holstein, Ruth calculating acres of waving grain, pitchers of fresh chilled milk waiting on the old tile counter, sweet Czech dough rising on the stove.

While Drew rallied his resistance to all those trying to pull the land out from under him, what was I to do? I felt a rising panic, seeing my plans for a country home slipping away. When was I going to see my girls? Where? If I was thrown out of the church's house, if the old homestead up the road was put on hold to me, where would I be? Where could they find me? I felt suddenly dispossessed, both of them and of a place to welcome them. I needed a halfway house, a stopping place, a shelter with walls, front door, deep shady yard, where they could come. A place they could hang their spare T-shirts and call ours.

Eben's cash was the one card I had to play; so I played it. I got a copy of a glossy real estate booklet, "The Home-finders' Guide," complete with photos, addresses, asking prices and salient information about available locations. Each listing the basics (bedrooms, baths, square footage), each tagged with a come-on comment. As it turned out, it was easy as pie to buy a house that a bank had paid its own note on for a couple of years.

First of all, it was a revelation to find that every house in town was not a ranchstyle, because that was all you ever saw: luxury ranches, like Mary Virginia's, authentic ranches, like the parsonage, ranchettes with carports, like those in Birdville, cutesy red-and-white barn decor ranches where doctors lived. Every house in town a low-slung, low-ceilinged ranch. Yet here on every page of the realtors' guide were options from the past. A bungalow with shingled roof and dormer windows ("completely restored, must see to appreciate"); an all-brick Tudor ("nice older home, near hospital"); a Victorian two-story ("beautifully updated and maintained"); an arched and columned Greek Revival ("an antique lover's delight, large rooms"); a Colonial with gallery porch ("lots of charm, formal dining"). What a wealth of choices!

And, the amazing thing—somewhat analogous to connecting dots and seeing a figure appear on a page—was that when I'd circled all my choices on the city map, the locations were clustered within walking distance of one another. I'd found a neighborhood. One that, in ten years of living in Waco, I'd never set foot in. It was as far to the east of Heart of Texas Fairgrounds and the middle school and high school as we were to the west, about a mile. An older area, clearly, and one with no cross streets, no through streets, so that unless you were going home or to visit kin, there was no occasion to find yourself on its tree-lined streets. Trees large enough, and old enough, to have been worth the asking price of the houses alone.

With a realtor at the wheel of her shiny son-of-Pinto red Ford Escort, I set out to look at all the treasures I'd marked. She was a nice lady of my general age with a shaved neck and wedge bangs, gold triangles weighing down her earlobes, and a snappy red tailored suit; and when she eyed my dilapidated Firebird and said, "Those muscle cars look like they're speeding when they're sitting at the curb," I knew we were going to get on fine.

I said it didn't bother me at all if she lit up in her own car. My mind was on what I was going to find: afraid that my picks, without the cosmetic photography, would look like slumlord specials. Or else be buckling on their foundations after several decades of Waco weather, expanding, contracting, heating, freezing, being battered by hail and lashed by winds. Or that I'd find just that inimitable something that makes a neighborhood feel down, gone, depressed, the victim of generations of renters who move through homes with the disregard of squirrels in an attic.

None of that turned out to be the case. I loved the streets. I loved the houses. I wanted to stop at every second one so the red lady could look it up to be sure it wasn't also for sale.

Urging her to park and have another smoke, I pried a little information about the area from her.

"It went downhill for a few years after it became mixed," she said, eyeing me to be sure we were speaking the same language. I nodded. I knew she meant blacks, blacks who had moved in at the same time the black and white school systems had merged.

"Lots of folks had bought on spec, to rent out or sell quick, prices were high, everything was selling, real high. Then after the oil crash and then the stock crash, there was wholesale liquidation. People owned three or four, thought they'd make a killing, were glad just to get out from under the notes. The banks foreclosed but they were trying not to go belly-up themselves. Then, few years ago, families began to buy back in. Lower mortgage rates, lower asking prices, good solid homes, and by then the area was multicolored. You following me?"

I was. The same thing had happened to the schools. A

lot of panic when black faces first appeared in the halls
and on the playing fields, but then, by the time the influx
of scientists from the Pacific Rim had arrived, the mathe-
maticians from India, and the postinflation waves from
interior Mexico, plus islanders of all sorts—from Cuba,
Haiti, Dominican Republic, St. Croix, Puerto Rico, Britain, Manhattan—polyglot seemed the norm. Every school
became a mini-UN, every class a geography lesson, every
extracurricular activity a multicultural experience. Apparently the neighborhood had followed suit.

It was clear by the time I was house shopping that the
area was mixed and stable, well built and conveniently
located, and generally pleased with itself. And it showed,
in the well-tended yards and face-lifted homes.

I almost bought "completely restored, must see to appreciate." It had a claw-footed tub in the bath, a nearly
new roof, and the original front door, circa 1915. It had a
small porch, the dormer windows, and a working fireplace, laid, for effect, with mesquite logs. (The central air
was going full blast; it was already eighty-nine degrees
outside.) The rooms were large and the ceilings high. The
problem was there were only one-and-a-half bedrooms, one
bath, a living room and an eat-in-kitchen, as the realtor
in red called it. If the girls came for the weekend—and the
closeness to their schools made it a lure in that way—where
would I put them? Plus, if I was going to run my SAT study
course from the house, and I'd have to, that would have to
be quartered in the living room or the tiny bedroom. But I
didn't like the feel of that; it would have the aura of a counselor's cubicle. (Houses of that vintage, which included the
parsonage, all had apparently had nurseries.)

It was only that fact, the small size, that made me take
a look at the "beautifully updated and maintained" Victorian two-story. I didn't like all the gingerbread trim in

the photo, plus it was listed at $48,000, more than I could swing. But it was just around the corner from the bungalow, and we decided to walk, so I could get a feel for the area. Also so the realtor could have another cigarette without smelling up her car. I can't say I fell in love with the place at first sight; it was, to be charitable, an eyesore from half a block away. Someone had added a lot of junky additional trim: latticework over the bay window, tacked-on boxes filled with plastic flowers, some scalloped Swedish-looking panels on the gabled roof. Plus the outside had been painted robin's egg blue with pink trim. "No," I said, "not possible."

But my guide had her keys out; she knew I was going to buy the house, probably by the strength of my protest.

One of the problems was, being the only Victorian on the block, it stood out like a sore thumb. The other was the extra frosting on the already frosted cake, the extra gilding on the already gilded lily.

"Picture it gray," the lady in red said, her gold triangles swinging as she cased it up and down. "Maybe white? Look inside. It's a find. One of a kind."

Inside had its own problem. Someone had walled up the fireplace and put a potbellied black stove four feet out in the living room. But apart from that, it was a dream. Ten-foot-high ceilings, hardwood floors rubbed smooth, wide stairs curving over a half bath, a generous dining room that could serve, with the proper table, as a work space for students, sunny, airy, grand, a kitchen with a gas stove that looked about the vintage of the house, 1885, and a bulky refrigerator not much younger, and behind that a storage area that had once been the "root room." Upstairs, a full bath and two large bedrooms on one side of the stairs, plenty of room for the Taits and Bledsoes both and, over the kitchen, a third bedroom with an adjoining walk-in attic space. (This had a trapdoor and wall ladder down into the root room, like a secret passage.)

"There's a four-hundred-sixteen-dollar-a-month note you can assume," the realtor said, confident, blowing smoke.

"I can put four thousand down. Get rid of the potbelly and I'll take it."

"Asking is forty-eight."

I looked out the bay window; what a room for reading comprehension. There was a Chinese tallow tree high as the house in the front yard. Definitely a *redbird* tree. "It's been sitting empty," I bargained.

"A year."

"More like three."

"It's possible."

"They shouldn't have junked it up with the alpine-awful trim."

"Who knows? Sometimes that sells."

I studied the patent latch, the machine-made screws, the rim lock, all late nineteenth century. I knew that stuff because Drew made such a big deal about how the farmhouse, which was old enough to be the momma of this one, had hardware and trim that dated back before mass production: mortise locks, pointless screws, latches made by blacksmiths. It made me smile to think that this house built in 1885 was too modern, too new, for Drew's taste. But the thing I liked about Victorians was their exuberance for what industrialization could do, their love affair with the steam-powered scroll saw, their finials, canopies, brackets, vergeboards: advertisements for the Machine Age.

I restated my offer. "Four thousand down, get rid of the potbelly, let me assume the note. Tell the bank you found a sucker at last for the blue cuckoo clock."

"It might be possible." She put on her shades, and we went at a trot to her Escort, where she used the car phone to get things primed back at the home office. While she drove, I drew a little map on the back of my "Homefinders' Guide" so I wouldn't get lost: Huckleberry to Mulberry to Blackberry to Hackberry. Then straight down Hackberry to the Heart of Texas Fairgrounds, the schools and Lake Shore.

At the red lady's office, I listed the parsonage as my present home; Shorty's as my place of business; my income as $20,000 a year, invented on the spot; Theo and the bank that handled Eben's money as financial references. It wasn't solid enough to get a loan on a doghouse, but to pick up a note that the bank had been paying itself for a few years, it might float.

After my guide got back in her Ford, off to show a nice place in the Oak Hurst area to a family of newcomers, I drove back to gingerbread heaven, down Hackberry to Blackberry to Mulberry to Huckleberry, just over a mile. I sat at the curb, car door open, looking at my new home, a structure not unlike the witch's house in "Hansel and Gretel." I was squinting, trying to picture it elephant gray, when a car squealed to a stop in the middle of the street, a beat-up, block-long metallic brown Olds, so rusted out it was hard to tell where real metal met its imitation, and so low to the ground (springs not even a nascent memory), its tail pipe dragged the street. A heap not even Drew would have been inclined to recycle.

A couple of hoods got out, waved a thanks, and sidled over to where I was sitting. One had on a gaucho hat, shaved sideburns, red Nike solo flyers with laces loose, shorts, and a T-shirt that read BE A DICK: PLAY HARD. The other, whose dark hair was slicked back and rubber-banded, wore black hightops, black shorts, and a black T that said WISH YOU WERE HERE, with a wide arrow that pointed straight down to his crotch. A couple of winners. I would have been nervous, but it was daylight, and despite the tough outfits, these were kids. Maybe they'd been crashing in the vacant house.

"How's it going, Cile?" the one in the gaucho hat said.

"You buying this place?" the one all in black asked, leaning on the car door.

I wouldn't have believed it, except that voices were like fingerprints, dead giveaways. It was Trey and Jock. Trey in the hat; Jock with the pigtail.

After a moment of total shock, I leaped up and gave them hugs. "You guys? Is it really? My eyes say Quit your kidding, but my ears say Yes."

"It's us." Trey pulled off his wide-brimmed hat so I could see his red almost-Mohawk hairdo. "We hitched a ride after you when we saw you getting in your car. One of your GYN jocks told us you and the preacher had split. Like we didn't have our own inside source. Like she was right, naturally, since nobody actually says anything to anybody ever at our house."

"No offense—but what's with the punk outfits?"

They looked proud of themselves. Jock said, "We turn the shirts inside out for class, not to freak out the pedagogues. They used to make kids wear their clothes right side out, then they were sorry. Now they leave us alone."

I gave them a grin. These cute boys. Who would have thought? "You know exactly what I'm trying to say. Your mom and dad don't see you looking like this, I know they don't."

Trey gazed at his red boots. "They don't see what they don't want to see. See, we come in and put on our tennis whites, wear them till we go to bed. Mom's not up when we leave and she's not around when we get back, Dad's not there, all they ever see is at supper, or we're going out, and we've got on our tennis whites. Wearing tennis gear you could rob a bank or snuff a herd of bluehairs and nobody who saw you would believe it. Not them, Officer, they had tennis rackets."

We wandered over to look at the blue monster. I was remembering Drew's description of his boys at home; it made me happy, how in control they were of their world. Maybe they always had been, bouncing up and down in my living room, getting grape-juice lips. I put my arms around them both, making a sandwich with me in the middle, and they didn't pull away. They were both taller already of course, although not yet caught up to my girls.

"What do you think?" I asked them.

Trey dropped his gaucho hat on the sidewalk and went over to the bay window. "What early primate put up this jigsaw plywood?" He pulled at the latticework, loosened it, began to shake the flimsy window boxes with their plastic blooms.

"I was thinking of painting it white—"

"Naw," Jock said. "White elephant."

"These old places"—Trey continued to pull on the loose trim—"were dark. Victorians were always dark. Somebody crudded it up. Hey," he said, suddenly tugging harder. "I think, yeah, this is, you know what, this is siding. This whole blue stuff. I thought that, because the boards should be vertical. What this is is a Carpenter's Gothic, and they had vertical boards. I think, if we can just—"

"Wait." Jock stopped him. "Odds." He stuck out his hand for a slap, dressed all in black, with his outrageous shirt.

"Odds," Trey said.

"Mustard. Dark mustard with plum trim."

"Good, bro." Trey shut his eyes. "I'm gonna say rust, no, maroon, no, rust with cobalt trim."

"You're on."

Both of them went to the corner of the house, picking up the FOR SALE sign out of the yard, using its stake for a lever, prying and pulling until I was afraid my new place was going to have a hole in its side before it was even mine.

Jock peered down into the crevice where they'd pried the siding. "Excellent."

"Look at that." Trey waved me over. "Panoramic."

Behind the baby-blue trim, I could see a glimpse of weathered brownish-red boards, and, at the corner, a darker, more purple color.

"Rust and plum," Jock said. "Tie."

"Tie." They slapped palms, then let the siding flap back into place.

"How'd you know?" I asked them.

Trey said, "Age, pitch of roof. Should be vertical boards. Good lines under there, basic Carpenter's Gothic. We're probably going to be architects."

"We came to take a picture of your place," Jock said. "Make you up some flyers. Your kid Martha said you were going to be coaching the SATs."

"We better wait." Trey tugged at the siding again. "It'll take us tools and ladders to get this off."

Jock checked his calendar watch. "Saturday? You going to be here Saturday?"

"Sure." At least I could be here, standing in the yard. I thought I could. How immediate was immediate occupancy? Would they up the price if the deal wasn't closed and they saw there was some dark Victorian prize under the Swiss doily work?

"We better wait," Trey said. "Wait till she's got her stuff in here. Possession and all that." He looked at *his* calendar watch. "Couple of weeks will be plenty of time."

"You were going to make me flyers?" I was really touched.

"Yeah." They looked like it was no big deal. "We do the posters for the middle school. We hang out in the graphics lab; do posters for games, fairs, that kind of stuff. I guess I'll be doing that at prep school next year, if nobody else is doing it already." He looked glum.

"You're sweet to do this."

"Sign us up in a couple of years, summertime?"

"For free."

"You going to do PSATs?" Jock asked.

"I hadn't thought about it."

"Think about it." Jock put his hands on his head, rocked up and down on the balls of his feet. Probably it was reflex action, being around me. Dance time. "Kids freak out before the PSAT. Your whole life flashes before you. Destiny is set. Futures tumble."

I looked at *my* watch, a Timex, trying to compute if the girls would be getting home from practice.

Trey rubbed his face. His freckles had blended together into a spotted golden tan. A mighty handsome boy. Both of them. "You and Dad going to get together?" he asked.

Jock came close enough to my shoulder to brush against it, leaning his head in as if to hear the answer.

"Your dad," I said, as lightly as I could manage, "is just an excuse, the best ruse I could think of, to get you guys back in my life."

They had to step on their laces over that.

"Can I give you a ride in the Firebird?"

"Let us off at the Fairgrounds," Trey said. "We'll walk to school. We've got our tennis stuff in our lockers; things have got wild at home, so we're playing defense."

"Thanks," I said. "For everything."

EBEN SAT IN the armchair; I pulled the footstool so I could lean against the wall. My hands were tucked, palms together, between my knees. I felt myself sweating in my frayed terry-cloth robe, nervous.

He was massaging his feet, his black socks still on. It was Saturday night; he'd stayed late at church, preparing his Easter sermon. Now he drained his cup of tea, forgot, started to take a sip, set it down again.

The blue willow pitchers, my mother's, I was taking with me to the new place; the will and document box we used as an end table, his father's, was to stay.

"We have everything in place for tomorrow," he said. "The Korean congregation is bringing lunch. There will be an egg hunt for their little ones and ours in the play yard."

Perhaps he was being kind, letting me know that Easter was different for all of us this year. I squeezed my hands, then exhaled and inhaled slowly. "Are you still doing Luke?" I asked.

"Yes, twenty-four forty-four not twenty-four twenty-five."

I wondered at the change from "O fools, and slow of heart to believe all that the prophets have spoken" to "All things must be fulfilled which were written . . . in the prophets." I loved the language of the first, wished I was going to hear the distinction he was drawing. Perhaps, on

some level, he didn't want to be calling his congregation
fools, reproaching them for being slow to believe what was
happening to their pastor.

"I'm sorry not to hear you," I said.

"Are you?"

"I'm going to miss the church."

"This is a fine time to decide that."

"What would you have done if I'd not made the first
move to leave?"

He kneaded the ball of his right foot as if the knots
therein were of immense interest. "I'm not following you,
Cile."

"Would you have asked for a divorce?"

"Sued you for breach of affection, you mean? Hardly.
My choice would have been, has been, to cause as little
public furor as possible." He put his feet on the floor and
lifted his thin hair with his fingers.

"Do you not know that I know about Jae-Moon?"

Hands on his knees, he wore his sagacious face, trying
to suggest that he'd seen this coming, that it was all part
of a plan. He met my eyes. "That is hardly the same."

"As what?"

"As a very conspicuous public affair between two married people."

"You mean because she's not married? Or because you
haven't made love to her? Which? Which, Eben? Or because you're more discreet? Or because it was foretold in
the tea leaves that you'd end up together?"

He crumpled. "Nobody knows."

"Everybody knows. Theo, my favorite stepmother, told
me. The girls told me."

He paled. "How could they?" He hesitated, recalled,
"I gave them permission to mention the computer."

"Just talk to me about her, Eben. Just tell me about it,

that's all. It may be your style to stand up in the pulpit
and tell everything, but it's not mine. I'm not showing up
at your Easter service making sure they all know. I just
want to hear it from you."

"Let's have our oatmeal."

In the kitchen, he put water on to boil, got our bowls,
spoons, wheat germ, skim milk. He found a peach I'd left
out for us, and sliced that on a saucer.

When it was ready, he put the bowls on the dining
table, as far away from the children's hearing as possible.
I was going to miss this house. Miss being a family; miss,
even, being a preacher's wife.

"Dr. Song," he began, "as she was to me in the beginning, pressed me to reexamine the words I was using to
proclaim the message. She made me see that the message
could not be received if the words insulted my listeners. It
was, she insisted, as if I shouted to blacks from the pulpit,
'Jesus loves you, niggers.' " Here he lowered his voice to a
whisper. "Put in that way, so blatantly, I could see the
point. Who could open her ears to words addressed only
to 'him'? There was more. I asked her to go over my sermons with me. I had not seen before the various biases of
the words I used, the words I selected from the lessons and
text, and those I wrote myself. I began to open my ears,
to make changes." He ate his cereal, seemingly unaware
that his face was wet with tears. "It began in that way."

"Then?"

"When I was tempted, I recalled that first Easter that
you saw your old boyfriend again and my realization that
if I lived with you for fifty years your face would never
look that way at me. I recalled that, and gave myself permission."

"How could you have brooded for ten years about
that? Drew and I didn't do anything, didn't see each other
until—"

"I don't want to hear the timetable, if you please."

How was it possible I was again, still, on the defensive?

"Will she want children?" I made an effort to bring us back to the present.

"I think not. She is thirty-five; by the time it would be possible, I will be fifty. The commute from Austin to Dallas, living here, has not been easy for her."

"Why did she move here?"

He flushed. "Her grandfather had been converted by mine; she'd heard that I, his grandson, had a church here. She is a very committed Presbyterian."

"That's nice for you." By implication he meant as compared to living fifteen years with a heretic. I could feel anger rising. What a rotten idea this talk had been; some idea I'd had that we would tell the truth, the whole truth, the gentle truth now that we were parting.

"It is a gift to the whole congregation," he said solemnly.

That did it; boiling temperature. I took slow bites of oatmeal and peach. "How's that?" I asked, giving him the chance to say what a drag it had been to have a wife who had her doubts about the Lord but loved the church. A chance to talk of infidels and infidelity; to throw the first stone. To cite the business about the mustard seed and the talents.

"It will be an enormous financial boon to the church budget. We will be able to pay the utilities and repairs on the parsonage, thereby freeing money for general accounting. Jae-Moon intends to pay for the children's education, as well as pick up our medical bills on her insurance. It will provide a substantial financial relief for the church."

"You never said you wanted me to get a job."

"Not once did you offer to resume your tutoring or make an attempt to go back for the teaching degree you once considered. From the day we married you have not contributed one dime to the running of our household. Can you not comprehend the strain this was for me, the drain? Unable to give to the church because every penny counted."

"No. No, I thought the point was the church got both of us for the price of one."

"But what did they get of you? Did you teach a Sunday School class? Participate in an outreach group? Attend adult classes? What, Cile? It comes as no surprise to me and will come as no surprise to the congregation that you are marrying a very wealthy man."

"Lord."

"Could you please, on your last night in this house—"

"Lord, yes, you bet." I dug the peaches out of my gummy cereal. "Would you like the girls to live with me?"

"You gave your word when you took my check; you gave your word to them. They are entitled to remain here. Besides, they don't need to be subjected to the disruption of relocating in your obviously temporary lovenest."

"So it was money all along? That business about her helping you with the sermons, opening your eyes to your frailties, about me lighting up when Andy popped back into view, that was just filler, rationale? Is that it? You saw where you weren't going to have to have the little tears in your suits mended by hand, the smudges on your white shirts fixed with chalk. Saw where you weren't going to have to grow old eating endless bowls of my potato soup."

He busied himself with his oatmeal, making no answer.

The world had gone nuts. Everybody had dollar bills for eyeballs. Here I'd kept myself tied to this supposed job of preacher's wife for most of my adult life, for almost half of my whole life, and all the time Eben, and maybe the whole lot of the friendly folks with their debates on the predestination of the common cold, were thinking what a drag it was, not to have a woman in the parsonage who was making real science-corridor bucks. The worst was, probably the kids felt that way, too. Here they were suddenly getting a computer right in their home; doubtless other marvels would follow soon, a VCR, a camcorder, a CD player, a microwave, a sauna where the large linen closet now was (filled, still, with my faded glory days formals, courtesy of the younger Mrs. Dr. Croft, now the older Mrs. Dr. Croft).

It had been a mistake to finish out the week here. Once I'd got the house cleared—with a lot of help from Shorty and Theo, who'd separately talked to the bank, testified to my solvency, to my trustworthiness, to the idea that turning down a preacher's ex-wife would look shoddy, to the fact that the bank was unloading a lemon on me anyway, to their willingness to cosign my agreement if need be—I should have camped out in my "beautifully updated and maintained" Carpenter's Gothic.

My mistake was in wanting one last Saturday night with Eben, hoping to provide us both with a decent farewell. To let us shake on it, part with grace, wish each other "Godspeed." Give each other permission to leave.

"Eben," I said, looking at him. "Don't do this, to you or to me. Don't do this to the lovely Jae-Moon Song, who is full of love for you. You insult us all. Putting a price tag on my actions or yours."

"The ministry is not what I expected," he said, wiping his eyes. "They do not want what I have to offer. No one is troubled by lack of faith; they want a new roof. I am the city's authority on interfaith marriages, unions of Baptists and Presbyterians, yet not one single member of the larger fellowship will step forward to offer help when they learn of my own mixed union."

"You want them to pull out their hair with disbelief;

cry out in their wildernesses." The sad truth was, as I knew, they wouldn't even care.

"As always, you exaggerate." He rinsed his bowl, got a glass of milk.

"Finish, Eben."

He spoke from across the room, the old son of an old man, in his sock feet, his trousers rolled, gray braces dangling. "It was the church's deceit, not yours, that made me turn to her."

That was benediction enough.

The kitchen clock said it was already Easter morning.

W E HAD BREAKFAST together, the four of us. I'd put out a bowl of dyed eggs, red and yellow, and a vase of yellow tulips bought on the street. I'd made creamed eggs on English muffins, thick sausage patties, and peach coffee cake dusted with nutmeg. My farewell. Even fresh-squeezed orange juice, which took a whole sack of thin-skinned Florida oranges.

The girls looked devasTAITing, so grown-up, in their church clothes. Martha had woven a green ribbon into her French braid, and Ruth had tied rose bows on her nosegays of hair. Both had pinker mouths and pinker cheeks than they wore to school. And both were being extra polite to their departing mother.

Maybe they felt relief that there would be no egg hunt–brunch with the Williamses. They'd never had anything to say to Trey and Jock anyway (although I now had a better idea whose tongues were tied and why). But I didn't feel relief; I felt heavy in my chest. Eben was getting to have his church service, his egg hunt with the sister congregation, custody of Lila Beth for the day, plus he'd prevented me from having Easter at her house.

Waving them good-bye, I felt sick at heart. When Ruth and Martha asked what I was going to do, I said I was going to the downtown Presbyterian church, the big two-thousand-member one, with Theo. In fact, she had invited me, saying that not being a churchgoer naturally didn't apply to Easter Sunday, and that of course she was going to hear that "Hallelujah Chorus" and see the half-acre of banked lilies. Why didn't I join her? Shorty was engaged in the final rounds of a serious yellow catfish competition.

But I'd told her no. Even though they had been great, had helped with the house, as well as helped with the loss I was feeling in all directions, I wasn't ready to see people from that part of my past.

Drew had been absent and silent. He'd called me once, after I'd first seen the alpine eyesore, and advised me against even renting in that neighborhood. "Rough," he'd said, "not safe. Mixed." When he could find his head, he said, get himself back on the track, he'd help me rent a place, till we could work things out, on the lake. Lots of nice condos. No, not the big lake; downtown, Lake Brazos. Lot of new places popping up, not bad addresses.

I couldn't think of a better indication that he was doing worse than bad: hearing words like *condo, nice, new* spring from his lips. What on earth was happening to him? Where had he gone? Was he coming back?

We agreed to meet at the farm on Tuesday. I almost said, That old place? But he didn't seem in the mood to take it as a joke or even to hear it.

Naturally, I'd wanted him to be delighted about a

house with an ancestry back to 1885; wanted him to de-
clare it a vintage year, treat it the way he did my clunker
of a Pontiac: having potential. But I could understand if
my moving anywhere seemed like defeat, because it did to
me, too. My moving anywhere but the farm. I still found
it hard to believe that he wasn't going to show up tomorrow and help me load a U-Haul and drive right up there,
picking up a sack of barbeque to eat on the way.

But most of all I wanted him to remember how badly
I'd wanted to go to Lila Beth's for Easter breakfast.

"How're you doing?" he'd asked on the phone, after
talking the whole time about the federals and conjecturing
all sorts of scenarios in which his mother was in cahoots
with them, had put them up to the whole supercollider
project as a way to take his land away from him.

"I bought a copy of *Hot Words for the SAT*," I told
him. "The three hundred and fifty computer-generated,
most frequently used words." I'd flinched a little using the
word *computer*.

"God, Cile, how can you even think about that stuff
now?"

My plan, after Eben and the girls left, had been to pack
clothes while everyone was at church, then take a drive
during the Korean egg hunt in the primary class play yard.
But the minute the house was empty, the parson's house,
I fled. Got in the car and drove. Luck was kind: Eva Lee's
stucco-fronted barbeque café across the Brazos was open
for lunch. It was filled with men having barbeque and
chicken-fried steak, black-eyed peas, red beans, rice, cole-
slaw, peach cobbler. The woman at the window seemed
glad to pack me a takeout. Maybe she saw I was ill at ease
in the crowded café; maybe she was ill at ease for me.
(Why wasn't I in church where I belonged, like the wives
of other men?) I got an order of pork barbeque—the third
best in the state, according to Drew, who ranked it behind

a stand in the hill country near his boys' camp, and a shed on the farm road west of West—which came wrapped in butcher paper so that the grease showed right through. I got bread and pinto beans, and coffee. Hot food for a clear blue hot day. I liked that.

There seemed to be only one place to go for an alfresco solo picnic, and I went there. To the Greatest Little Horseshoe Pits in Texas. This spread of pits, two dozen of them, taking up about the space of a miniature golf course, was stretched out along the Brazos in a low meandering park before it met the north fork of the Bosque, which ran below steep white chalk cliffs. There was not a soul in sight. Redwood tables were scattered under moss-hung live oaks, and gravel trails wide enough for cars ran along the shore. There were no boats on the river. It was as if everybody in north central Texas had decided that it wasn't right to be out in public during churchtime on Easter Sunday.

The area looked old enough to have been the home of tournaments back when blacksmiths hammered out iron shoes. The placid river too calm for Shorty and his trotlines.

I used to bring the girls here once in a while, letting them run along the trails until they wore themselves out. This was the same land that rolled up toward West and the farm; it had the same rich soil, the same grassy pastures. What were we going to do, Drew and I, if we didn't end up living at his grandparents' place? So much of our hope was bound up with the life we'd planned to live together there.

Pulling one of the benches out into the glare, I sat and sunned my legs, eating my pork with my fingers, moist and smoky, with a burnt crust and tangy-peppery sauce. I didn't see how there could be two better barbeques than this anywhere.

I knew why I'd instinctively picked this spot today: so

I could look across the wide still water up the cliffs to Lovers Leap, a promontory all but lost in the thick foliage of spring. Just behind it, lay a vast wooded park which ran from the start of the bluffs down to the river bridge, its elegant acres once filled on Sundays with strolling sweethearts, family reunions, and church picnics. Abutting the park was an area of large homes, fine old places with rock fences and deep private lots, many with streams and footbridges, bordered paths, horse barns, tennis courts. One of these, a stone's throw, or at least a horse's canter, from Lovers Leap, was Lila Beth's.

The neighborhood, when I'd first seen it ten years ago, seemed a remnant of yesterday, with its streets named for old Texas families—Baker, Frost, Rice, Austin, Houston—and its grandeur. Its property values were yesterday's back then, also, for times had changed and nobody went into the park after dark; teenage gangs terrorized certain sections, vagrants slept under trees. Many homeowners had sold; others pulled back and made fortresses of their homes. But Lila Beth had remained, swearing the only way she was going to leave was in a pine box.

"Put a detention center in City Park, put in a reformatory, put in a halfway house, put in a detox center," she'd said. "You can't drive me out. This is my home." Gesturing to indicate that every rock of the old place—in her lined walkways, her azalea gardens, her streambed—she'd put in place by hand.

From the first time I'd walked into her house, that first Wednesday when she'd asked me over to meet her daughter-in-law, to get my babies together with her grandbabies, to make me some extended part not of the church family but of her own family, she'd been the nearest thing I'd had to a mother since I'd lost mine. Very different from Celia, I knew; a lady in a sense that my mother couldn't abide. Reserved about the very matters that my mother was open, assertive, impassioned about. Talking with me only of those daily matters of my life, hers, the parish's. Yet nonetheless, in that way some women have of opening their hearts while keeping their arms to themselves, she had embraced me when I came to town, and I was grateful still. It stung my eyes and tightened my chest to look across the flat river up the bluffs in the direction of her old rock home. How could she, out of all the rest, have turned against me?

Being on this side of the river was a compromise with myself. I was not going to drive by Lila Beth's to see who might have been invited in my place, yet I intended to commemorate that decade of Easter Sundays in some way.

I'd gone by her house surreptitiously once, the Monday after Drew, then still Andy to me, had turned the corner of her dining room back into my life. I'd driven, that next day, up through the park, past the city's faltering attempts to keep its public grounds in use, past a new senior citizens' center, past a new playground for day care, past Miss Nellie's Pretty Place, a wildflower preserve erected by a congressman for his mother, with a columned terrace above a fountain, designed for civic functions. All with not a soul in sight.

I'd wanted one glimpse of Andy/Drew again, knowing that it was idiocy, that he wasn't going to be at his mother's house on a Monday morning. Just wanting to see where he'd been, drive by the curb where his fixed-up pickup had been parked. On some level I was tempting fate; gambling that if he was thinking the same thing, then we'd end up together in the park, falling into one another's arms at Lovers Leap, like the teenagers we still were in memory. Making love, which we had never done, right there on the ground, a ground grown green and soft, no twigs, nettle, snakes, rocks, ticks; no rough patrolling gangs. A schoolgirl fantasy.

What had happened actually was that the Firebird had had a flat. I'd got quite lost, driving first into one circular picnic area and then another, consulting my map, unable to tell even where I was, much less what old bridle path came out into the fine homes so close at hand. I was turning into another circle, straining to read a faded wood sign ten feet away, when I felt that awful thunk and the car twist in my hands. I looked around for help, and saw three black boys bending close together, smoking something, and, closer at hand, two middle-aged white men making out in the grass, completely oblivious to my car. The idea of getting out and approaching either group terrified me. As did having a flat in a location I couldn't explain to anyone. What on earth had I been doing there? Even as I turned the car around against its will, I constructed an alibi: I'd been looking for Miss Nellie's Pretty Place, to see if the wildflower trail was something my girls would enjoy. (At two and three years old?)

Meanwhile, I headed back down the hill as best I could, descending the sharp turns, riding on a rim, until I got in sight of the senior citizens' center. There, I pulled over to the curb, wiped my face, cursed myself, and set about to change the tire. I was putting a very uncertain jack under the back bumper when a black man and two teenage boys pulled up in a car and got out to help. He was a probation officer; they were his charges for the day. In return for community action hours, they had my flat changed in two minutes, and told me the spare was only going to last about six minutes more at best and I'd better get to a station. The man—small-world department—later turned out to be the daddy of Sugar and Baby Bledsoe. (I'd always thought he had his own ideas about what I'd been doing up in City

Park on a Monday morning, but if so, he'd never mentioned it.)

Later, after the Czech Fest, when Drew and I were lovers, he told me that the morning after that first Easter at his mother's he'd been wild to see me and had driven to the parsonage, reasoning that, after all, it had once been his other grandparents' house, and that he could just drop in on me and ask if everything was going all right. Say that his mother had sent him to check. Any problems with the roof after the last storm? How was the water pressure in the heat wave? But no one had been home when he knocked.

I didn't tell him about my foolish trip up through the park, headed for Lila Beth's house. It scared me too much to think about how close we'd come to a lover's leap ourselves. What if we had run into one another that day? Babies only toddlers; marriages as fresh as laundered diapers; ourselves still not yet who we were becoming but no longer who we'd been. We could have broken lots of hearts. It had been too close a call. A couple of calls too close.

I'd forgotten to get a spoon for the pinto beans, so I ate them with my fingers, squinting into the sun, which was now directly overhead. I put the rest of my lunch in a trash can, then took a little stroll. Up the river from the horseshoe pits was China Spring; down the river, the city of Waco. I wiped my hands on my skirt. Getting myself here, looking up at the beautiful white limestone walls, was a way to keep from being there, in that fine old faded part of town where I was no longer welcome.

Somewhere on that rock-lined hill with its meandering creeks at Lila Beth's house were eggs dyed a decade ago, unfound by small people, eaten out of their shells by raccoons, the shells becoming part of the paths, the ground, finally the streambed. Somewhere on that hill were four young children we had left intact with their families, their little faces full of trust.

If not a "Hallelujah Chorus," it was at least some cause for rejoicing.

I 'D CALLED AHEAD, to see if I could come by to say thanks in person. "Miss Moore, are you receiving today?" I asked when Theo answered.

"Come for lunch."

"I can't wait. I'm ready to go all the way, try it with olives."

"It takes you a while to come around." She sounded tickled.

I stopped at the bookstore on Lago Lake Drive that carried all the Save the World gear the girls adored. I got them each something called a Reusable Lunch Bag, which looked just like a paper sack but was made of waterproof fabric. These I'd put back for their birthdays or maybe Earth Day. I got Theo a Recycling Center: three portable, scrubbable bags that slipped down onto a tubular plastic frame. To my untutored eye, it looked a lot like a triple-sectioned magazine rack. It set me back seventy bucks, a week's groceries, but I was making a gesture. And that was small cost for what she'd done for me, using her best teacher-intimidation tactics on the bank. Although in truth

I wasn't much of a risk; if I defaulted they were in better shape than they'd been, plus the gross siding was going to be gone from the dark-hued exterior, which would up the chances of resale.

At the door, Theo wrapped her plumpness around me, her flour-sack flowered dress of the day a lavender-with-green, her tiny heels bottle green.

"Nothing like a prospect of becoming a stepmother yourself to make you show a little respect," she said, taking my present.

"You think that's it? Not just me getting more decent in mid-life?"

"I think that's it. Next thing you'll be calling me *Mom*." She watched me warily, ready to dart off to the sandwich counter if I took offense.

Had she wanted that? All this time? What an idea. What an idea that had never for one moment occurred to me, not in the twenty-plus years she'd been married to my daddy. I hadn't called my own mother Mom; in fact, I'd thought of her in rather romantic terms as Celia for most of my recent life.

"Then you'll have to call me Miss Tait," I said. "The SAT teacher."

That broke the tension and she swept me with her into the kitchen, where Shorty had a ruler out and some sinkers on the table. It was gusting outside, whirling dust devils whipping across dry yards and parking lots. I asked him was that why he was home, or was it just Monday? It seemed to me that fish weren't going to notice low-visibility ground conditions.

"Late in the year for a duster like this," he grumbled. "Weather gets itself tied in its own tail. I remember the big dusters of '56 and '71, buried cotton crops right in the ground, buried cars, you couldn't see your hand in front of your face from Dallas to the Rio Grande valley. Street-lights stayed on twenty-four hours a day."

"Drew thinks if they lose the grasslands to the atom smasher the dust bowl will come back."

"He's worrying himself about his bluestem to keep his mind off his momma, if you ask me. The government's got no interest in uprooting the ground, they just want to tunnel under it. You tell your boyfriend they'll just lease up what they need, dig in. Tell him that it's like the perio-dontist telling me he was going to reposition my gums. They used to say 'long in the tooth,' now they say 'reposi-tion the gums.' You tell him that the feds will just reposi-tion the topsoil; leave him a little long in the sorghum." He wheezed and wiped his eyes. "Coming right in here under the doors, see that?" He got out a handkerchief and blew his nose.

"I stopped by the Greatest Little Horseshoe Pits yester-day. Nobody there."

"Used to throw a few there, when we first moved. Not lately. Horseshoes'll come back, now we've got a president playing. Trouble was, too many flip-pitchers and not enough top-pitchers messed up the game. Too many people entering tournaments who thought averaging ten percent ringers qualified them against folks averaging eighty per-cent all their lives."

While Shorty ate his Garden of Eden, Theo and I at-tacked our Double Cream Cheese with Sliced Olives on White. She'd been pleased with the Recycling Center, which now sat conspicuously inside the back door, for handy separation of glass, aluminum and plastic.

"Your hometown girl won her runoff for governor," I said. "You did good. Congratulations."

"Congratulations to the great state of Texas. Now, if she can beat out that good old boy who's pouring enough money into the campaign to build the Hubble telescope, we'll really have something to celebrate."

"What're her chances?"

"I think if the people of Texas vote in a cowboy who is known to have 'honey hunts' on his ranch, by which I'm talking inviting your friends and clients to drop by and paw around in the mesquite for prostitutes, then we are not only not heading into the twenty-first century, we're heading right back to the nineteenth. It's pitiful."

I got out a glossy paperback with fiery red and yellow script that said *Hot Words for the SAT*. "I really came by," I told her, "because I think my career is over before it got started. There's no way I can teach this stuff. None of it makes sense to me. The definitions they give—I don't know where they found them. Pocket *Webster's* maybe. I looked in the *Oxford,* just to be sure I didn't have amnesia of the vocabulary." I handed her the paperback. "You know what I call proportions, this is to this as that is to that?"

"Analogies."

"You cheated and looked."

"What about them?"

"Just let me read you this. *'Peripheral* is to *cardinal* as *loquacious* is to *laconic.'* I'm giving you the answer. You tell me how on earth *tangential* is to *fundamental* is the same as *running off at the mouth* is to *can't get a word out.*"

Theo waved a hand, as if to say this was nothing to fret over. "You're working too hard at it, girl. Give it a quick glance; say 'shallow is to deep' and go on to the next one."

"Panoramic," I said.

"You've been hanging out in the halls at school."

"Panoramic is to *excellent* as *awesome* is to *wow.*"

Shorty scrunched up his eyes. "No wonder we got drop-

outs hanging around on the streets and in the parks, this is
what they learn in school."

"You want iced tea?" Theo asked me.

"Please."

"I made a pie, on account of you were coming and
your daddy is stuck here until the duster blows past."

Shorty waved a partially chewed half of his Garden of
Eden at me. "It's not the fish get dust in their eyes; it's not
the bait, either. It's us don't want to sit there polluting our
lungs, coughing into a wet hanky." He reached out and
ran a finger down my cheek. "Fine as sand that stuff, coats
everything." He wiped his finger on his handkerchief,
wiped his nose. "We got lines set out on the Brazos, too
many folks crowding up the North Bosque, heavy traffic.
If we ever get a little rain, we'll have ourselves a catch.
Saturday we weighed in with six hundred pounds; Sunday
they all had lockjaw."

I couldn't believe coconut pie on top of that sandwich,
with meringue that was higher than the pie and almost too
sweet to eat. Powdered sugar in it, Theo said, a little real
vanilla.

"Overdose," I told her. "How can you go back and
teach after a lunch like this?"

"Fuel."

I took a second bite cautiously, deciding that three
would induce coma.

"I've got news," Theo said.

"What's that?"

"I'm going to be hug dancing with the gifted and talented next year."

"The Academy? That's great. That must be a feather,
to get to teach in the prep school within the high school.
But, hey, don't say 'gifted and talented.' There's no test
screening, no teachers picking the knowbots from the early
primates. 'Those who can take it can take it,' right?"

"You *have* been hanging out in the halls."

"My girls are counting on it."

"I thought I'd been passed over. Forgetting that it takes the administration months to get its act in place. They called me in this morning; handed me a letter. I was late to class. Going to have first-year students."

"Teach English as a second language?"

"Just about the truth."

"Congratulations."

"You didn't think much of my teaching."

"Come on, Miss Moore, let's don't plow that field again."

"I was trying to get a few general ideas in your head, but you were always making things complicated."

"That's true," I admitted. "I'd have to say that *cardinal* doesn't actually mean 'fundamental'; it means 'on which something hinges.' You have to get that idea of hinge, of the point at which something turns. Which has got zero, not one frazzling thing, to do with any possible definition of *laconic*. It's a wonder I got out of high school."

"You weren't the easiest student."

"You want me to say I'm sorry, Mom?"

Theo blushed like a kid, gave Shorty's arm a poke, filled her mouth with a hunk of gooey custard pie. "I wouldn't mind that," she mumbled.

"The girls' friends, the Bledsoes," I said, to give us a chance to come up for air, "call the Academy pupils the *nesters.*"

"Whatever they call them, the program is going to go. Not because of the parents who want their kids in it, but because of the parents who want the brainy foreign kids out of their kids' classes. There've been a lot of mothers and daddies griping—what put the program on the boards in the first place—that the kids from the Pacific Rim were ruining the curve, acing all the tests and scores." She stopped short, took off her glasses. "Hey, nesters, I get it. Prep school within the system. That's good." She made a mental note, I could see, the way teachers did. "The point is, kids can stay out and make all A's again, they have that choice, or kids can apply and compete."

"Sounds like a *cardinal* point to me."

"That's what it *hinges* on, all right."

I gave her a smile and took a third brain-alerting bite of coconut pie.

"How's your boy doing?" Shorty asked me, indicating to Theo that it was Dr. Pepper time.

"More ice?"

"New glass."

"I don't know," I told him. "I'm going up to see him tomorrow."

"You want me to have a talk with him?"

"No thanks. You helped me get a roof over my head; you can't browbeat him into making an honest woman of me."

"Just say the word. I'm always here, if I'm not there." Wheeze, wheeze.

T HE AMAZING THING about driving up to the farm on Tuesday was that I didn't have to hurry home, not the way I used to. I was halfway moved into the place on Huckleberry, which was due, in a couple of weeks, with a little help from my friends, to emerge its former dark and gracious self. The potbelly was gone, a not very well-matched circle of hardwood fitted into the hole it had left. I was still partly at Eben's, with all of us treating me in the manner of a visiting relation who's overstayed her invitation.

But at least everyone knew I was seeing Drew, that we were sometimes at the farm together.

The duster had left tracks along the road, almost as if tree branches had been dragged along the shoulders, or Czechs with brooms had set about to tidy even their countryside. Dust was still in the air, a faint haze, fine topsoil far from home, some part of west Texas blowing our way. A couple of bluetick hounds chasing turkeys through a field stopped to shake off silt that settled like a sigh on their backs and the surrounding stalks.

The truth was, I was nervous. The crazy eagerness I always felt barreling up the road to see him was still there, that lurching in the stomach, the feeling of sex running like a current up my legs, making a flush across my chest. The feeling that I was not going to be able to wait—for it, for him, for the sound of his belt buckle hitting the floor, for that old quilt-covered double bed. It made me giddy, a haze in front of my eyes worse than the dust. But, in addition, I was scared.

What if—I didn't know how to finish the thought. What if Drew didn't want it, me; what if he was out working on his bikes when I got there, suggested we go into town to eat, said maybe we should wait a few months to get together, until his mother, or Mary Virginia—I got myself in such a state I had to pull over on the side of the road and lean my face against the steering wheel. Breathe a little. Locate the old hounds running around chasing a little swirl that had risen between their paws, snapping at it with their jaws.

When I parked the Firebird by his pickup, I could

hardly brake and turn off the ignition for nerves. For just a second I felt as if the car was going to slide right on into the shed, nose the wide doors off their hinges, come out the back and keep going right into the field of clover, the bluebonnets and primroses gone.

Drew was working on the bikes. He had them both out, the Western Flyer, mine, the Schwinn Black Phantom, his. Shiny as if they were in a showroom. He was oiling them, and looked to be fixing a loose chain. "Whoa," he said, getting up, wiping his hands on his jeans.

"She saw the barn and bolted," I told him, getting out.

For a minute we stood there, six feet apart, both of us trying to read what was going on, looking, scanning. Then we were holding on and it was just the same again.

I didn't talk or think until we were out of our clothes and had done it on the bed and again on the feather pillows on the floor, and were too winded to get back up on the bed. Lord, I'd been so terrified.

"God," Drew said. "The way you looked driving up, like you were going to run me down. Like you were not even interested in stopping. I've been nuts to see you; getting hard just walking down the street, like some kid who hasn't got control over it. I thought I'd die when you walked out of Circleburgers and never even looked back."

"Me, too," I said. "I was afraid you didn't want to see me."

"How could you think that when I'm messing up my whole life and all my granddaddy's acreage so we can be doing this every day of our lives?"

"That's why, that's because. Because you might be mad about that; because you might decide this wasn't worth it."

"What is this *it*—? Worth *it*? We're talking about you and me. And damn straight it's worth you and me." We kissed, then put the pillows back on the bed and got into our clothes. "I don't know what's got into Mother. Some ant's up her ass."

"I had an awful time Sunday."

"What happened?"

"Not being at Lila Beth's. Not having brunch there one more time."

"Lot of fun that would have been. The preppies in their Sunday suits pretending they cared who found the golden egg, Mother looking at me like I'd got fleas, Mary Virginia talking about what a bummer that ParkGate was going down the tube, all her sister's hubby's money going with it, thirteen swimming pools or thirteen golf courses, thirteen somethings. And all that's on my mind is that I'm about to lose my granddaddy's land, which is suddenly valuable because the Austin chalk formation is easy to tunnel under—"

Did he mean that's how it would have been Easter, if we'd all gone? Or that's how it was? Had he gone to Lila Beth's with them all? Had he gone to the Episcopal service with Mary Virginia? Sat by her? Did he still live with her, with them, as if nothing had happened?

"Let's eat." He pulled me against his chest, kissed my neck.

"I didn't stop for kolaches, I didn't even bring butter. I was a wreck; all I could think about was getting here."

"Yeah, I didn't pick up steaks, same thing. What the hell, we don't have to hide out here. Let's go into West and eat at Vlasek's on the square."

Vlasek's, the old café in the center of town, with the ancient sign in the window that said WHEN YOUR ONION RINGS ANSWER IT HERE, was now sandwiched between the Orient Express Chinese takeout, and Eata Fajita Mexican fast food.

On the square, we saw the drab green fifties pickup I'd told Drew about, pulling away, heading out of town in the direction of the milo silos to the west. No sign of the fancied up Model A I'd seen parked at the horse posts last time.

"Let's get to-go," Drew said. "I'm too antsy to sit in there."

We stood at the counter, reading the menu, trying to get our appetites up. We got half a dozen big hot links, juicy sausage baked in bread dough, and half a dozen baby hot links, plus a quart of local milk. It was too early for the lunch specials.

In the truck, riding around town, we ate a couple still warm, taking turns drinking from the glass milk bottle, getting mustaches, trying to celebrate because we were out in public. The yards were still full of CZECH YOUR BALLOT signs, and the Old Czech Corner had its crafts set out in the window of its restored nineteenth-century quarters.

"Let's go back," Drew said, turning and heading east without waiting for an answer. Out of town, we were into rolling fields, with not a tree in sight except those planted, like Drew's pecan, by a farmhouse, or in a clump down by a stock pond for summer shade.

"Some granddaddy of mine," he said, "dug out the first tank in these parts, did you know that? With a scraper of cowhide."

We passed cozy roadside homes with grape arbors and stands of phlox as high as the doors.

"Did you hear back there?" he asked. "Man in Vlasek's said the phone lines were out again in the whole town. Third day in a row. Fire ants eating the cables, everybody knows that; he was claiming the trouble was they dug a trench in the wrong spot."

He turned the radio to the Best Country in the City,

and we heard Charlie Pride singing "Let's Fall to Pieces Together." "You can say that," Drew said.

It seemed to me he was running, riding around, going out, coming back, in order to avoid talking. Maybe that wasn't right; maybe it was just his way of dealing with worry. I hooked a couple of fingers in his belt, sitting close in the high cab of the truck, the sack of hot links between us.

"—alone, we're better together—" Charlie sang.

I hadn't been wrong; something wasn't right.

"You get over the idea of renting a place in the Berries?" he asked, making a point of staring down the road, in case a combine or tiller sprang into view.

"I was never renting; I bought a house. I tried to tell you. On Huckleberry. It's walking distance from the schools. So students can find me without having to draft their carpools or their folks. My own kids can walk."

He took his eyes off the road, steering with his left hand, his elbow resting in the window. "Bought? You're kidding. That's no place to buy. It's rough. It's mixed."

"*The whole world is mixed,* dickhead." I borrowed Sugar's word.

"The preacher help you get it?"

"My folks did a little bank work."

"Shorty and Theo?"

"Daddy and Mom, these days."

"I've heard everything."

"Any birdhouse in the storm."

"They seen the place you bought?"

"No, but they've seen me."

"Where'd you get the money? I thought you said the parson was only kicking in five thou period. Cile, what's the matter with you? I thought you'd rent something temporarily, while Mother and Mary Virginia were waging

all-out war on my future life and the dreams of my ances-
tors, and then we'd be up here. The way we said. You
changed your mind? You want to live in the city? You
want to *date* or something?"

"Date?" Was he mad that I was going to have a place
by myself? What was going on? "You mean you? Or you
mean date-date people? You early primate—" This time I
borrowed from Drew's elder son. Vocabulary enrichment.
"What're you talking about?"

"You don't want to live there, in the Berries. Any place
there you can afford, you don't want."

"It was built in 1885. Old, it's old. It's a Carpenter's
Gothic. I have it on good authority."

"Falling apart, something that age. Nobody's kept it
up."

"I thought you'd be glad. I need somewhere in town I
can teach. You said you had to keep your office in town.
I'd thought we could—"

"When did I say that? I don't see why I can't run things
from up here. What am I going to have to run, anyway?
I give up the acres, the mineral rights, the riparian rights,
the access roads, the topsoil to the dusters, the innards under the soil to the *federales*, what's to manage? The bikes
I can handle up here."

What a carful of hurt feelings, his, mine. Why don't
we fall to pieces together, as the song said. A cluster of
Maine d'Anjou cows looked solemnly at us through a
shredding cedar-post fence. On the other side of the road,
Holstein, neat and long-headed, chewed in a mannerly
fashion. Did the two breeds consider themselves the same
species? Did they like one another's looks? Was the buffalo
grass greener across the road?

"You want to try them out?" he said, pointing to the
bikes, back at the house.

"Sure."

We got on the bikes and rode, panting slightly because of the strain of loosening the chains, stiff from being long unused, around the drive, then out onto the dirt farm-to-market, then back in front of the shed.

"We can take a picnic—"

"Yeah."

We went in and sat at the kitchen table, dumping the rest of the hot links on a plate. Drew put a pot of enamel-chipping coffee on and we filled the blue-veined tin cups, sat in the Stickley chairs, stared at the BUY FROM THE PUMP sign.

"Lord," I said, "we're a mess."

"I know it. I know we are. I don't know what's the matter. I was mad coming up here, mad all the way through, and when you showed up you just seemed to be asking for some of that mad to land on you. I saw red, I mean it, bright red sheets just the way they say, when you said you'd bought a house. Imagined you going at it with somebody else, even though I knew better. What do I think, I own you? You can't make a move without asking me? We talk about moving up here and I'm killing myself to hang on to this place so we can move into it, and then you go buy a house." He got up and poured his coffee down the sink. "It still makes me mad."

"What's happening with you? Is Mary Virginia saying no?"

"Mary Virginia has not yet said *uno* word about the fact that I'm all but gone. That I've told her to get a lawyer. That we are finished, through, that we aren't married anymore."

"Did you go over to your mother's Easter?"

"That was a command performance, after the parson's egg hunt."

"Are you still living at home?"

"What is this? Is this a cross-examination? Are you saying I should have moved my straight edge and collar stays here? Are you? Or what?" He poured us a fresh hot stomach-jolter of coffee. "You think that would help? Get my point across? Move myself up here? I'll do it."

"I mean maybe Mary Virginia doesn't really believe you're leaving." I made fists, mad myself. "Maybe I don't."

"Mother says that Mary Virginia will sell all the acres she can for all the money she can get; the land's gone, last count, up to seven thousand per." He looked wild.

I reached out and touched his brick red face, his brick red hair. He was wearing a pickup red cotton shirt. No wonder he and I were seeing red. I wished we weren't picking at each other, sitting two feet apart and losing each other. "We could go dancing," I said. "If we can go to Circleburgers and Vlasek's, we can go dancing."

He brightened at that. "Yeah. We don't have to drive ourselves nuts, do we? I mean we can go out, not out-out, not flaunt it where all the bankers in town can see, but, yeah, out. We can go out. We can dance our brains out; maybe that will shake our heads loose."

"We could drive down to Round Rock and see if any of those little dumps are still open. Nice pickup bands, sawdust on the floor."

"Not down there. Not that far away; I need to stay on tap. We'll think of something. Wrong time of year for Czech Fest." He gave me an old-Andy look.

"There must be places around West, out in the country. Some dance hall next to a Meetingside Church of Christ?"

"Cinco de Mayo, that's just a couple of weeks away. Cen-Tex Hispanic Chamber goes all out for that. Firing cannons to reenact the Mexicans stomping the French. Little kids dancing in costume, big *folklórico*. There's always a tent where just plain people can polka and do a little country. I remember because I used to go every year, looking for you. Dragging the boys with me, who didn't give a bat's eyesight for the Mexican hat dances; giving them ten dollars to eat their way through sixty taco and chalupa stands."

"I know, I used to take the girls. Looking for you."

"You ever think, what if we'd run into each other five years sooner?"

"Sometimes."

"The thing is, you know, Cile, that I'm kicking myself for taking so long, the way it turned out. If I'd come home, right home, that night after the Czech Fest and cut out, before the supercollider was even a gleam in some crazy physicist's eyes, when all that land was still too far south for Dallas to expand into, and too far north for Austin, and Waxahachie hadn't even been invented, and the fastest way to bore my mother and my wife was to get off on the subject of grass, talk about the difference between windmillgrass and big sandbur, saltgrass and indiangrass, cottontop and silver bluestem, I could have got my gear out of there and they'd have said, Good riddance to small potatoes."

"Not if it's me Lila Beth is mad about."

"Yeah, she said that. I don't know. I always thought she preferred you. Mary Virginia was never her kind."

"Let's try the feather pillows again," I said, starting to unbutton my shirt.

"Let's try the bed and then the feather pillows."

ARTH DAY WAS perfect: sunny, calm, blue, clear. Weather, in an ecological mood, had taken a holiday in Waco. My girls, who were running in the six-mile benefit marathon along the lake, came by looking frisky as young heifers. A comparison I didn't confide to them, being happy to be included on their itinerary.

Barbara Bledsoe was going to pick the four girls up from my place and take them to the start of the run, which followed the west side of the Brazos, crossed the suspension bridge, came down the east side, and ended at the park by the Austin Highway bridge. My two and her two wore identical T-shirts, the theme of the day having eclipsed private concerns. These had a banner saying THINK GLOBALLY / ACT LOCALLY, and, under that, listed in order, the top ten threats to the earth: global warming, ozone hole, air pollution, water pollution, garbage, rain-forest destruction, ocean pollution, topsoil destruction, toxic wastes, endangered species. I asked them to see if they could find just a STOP TOPSOIL DESTRUCTION T-shirt for me, man's large.

They'd carried in a stack of posters that read BAN THE BOX and WRAPPING IS A RIPOFF. The posters were on stakes, and looked as if someone had taken the campaign posters from the recent runoff election and covered them with a fresh message. A new form of recycling. After Earth Day maybe they would be used for the general election, and then for other topical movements: blocking bulldozers in Tasmania, saving the Belize coral reefs, planting trees in Kenya, putting down roots in the Amazon. They also had literature on Earth Day, pamphlets proclaiming this a grass-roots movement. I took two, thinking I could make Drew a birthday card with *grassroots* cut out and pasted front and back.

"I did a paper on tropical forests," Ruth told me, "for school. Did you know that the problem is that tropical forests have infertile soil? The nutrients are all in the vegetation. That's why they can't clear the forests without letting all the species die. I got a quote from both candidates for my paper. He said, 'What's that, little lady?' and she said, 'Tropical deforestation is an unparalleled tragedy.' I mean, I didn't talk to them directly, just their offices, but still—"

"I'd like to see your paper," I said.

"Sure. I'm going to print it out when I get it back. I didn't want to do that, you know, until I saw the teacher's comments."

Print it out. Right. The home computer center. I'd forgotten.

"Momma, what're you going to do?" Martha sat on the bare living room floor, uneasy. She didn't like my being here. Being up there where nice old Drew had a pasture full of bovines was one thing, something she could explain to herself: I was an outdoor type, a nature lover the same as she was. But sitting here in this more or less empty house, with no man in sight (although she'd never have said that out loud), made her nervous. Younger kids than she and Ruth would have climbed up and down the secret ladder ten times by now; younger kids would have thought that tearing off the outside of the witch's gingerbread house was a lark. But I reminded myself that *teen* was a word that originally meant hurt or injury. So why was I surprised that these girls of mine, turning thirteen and fourteen, were *teening?*

"Do?" I answered my youngest. "I'm going to be tutoring kids for the SAT—if I can figure out how to get the answers myself." I told them all the analogy I'd talked about at Theo's. They all got it; it wasn't a big deal. Explain it to me, I said. Oh, vague hand gestures, you know, *peripheral*, out there; *loquacious*, out there. *Cardinal*, that's just one or two main points, right? *Laconic*, you just make the main points, right? Clearly, I concluded, a little learning is a handy thing.

"I mean, Momma, I thought you and Drew, I thought you were going to live up at the farm. You said—"

"I did. But divorces take time. His especially."

"Oh." Martha fiddled with the stack of BAN THE BOX posters, as if she didn't know what to say when presented with this grown-up reality. A problem I shared.

"Can we sign up, Mrs. Tait?" Sugar Bledsoe was stretched out on her back on the floor, flexing her calf muscles.

"I'm counting on it."

"That score follows you all your life; it's your social security number. You do bad on it, you're brain dead as far as schools are concerned."

Baby, who was sitting cross-legged, flattening her knees to the floor to stretch her inner thighs, said, "You brain any deader we gonna put a lily in your hand, close your eyes."

"I'm going to close your eyes, you tree stump, if you don't cut out that kind of talk." To me, Sugar said, "Pardon, Mrs. Tait, I'm using peer parlance here."

"The SATs," Baby went on, "they full of words like *iconoclast* and *sequester*. How'm I doing, Mrs. Tait?"

Sure enough, I looked them up in my *Hot Words* and read aloud. " 'Iconoclast: a person who attacks cherished beliefs or established institutions.' 'Sequester: to keep away from others, to segregate.' " I looked at Baby. "How'd you know that?"

"That's policemen's talk: 'We gonna sequester the iconoclasts.' "

Sugar rose up to her almost six-foot height and walked over and put her foot on Baby's head. "You are a losing proposition."

Baby, laughing, said to me, "She mean I am *intractable*."

"You are *recalcitrant*." Sugar did squat thrusts in Baby's face.

I tossed the book in the air. "You two've got it memorized."

"We going to turn down Brown and go to Yale."

Ruth, who had wandered off upstairs, came back, tugging at her puffs of hair, making elephant ears. "Lots of space," she said. "You planning on us staying here?"

"I'd like that."

"You getting any furniture?"

"Theo has some 1920s horsehair stuff in storage, she says. Things she packed away the minute Shorty proposed."

"That's my granddaddy," Ruth explained to the Bledsoes. "The only one I've got. One grandparent. That's like back on the frontier or something. Everybody I know has about ten or twelve."

"You've got Theo."

"Does she count?" Ruth asked.

"She's to me what Jae-Moon will be to you."

"What do I call her? She teaches at high, right? When I see her in the halls or something."

"She's teaching in the Academy program."

"Really?" Ruth didn't know whether this was bad news or good. I couldn't help her there.

"She'd like 'Grandmom,' I suspect. Not in the class-room."

"Really? I thought she was kinda—not too involved with you, you know?"

"No, that was me." I gave her a big smile, which went sailing over her head, but was a joke between me and me, and this was my house.

"What I mean, is—" Ruth wandered out into the hall, came back in, clearly working up to something. "We're supposed to start staying here on the weekends."

I hadn't got that in my head. Had thought that applied to down the road sometime, when I'd got the rest of my life straightened out. I'd thought I'd be so glad to see them when they walked this way after school, instead of walking the other way to their dad's house. And I'd thought how much I was going to miss hearing them argue every day about their genetic cow projects and their trees-per-acre saved by vegetarians. But I hadn't got around to realizing that even as we spoke now Eben and Dr. Song were counting on having the parsonage without its daughters on the weekend. "So," I said, "I'll need something for you to sleep on."

"Momma, we need *soap* and *towels* and *sheets* and *food*." It was just this side of a wail. "There's nothing up there; there's nothing down here. Bulletin to the short people."

I wondered if I should offer to put them up over at Theo's? My newly reconstituted mom might love nothing better than tucking them in the Guest room, ha, ha, and packing coconut custard pie into their long lean frames. "Two weeks," I promised, "I'll have all the comforts of home." I tried to keep my tone light. Not to shout about how I was doing the best I could as fast as I could and how did they think I was suddenly going to materialize a life-style as secure as the one they had, not to mention the high-tech, high-priced spread they were about to be acquiring.

Martha dimpled in my direction, sensing with her younger sibling's radar that Ruth and I were chewing at the very edges of hurt feelings. "Daddy and Jae-Moon are taking us out to eat for our birthday. We're going next Saturday, because Daddy can't do it Sunday. So maybe we can come see you and help out with the house the next weekend. How about that, Momma? Then you could look at—Granddaddy's wife's things, and everything. Okay?"

Right, their birthdays. "I got you something," I remembered. Getting up and carrying out the pitcher of lemonade I'd made for them (custody of the pitcher being one of my big coups). From my bedroom upstairs, which had at this moment a sleeping bag on the floor (and, in the attic, my old formals from the younger Mrs. Dr. Croft), I brought down the two washable fabric "paper bags" I'd got the girls on Lago Lake Drive.

"Sorry," I said to Baby and Sugar, "none for you."

"*Disparate*," Baby said. "*Malicious*."

"Dickhead." Sugar punched her so that she rolled over on her back, then went into a somersault.

"Thanks, Momma." Martha looked touched that I'd got something for them, anything at all, most likely.

"This is neat," Ruth said, folding it over and Velcroing it shut, holding it up to show that it was a reusable clone of a real lunch sack.

Martha came over and gave me a squeeze, and her cheeks were damp. "I'm doing a paper," she said, "on the animal genome project at Texas A & M, the one using Brangus cattle. My teacher said that was of general interest because in current events they talked about that France has banned beef from Britain because of mad-cow disease. And she let me do it because I was the only one in class who knew what that was, bovine spongiform encephalopathy."

"That's great." I squeezed her back. "I bet you can feed your new machine a lot of material and get a whole lot of data back." Was my voice just barely tinged with that nebulous negative, jealousy? I tried my best.

"My teacher said I could submit it for the public awareness essay contest, if it turned out to be good enough." Martha nicely sidestepped my comment.

Past her shoulder, I saw Ruth frown and bite her lower lip; my tone was never lost on her.

Barbara Bledsoe, who had written down my directions from the Fairgrounds—Hackberry to Blackberry, Mulberry to Huckleberry—honked out front, right on the minute.

The four girls picked up their stacks of BAN THE BOX and WRAPPING IS A RIPOFF. Lined up going out the door, in their THINK GLOBALLY / ACT LOCALLY T-shirts, all in a sort of faded wishy-washy, one-world green, with the ten worst threats to the planet listed in order, plus pictures of dolphins, forests, lakes, tires, garbage sacks, all moving with the curves of their breasts and the thrusts of their shoulder blades, they look like some brave new peace corps, larger-than-life size. Awesome.

"Good luck in the race," I said to them.

Then, as I waved, and they clambered into the idling new Olds, I heard Sugar say, "You can stay with us until your mom gets her place fixed up."

HAVING TAKEN A week off in celebration of Earth Day, the weather let loose its entire repertoire of tricks. The Hubble telescope, according to the paper, opened its eye to golf-ball-size hail; baseball-size hail was reported east of West. Funnel clouds and tornadoes descended across the county, the National Weather Service Station in Waco reporting sightings on the North Bosque at 3:55 p.m., the South Bosque at 4:25, China Spring at 4:27, east of the traffic circle at 4:52. Sirens met themselves going and coming, sounding like a barbershop quartet overharmonizing. Temperatures dropped overnight from the high eighties to the high forties. After the hail had landed like meteorites on the dusty ground, twisters had picked up the whole and made flying mud pies of it, and then north central Texas was hit by the worst flash floods since the twenties. The paper carried daily photos of the swollen Trinity, the Brazos's sister river to the east. It carried stories of Dallas County sustaining millions of dollars in property damage. But mostly it carried pictures of Dallasites in rowboats, Dallasites stranded on rooftops, Dallasites gazing from treetops down at drowned Cadillacs.

Deaths of humans and animals made the news. An unidentified woman drowned south of West when a flash flood washed out the two-lane farm-to-market. A couple was killed in a pickup when a bridge gave way and they were washed downstream. Teens capsized on an outing to Save the Marshlands. A seventy-year-old man was swept away on the bank of the Trinity, fishing line in hand. Five hundred dairy cows drowned as thousands of acres of farmland were inundated.

Rescue workers—Red Cross and fire departments—met further obstacles. Water pressure punctured an oil line and the surface of the river became an oil slick. The high water brought out poisonous snakes by the thousands, seeking higher ground. Fire ants swam on the surface of the bloated water, decimating everything in their path. Power lines were down; lightning ignited a 220,000-barrel tank of gasoline.

Then it hit the Brazos, and prurient readers stopped telling Dallas jokes. Thirty horses went under not far from Horseshoe Bend. All fishing docks closed. Flood control measures went into effect. And, extremely locally, meaning at my house, awful-alpine trim stayed in place, and it was too wet to move furniture or even to look at Theo's castoffs in storage.

The flash floods, especially the story about the unidentified woman on a two-lane south of West, brought back to me the spring when an unidentified woman drowned south of Wimberly: my mother.

I'd been home alone, excited by the freedom at first; wondering what would happen if I called my boyfriend, Andy, to come over. But my daddy had gone fishing up at Lake Travis, which was sure to be flooded, too, and might at any minute pull into the drive. He was usually tanked on beer in those days, and fairly out to lunch when he wasn't actually in his hardware store gossiping with his customers. He acted as if he thought I was still about ten; and I suspected I could have told him I'd been riding my bike if I stayed out all night, and he'd have believed me.

There was this pairing of opposites at home that I couldn't get a grasp on, with him like that and my mother always talking about teenage pregnancies and the unwanted babies nursing up and down the southern counties of the state. I imagined she'd have secured the pill for me if I'd asked.

She'd driven off that morning before school, waving to me, looking lovely as a film star (looking much like my daughters now, the thick hair, full lips, deep-set eyes, but dark where they were fair). Driven right out despite flash-flood warnings on the radio, and the low-water crossings outside Austin already underwater.

I didn't consider my mother foolish for heading into it; I never thought her foolish. It seemed to me dedication: an activist on the front line of defense, standing for her rights. Even after Dr. Williams's office had called in the afternoon to say the clinic at Wimberly had been canceled, I didn't think her foolhardy to have gone.

When she didn't come back, when I didn't hear from Daddy, I turned on the television to get the news, having some halfhearted desire for drama, to have my family caught in the middle of the storm, everyone scared to death, us reunited in the downpour. Daddy, maybe, sobering up, losing his beer gut, getting his head out of the bait bucket long enough to notice we were around; Mother, frightened, chastened, sticking closer to home, perceiving that I, while not sharing the vast problems she daily battled, nevertheless had a few small needs kicking around.

One of the camera shots showed a swollen creek, an uprooted tree, the bumper of a submerged car. This flashed on the screen, held, flashed off, and the commentator reported that an unidentified woman had drowned on the road to Wimberly. I tried calling the bait shop up at Travis, but the lines were down.

By eleven that night, I was on the verge of frantic. I

didn't know who to call. Andy never came to mind; I couldn't imagine calling his house in the middle of the night; it would appear as if I was presuming on his dad's connection with my mother, asking for some favor that was out of order. Finally, at midnight, I decided that I'd call a teacher, late as it was, on the excuse that I might have to miss school tomorrow, both parents and their cars being gone; that I'd pick up my homework assignments from someone later. My favorite teacher, Mr. Johnson, taught Civics, but when I looked up Johnson in the phone book there were four pages of them, and although I knew he was called Ed, there were eight Edwards plus Edwins, Edgars, Edmonds, and E.A. through E.W. I also liked Mrs. Brown, my Texas History teacher, but she was married and in those days only the husbands' names were listed in the phone books. So I decided it had to be Miss Moore. She was right up there with my all-time unfavorites, but I knew her name was Theodora and there couldn't be many of those, and she was unmarried. Then it was fairly common for women to put only a first initial—this was to discourage obscene callers, but since no man ever listed himself that way, it was a giveaway—so I expected to find T. Moore. But there she was, Theo Moore, and I thought that pretty clever: sounded like a man, but was clear to anybody looking for her.

"Miss Moore," I said, "I'm sorry to disturb you so late, this is Cile Guest, in your senior English class—"

"Why, yes," she said, sounding very sleepy, a new concept for Miss Flour Sack. I'd assumed she never slept.

"I'm calling because, well, really, I'm not sure I can make it to class tomorrow."

"Is anything wrong?"

"My mother's down south of here and I'm afraid that—that she's drowned." I hadn't meant to say that, or maybe I had. Maybe I needed to tell someone.

"Tell me about it." She was alert now, and I could imagine her making notes in her large curling script on a flowered notepad by the bed.

When I finished, including the part about seeing the bumper of the car on TV, she asked, "Where is your daddy?"

"He went fishing, took off early. Said the rising water made the fish bite." I didn't know why I was telling her all that. Stuck a six-pack of Bud in his car and had probably stopped off somewhere and was on his sixth six-pack by that time. Probably Mother was trying to let us know she was fine and had stopped six pregnancies before nightfall but she couldn't get through. I was talking too much, afraid to put down the phone.

"Now listen, girl, I better come over there. You leave and they won't know how to reach you. Just sit tight. I need to collect my wits, get my notes for class and something to wear. Are you doing all right? You want me to send over the police? No, not while you're there alone. We can call the Highway Department, they have those telephone networks. They can find a lost parakeet in the piny woods. Sit tight. Have yourself a glass of fruit juice, that's a help for shock. Now I'll be there in twenty minutes, you hear me, and I'll knock three times. That's so you won't be scared to open the door."

"Do you know where I live?"

"Why sure I do; I know where all my students live."

She came and got on the phone to the Highway Department and they wanted to know what my mother had been wearing and what she looked like, and within the hour we'd got a confirmation. She'd looked at me and slow fat tears began to crawl down her fat cheeks, and she nodded her head and then looked a question at me, and then said, "You better tell it straight to the girl." It took another hour to locate Shorty, stranded with a bunch of other fishing nuts, just as I'd guessed, in an all-night truck stop on high ground between the lakes, Travis and Austin. He'd seen the TV, too. It was six in the morning before the roads opened and he could get home—stone sober, his face a pasty white and his mouth sucking air like he was a catfish out of water.

"Nice of you to come over, Theo," he said, remembering they'd met at the PTA. "I don't know what she would have done, my Cile, here by herself. I thought I was going to go into cardiac arrest seeing that news item and wondering if she'd seen it, too. We owe you. We owe you, both of us do."

"She's my prize student, Mr.—Shorty. I'd have come anytime. I just wish she'd picked up that phone sooner. But it makes me feel real good that it was me she turned to."

The rest was pretty obvious: they were thanking each other and hugging each other and before long they were doing whatever it was that fat people did together under the covers, and then one day, what seemed to me like about two weeks, Miss Moore announced to me (actually they'd discreetly waited until I was out of high school) that she and my daddy were going to tie the knot. I think she honestly thought I'd be tickled pink. I was anything but. I thought him fickle and faithless and callous, interested only in his gut and what nice meals he was going to have. I thought her calculating and pushy and looking to get herself a man even though she was already on the other side of thirty-five. I hated them both, sobbing myself to sleep the night she broke the news.

Then, when I dried my eyes, took note of the clear skies, when I could read that a big hurricane with a name that began with B was squalling out in the Gulf without coming unglued, I looked around for Andy. But he was

gone. I called his daddy's office: disconnected. I thought
maybe his parents had divorced, so I went by his house: a
FOR SALE sign was in the yard. Then he seemed to get en-
closed in the other loss, wrapped up in it, as if the driving
rain had dashed all my past against a brick wall.

All of which old stuff meant that I couldn't land over
there in Birdville while the Trinity and now the Brazos
were wreaking havoc. I didn't want to see that it didn't
remind them of anything; that they weren't still tender on
the nerve endings every time a flash flood washed away
a car.

The deejay on the Best Country in the City was dredg-
ing up all his rain songs ("Blue Eyes Crying in the Rain,"
"Singin' in the Rain"), and my girls, when they came by
to see if I was surviving, since I couldn't move furniture or
remove siding in all this extravagant weather, showed a
rare flash of humor by both appearing in SAVE THE WET-
LANDS T-shirts.

It hadn't dawned on me, not once, wrapped up as I
was in reminiscence of a mournful kind, what the fact of
Dallas County's being underwater meant for Drew. And it
was days before he got word to me.

I checked with Theo—to say that the flooding was
messing up my move and to hear that it was messing up
Shorty's fishing—and she said, "That boy's been trying
to reach you. Wait a minute, I've got a number here.
Hang on. You're hard to get hold of. We were thinking
about you."

"I've been busy."

"You been avoiding us because of that woman drowned
on the two-lane up there south of West."

"Sorry."

"No need. You have a right to take care of old business
your way."

"Thanks, Mom."

"No need for that, girl. I know what you're feeling. The way things are doesn't change the way things were."

"That's deep."

"I'm practicing up for the Academy students."

"I'll come by to use your phone, mine isn't in, if that's okay."

"Too late for lunch. How about supper? Your daddy's sitting in there staring out the window, telling himself every hour on the hour that in the long run this is a big help. That when the water's high, baby fish that would usually be eaten by big fish can hide out in the grass and weeds underwater, bass and stripers. That five years from now he'll be fishing rivers of plenty."

"Sounds like he's in bad shape."

"He saw the story about the drowning, too."

"I forget sometimes he doesn't have a heart of fish bones."

"You forget a man never gets over his wife dying on her way to meet another man."

I looked out at the weather. "I forget a lot of things, I guess. Including that you were a big help."

"Tell your young man to come have supper, too. Shorty'd like to see him again."

"We'll see. He may be at the farm."

The number I got for Drew, which I didn't wait to use from their house, but called from a pay phone, since it was local, was his house, what I thought of, had always thought of, as Mary Virginia's house. I wouldn't have called him there in half a million years, but if he'd gone to the trouble to track me down, then I guessed I better use it fast. Maybe she was standing by his side and had to hear him say in my ear that he was sticking by his wife and wished I'd leave him alone.

"Williams residence." It was the Swedish contingent. Lord, what was I supposed to do?

"I have a call for Andrew Williams." I tried to sound like a telephone operator.

"Yes, ma'am."

Long silence.

"Hello." He sounded as if he'd like to bite nails in two.

"This is the party you've been trying to reach, sir."

"Cile? Goddammit, where are you? I tried the parsonage and that Dr. Song answered so I hung up on her. Then I checked your name with information, no listing. I couldn't remember your dad's first name—or if he had one—but I knew Guest, since that was you, and I knew Birdville, so I looked in the book and there were *Edgar and Theo* on Nightingale. I said it's got to be them. When I got your dad and asked him 'Where's Cile?' he said, 'Who wants to know?' 'Andy Williams,' I said, thinking that's how he'd remember me, and he said, 'You the boyfriend?' I said, 'I'm the boyfriend.' 'She's not here,' he said, which he could have told me right off. I asked him, polite, 'How can I reach her?' 'You got two arms, used to have.' He hasn't changed a bit."

I could imagine the conversation. "Why are you at home calling? What's the matter?"

"My in-laws had to get out of Dallas. They're at the farm, waiting for the waters of the Trinity to go back down so they can go home and reclaim their Park Cities' Georgian Colonial Second Empire Queen Anne homes."

I laughed, thinking of his boys: architects in training. "You ever seen their houses?"

"More than once. One style piled on the other. You'd have to see to believe. Quarter of a million they were running when we got married."

"Trey and Jock must have visited up there."

"What is this? What's going on? I'm trying to tell you that the locusts have descended on Granddad's property, and you're getting wet thinking about Romanesque English Tudor mansard mansions in Dallas."

"I'm getting wet because I'm standing in a phone booth at the corner of Lago Lake Drive and the Fairgrounds."

"There's a phone booth there? I can't picture it. Which corner?"

"While you're dry and snug and Olga the milkmaid serves you coffee from a silver service."

"Sorry. Look, don't get in a huff."

"Snit. I'm getting in a snit, trying to get some news."

"They're up there, that's what I'm trying to tell you. Mary Virginia's mother, her sister, her sister's husband, who is crying in his Beefeaters because he's lost more than the rest of us ever see in a lifetime. He's lost his—don't those phone booths have a door, honey, did you pull it shut?—mallard duck collection. Doesn't that sock it to you right here? Plus he and his partner, they're both named John, everyone in Dallas is named John, the women are named Bitsy. That's what Emvee's sister's named, Bitsy. That's what they call her, Emvee. Anyway, the Johns have lost their drawers on ParkGate for sure in the flood."

"Drew, wet feet here on Lago Lake. The South Bosque is over the tops of the banks and running down the street."

"Don't you hear me? I'm saying we can't meet up at the farm. We can't go up to the farm and everything is on hold, on account of the land in question being more or less under the waters of the Trinity at this point. I wonder if the supercollider people have budgeted in Flash Flood of the Decade costs."

"So Mary Virginia is there?"

"That's right, playing den mother."

"So you're here."

"I'm here. You're talking to me."

"I'm here, too. Why aren't we here together?"

"Where? Where can we go?" He was almost shouting at me.

"I have a *house*, Drew."

"It's for the berries, ha, ha."

"It's old; I thought you liked old."

"There's old and there's old. It's old, but not *old.*"

"My consulting architects say it's vintage."

"I can't remember if I put the bikes where they can't get to them."

"I'm going to hang up. I hate phone sex."

"God, honey, wait. I'm going nuts. I don't know what's going on. Them up there at the farm, trashing it, probably. Me down here baby-sitting these preppies."

"How's Lila Beth taking all this?"

"Has the flu. Can't come to the phone."

"What do you want to do?"

"I'll have to bring the boys with me Saturday, if I can locate them in this acre of mowed carpet."

"What's Saturday?"

"Cinco de Mayo. I guess you've been leading too busy a social life to remember."

"I am not dating. *I am not dating anyone including you.*" I took a breath, inhaled, exhaled. "Sorry about your eardrum."

"I get out of my mind, everything being nuts like this, them up there and me down here."

"I'll have my girls with me, too, now that you mention it. Weekend visitation has begun."

"If it's still raining, they're holding it in the Shrine Temple Hall."

"If not—?"

"Heart of Texas Fairgrounds. I thought you said you

used to go, looking for me. You forget?" His voice had an injured tone.

"I remember. That's in walking distance of my house on Huckleberry, my new old house." Mine did, too.

"We'll just meet there, okay? I'm not going to be able to call you. This took two days."

"We'll meet there."

"Where?"

"Rosa's Chalupas," I said.

"How do you know there's a Rosa's Chalupas?"

"I made it up."

"Nearest thing, then."

"Nearest thing." I didn't care if we were in the Shrine hall, or under a tent, or in a windowless beer joint or in the kitchen at the farm. I just wanted us dancing again, holding tight, moving to music.

"Oh, God, Cile, I'm steaming up this bedroom with its half acre of manicured broadloom."

"Visibility in this phone booth is one inch. So's the water in my shoes."

"I wish things would get back to normal."

"What time Saturday?" I asked.

"Let's go early, so we're not pushing through ten thousand people, but late enough so we can afford to feed the kids until the band starts."

"Five o'clock?"

"Five's good. I don't suppose the preppies will be having a tennis match in this weather."

"You know what?"

"What?"

"We had the four of them along at Czech Fest. That won't be bad, having them along again."

"Yeah."

I T W A S N ' T T H A T I forgot when
Cinco de Mayo was—the Fifth of May—
because that was Drew's birthday. The
big Four-Oh that he'd feared enduring at Mary Virginia's
hands—doing something outrageous, something extravagant being an obligatory celebration in her crowd. Fly your
original wedding party to Acapulco, have all the furniture
moved to a new house, have an entire rodeo catered in the
hill country. I knew because the younger Mrs. Dr. Croft,
who had already crossed that bridge, used to talk about it,
and because the papers there and here always carried features on the most novel parties.

What a relief that we were going to be together and
out in public with all our kids instead. That was enough
of a present, it seemed to me, although I tucked what I'd
got him, courtesy of the girls, in a cotton shoulder bag. I
was as excited as a girl on her first date, or at least her first
date with both sets of children invited along.

Mine were at my house, which we'd christened the
Gingerbread, the name pleasing the three of us. That
probably came automatically to us, giving it a name, our
having lived all their lives (and a lot of mine) in a house
called the parsonage. We'd got used to that. The Gingerbread was coming along. I'd managed to go through Theo's
storage unit, with her blessing and key but not her presence, taking out twin beds, which she'd used in Austin so

189

that her mother could come for her two-week annual visit (no wonder Shorty had looked good!), a love seat and two matching chairs with stuffed backs, wooden arms and legs. The kind of furniture that had *parlor* written all over it, in a ruby plush that was going to be right in keeping with the exterior colors of the house. The sort of furniture that Drew would doubtless label "old but not *old.*" No dining table. Theo had kept her small dropleaf (Mother hadn't been much of an eater), was using it in their bedroom in Birdville. A couple of shaggy-shaded lamps, which were a help. That was about it, but it meant the girls could sleep in.

From the parsonage, I'd taken the blue willow pitchers and the stool where I always sat while Eben massaged his feet at night. It was used to me and I to it, and I put it in my bedroom until I got a chair. That and the desk and chair from the private room, aka computer center, that had been mine in school. I also took both cow pictures, the stand of black and white Holstein with the soulful eyes and doglike ears, and the nineteenth-century primitive from Lila Beth of the orangy Guernsey with both jutting horn and sagging udders. And because it was my house, I hung them both at once, not giving a thought to the nail holes left for future generations, the larger one by the local artist in the dining room, the smaller one, painted on wood, over the mantel of the closed-up fireplace. I'd need a rug to cover where the potbellied stove once sat.

The girls seemed excited also. Ruth had put the rose bows she'd worn Easter on her hair and had a long skirt of the same shade and a plain white T-shirt on her ample bosoms. She looked so grown-up, her deep-eyed beauty reminding me more and more of my mother. Martha had again braided the wide green ribbon into her hair and had put on a sleeveless green T and long baggy cotton pants.

Her milk-fed cheeks were deep pink, whether from artifice or blush I couldn't tell.

Would they be spending the summer here with me? That had not been decided. Were we closer or less close than we'd been under the same roof? That hadn't, either.

"Soap, Momma," Ruth called from upstairs, wanting to wash her hands before we left.

"Look in the tub."

"Can I have some lemonade, Momma?" Martha asked, in the doorway to the kitchen, looking about, wondering where to find a glass.

"I made it for you."

Tomorrow I ought to make a pot of potato soup, a pan of corn bread. I'd have to return them for church, get them in the afternoon. We hadn't worked out the schedule. They'd forgot toothbrushes. Could they keep some here?

"How come Drew isn't picking us up, Momma?" Martha had asked about a dozen questions already.

We were pacing around, ready to go, having run out of anything else to do. The sun had come out, in a dazed way, the rains were gone, the air had a very light white feel to it, as if it had been bleached by all the recent activity.

"We won't all fit in the truck," I said.

That was true. It was also true, which I didn't mention, that he had yet to see my house, or even acknowledge it with anything but anger. This was building a storm center in my mind, but one I was resolved to keep banked on the horizon for tonight: his birthday, and our first appearance as a couple out with the kids, hers and his.

I admit I was eager for them to see us together, to see Drew as someone other than Lila Beth's grown son, to see him as someone dear to their momma. I'd let them help me get ready. I wore a skirt long to the ankles—I wanted a full circle for dancing—and a silk shirt, both a dusty lavender. Martha had tied a spare green ribbon around my waist, knotting it and tucking the ends in, and had smiled at the effect. They had such great amounts of nice thick hair, I think they'd have liked to do something more with mine, but I'd washed it and given it a rinse in steeped tea, and had finger-combed it dry. Plus I painted up a little, and they seemed pleased with that.

"We could walk," Ruth said, standing outside while I locked up, looking at the washed-out blue sky.

"Let's not. We'll be fresher if we take the Firebird." I didn't know how late it would be when we started back, how tired we'd be. Hoping, maybe, that Drew would follow us home, come in and have a cup of coffee, all of us together in the Gingerbread.

We could hear music and crowd noise as soon as we turned onto Mulberry; by the time we were driving down Hackberry, the streets were filled with people hurrying to the Fairgrounds. We parked a block away, so that I didn't have to maneuver the Pontiac into a line of cars going into the already-jammed parking lots.

"Where are we going to meet him?" Martha asked. She seemed to be holding her breath; her anticipation floated from her, like perfume.

"At Rosa's Chalupas."

"Where's that?"

"I don't know. I made it up; we were trying to pick a place."

"You mean you're just going to look around for him?" Martha looked crushed. "Maybe we won't find him."

"We're going to meet at the nearest thing."

"That is so dumb, Momma. That is really dumb." Ruth scowled.

"It is?" We stepped onto the Fairgrounds, which had been transformed into a Mexican marketplace, with maybe a hundred booths selling food, every fifth one selling beer, every tenth, iced tea and cold drinks. Hundreds of people were in costume, looking like exhibition dancers, and maybe they were, with sombreros, serapes, gathered many-colored skirts, ruffled blouses. Clothes you never saw anymore on anyone in Texas, most of all not on Cen-Tex Latinos Incorporated. All the signs were in Spanish, the only English translations being BEER and RESTROOMS. I looked around, liking the smell of corn and chilis, liking the very loud canned polka music that was coming from a dozen loudspeakers high in the air. Here and there we saw strolling mariachi players, carrying their fiddles, having a cold draft beer, waiting for their turn. We were early, despite the mob; the place had the air of a carnival before the rides really get going, before the barkers start shouting you in, before the lights go on on the Ferris wheel, when there isn't much to do but eat cotton candy and throw hoops over small-time prizes.

Then, right there, big as life, was ROSA'S CHIMICHAN-GAS. "That's it," I said.

"What if there's a Consuela's Chalupas?" Ruth had a wide smile on her face, as if she was suddenly getting a glimpse that this wasn't the dumb idea it seemed, some glimmer of how her momma's mind worked, or how her momma and this man talked to each other. It wouldn't take a future Academy nester to figure out that Eben Tait and I were never going to work out a system like this.

"*Rosa* trumps *Chalupas* because it comes first," I said.

"Does Drew know that?"

"If he has any sense." I smiled back at her. Maybe the tone also wasn't one she'd ever heard before, certainly not in reference to her dad.

"There he is, Momma," Martha said, squealing slightly, waving before I had the chance.

Drew was leaning on the far side of Rosa's, wolfing a

huge messy chimichanga, which appeared to be a tortilla platter with about twenty things piled on it. By his side, waving back at us, were Trey and Jock, dressed in tennis whites, their hair freshly blown, and, strain though I might, I could not spot where exactly the hair in Jock's dark pigtail had disappeared to or how Trey had managed to brush his to the front so his shaved sideburns didn't show.

"Buenas dias, señoritas," Drew said, and to my ever-lasting joy and gratitude, planted a big chimichanga kiss right on my mouth in front of our four big-eyed voyeurs. He then bent (not as far) and kissed the cheeks of both my daughters.

"Buenas dias," I said, shooting him a look that said he could bark at me in public phone booths all he wanted, and that I'd keep his bikes oiled for life.

"Ring Around the Rosy," Jock said, and he and Trey grabbed the girls' hands and they made a circle around us, then awkwardly stepped apart.

"There were two chalupa stands," Drew said. "Chico's and Carmen's."

"Rosa's was it."

"I know it." He took a sip of foamy beer from the paper cup in his left hand. "What if there hadn't been a Rosa's anything?"

Ruth answered before I could. "Then we'd have met you at Carmen's Chalupas."

"This person has a future." Drew looked impressed.

"We lost," Trey said, slapping his brother's hand. "We said food was the point; anybody's chalupas beat Rosa's anything."

"Naw," Drew said, sounding just like Jock. He looked around. "Where's the band?"

"First," Ruth said, "there's the pageant in which they reenact the Battle of Puebla."

We groaned.

"Then," she recited, as if reading, "there are performances by El Folklórico Juvenil and Las Hispanas."

"You reading from a TV monitor or what?" Drew asked her.

"There were posters all over school."

Trey and Jock looked at one another, tickled. "Good graphics, huh?"

"I guess. I remembered all that stuff. Did you make them or something?"

"We made them, and something." Jock was rocking up and down, whether because of my presence or the strain of being with his dad all decked out in his center court clothes.

"Let's rank the tacos," Drew said. "Serious study. No messy halfway stuff. A scale of one to ten. Every booth."

"We can't eat that many tacos, Drew," Martha said, her face dimpling and blushing at saying his name.

He noted both and slipped his free hand down her French braid, giving it a tug. "Says who?"

"We'll get sick." She had an attack of the giggles. This was a daughter I'd not seen before.

"Suffer for the sake of science," he said. "Just a nibble, honey. One nibble per stall. Winner will be notified."

My youngest moved as close to Drew as she could get without straight out touching him. Something like the way a puppy wags around a stranger. A new TAIT offense; or maybe it was defense. TAIT à TAIT with a new daddy.

Jock bounced in my direction. "Sun's out again," he said.

"I noticed."

"Consultation," he said loudly.

"Consultation." We went off to one side, where they couldn't hear us. "What'd you do with your pigtail?" I said.

He shrugged. "You just blow it out."

"I liked your other shirt better."

"Me, too." He squirmed. "You still want us to rip that crud off your house?"

"I do. How about next weekend?"

"If it stays clear." He looked over at Trey and they nodded at each other.

Drew had three paper cups of beer and I had one. The kids had two iced teas each, plus the boys split a beer while no one looked. We tasted every taco at the fair, or every one we spotted anyway. Until just the sight of one made me queasy. The winner was the one we all ate every bite of. It was a great idea and lasted us until finally the blaring canned music abruptly died, the stars came out and the evening began.

We suffered through all the exhibition dancers, all of us locating, cursing and using the white portapotties in their unsteady plastic cubicles. We ate our way through pralines— chewy, crisp and sugary, studded with toasted pecans.

Finally, when the pageant was over, and we were fed and-watered out, Drew asked, "Can we dance now?"

At which moment, as if on cue, a bandstand was scooted into place at the far end of the tent, on whose floorboards the Mexican hat dance and the flamencos had taken place. From the dark area behind the tent we could see musicians approaching with a shout going up around them as they walked by, young and handsome Latins, hair slicked back, gleaming black skintight tank tops and pants, with wide silver concho belts and high-heeled boots. The crowd, mostly young, those still there, began to chant and stomp, "Las Bambas, Las Bambas."

Drew and I stood and watched as two hundred people crowded out onto the floor.

"They must call that dance the Dog at the Fire Hydrant," I said.

"That's Las Bambas playing the lambada: heavy kettle." He looked the way I felt.

"Wanta dance?" Trey came up to me, extending a freckled arm.

I was touched beyond belief, although I wasn't sure what we were supposed to do.

I didn't need to have worried. He led me out, dropped my hand, and moved around two feet away, shaking his arms and legs in an agitated rhythm that I imitated without a lot of trouble. The music had its definite beat and we watched each other's feet.

"My turn," Jock said, shoving his brother out of the way. He got into it with vigor, flailing up and down, lifting his feet off the ground, flinging his arms. A natural.

What we were really doing, the boys and I, was the descendant of the minuet, although I'm sure that wasn't likely to cross their minds. Same distance between dancers, same nods and turns to your partner, same conventionalized movements, performed before an audience. Not like the waltz, which came later, where men and women touched in a sexual way, losing themselves as they turned round and round and round together. It might be that "heavy kettle" would become acceptable in this church town, that the Baptists could see their way clear to voting in social no-touch dancing the way these kids were practicing it.

When Jock took me back to our place on the edge of the dance floor, Ruth was standing there alone, looking busily at the crowd, while out on the boards Drew was shaking himself somewhat like a hound just coming out of a swimming hole. Martha was rolling back and forth, her chest heaving, her color high, her eyes closed. Oh my.

Then they were back, and he held out his hand to Ruth. "This one's for us," he said, and took my tall serious daughter by the elbow, then dropped his arms and began to move. An athlete, she was incredibly graceful, as loose and tight, as precise as when she was shooting baskets. She didn't smile and she didn't flirt, but the vibrations she was sending, by the very fact of being so controlled, registered on his face. He looked across at me and shook his head. Some girl, his look said.

"Now the old folks get their turn," he told the kids when he was back.

"Nice kids," he said.

"Our fault."

He held me so tight, his hand down on my hips, I could hardly move my feet. "The music of their generation is called hard listening," he said.

"This dance is hip coupling." I moved to him, with him, but was aware of the spectators on the sidelines.

"I'd like to get out of here," he said, "and do what this is a miserable imitation of. This isn't dancing."

"Think we could slip off and polish the side of your pickup?"

"It'll take me an hour to locate row 36B in the dark." He glanced over at his sons. "They took the lead, didn't they?"

"They did."

We quit after one number. At the edge of the tent, in the grass, but still in the light, I said, "I brought you a birthday present."

"Hey, that's right." He looked pleased. "This is what they mean by plowing the back forty."

I gave him the STOP TOPSOIL DESTRUCTION T-shirt and the birthday card I'd made with *grassroots* pasted front and back, and YOURS UNTIL THE COWS COME HOME hand-printed inside where only he could see it.

He turned his back, took off his white shirt, and pulled on the T. Black with bright green letters and a picture of a stand of grass, it looked fine with his jeans and boots. He turned around to show it off.

"We saw it already," Ruth said.

"We got it for you, Drew," Martha told him, starry-eyed.

The boys glanced at each other, at me, at their dad, looking stricken. "We're saving ours for tomorrow," Trey said, his words sounding slightly frantic.

"Happy Birthday," Jock sang, leading us at top volume.

The boys walked us to our car, that is the four kids walked ahead, more or less talking to each other, or at least all together going through the motions so that we could walk behind in the dark, holding hands.

"What'll we do with them when school's out?" Drew asked.

"What're we going to do with *us*, this week?"

"Circleburgers, Monday."

"This time you get to walk out." I leaned against him; he'd been so swell with the girls.

"This time I get to play the box. Twenty quarters, all on 'Let's Fall Apart Together.' "

"Eleven o'clock?"

"Ten-thirty. We can lean against the truck until they open."

"Hey, uh, just a minute," Jock said when we got to the car. "Consultation. I forgot, Cile, you know—" He made gestures in the air which I took to mean tearing off siding but which might have been just semaphores for help.

"Consultation," I said, walking him away from the others while Drew helped the girls into the car. I could see him looking up and down the dark street, seeing uncountable dangers lurking everywhere in the Berries.

"Listen," Jock said, "cross your heart."

"Cross my heart."

"Don't you ever tell I told, swear, I'll get murdered."

"Not a word."

He looked back at Trey, nodded. Leaning his head way over he said, "Mom and the grandmoms and Aunt Bitsy and Uncle John are all of them having a big surprise party for Dad in the morning. They all drove down tonight and are staying at Grandmom Lila's. They've been planning this since before the rains. They brought all the stuff with them, from Dallas."

"Lord," I whispered. "Have mercy."

JAE-MOON OPENED the door to me. "I am so glad to see you, Cile," she said, taking my hands in both of hers the way she had in church. "Come in. They will be out soon; they are cleaning their rooms."

The smell of sesame oil lingered in the air and something sweet and spicy. The parsonage had crossed the line from the potato to the rice belt. I was ravenous. I'd been such a wreck all morning, I'd had nothing but coffee, wondering what was going on at Lila Beth's or Mary Virginia's, what they were doing for (or to) Drew. I'd forgotten to eat, a sure sign of head-lapse.

My former home was unrecognizable. There was a long pink cloth on the dining table, pink and gray and black wall tapestries where my cows had hung, a sectional gray tweed sofa that made an angle with its back to the door, creating a cozy corner which faced a commercial-sized screen on which Korean police—recognizable by their Darth Vadar helmets—were beating rioters.

Jae-Moon seated herself and leaned forward, the pictures flashing, the sound off. She gestured that I should sit also. "It is dreadful," she said.

I made a noise in my throat, not wanting to get into trouble here.

"Everyone thinks I am connected to this." She gestured. She was in black trousers the color of her hair and a pale pink shirt. "They ask me how rough are the riot troopers? What are the unions striking for? What is the trouble at Hyundai? What is Roh Tae Woo's government going to do? They think because I am from there that I have never left there. Even in the labs they ask me questions." She turned her eyes from the violence. "Shall I turn it off?"

"That's okay."

She looked at me with the same all-over glow she'd had hearing in public that Eben was a free man; *joy* was too small and timid a word for her. "This will be better for everyone, don't you agree?"

"I do," I said, hoping she was talking about the passing of Eben from my life to hers and not the riots in Seoul.

"I think Eben will be happier with a woman who was raised in his church and believes in it. Don't you agree?"

I nodded. She said his name e-BEN and not EB-en as I did. It made me think—one of those digressions the mind makes in order not to focus on what's at hand—of a schooldays' poem called "Abou ben Adhem." *Abou ben Adhem (may his tribe increase)/Awoke one night from a deep dream of peace.* That was all I remembered, except the end. The angel revealing that, as God-lovers went, *Abou ben Adhem's name led all the rest.* Perhaps that's what Eben was looking for, a little rest and peace.

He might have grown tired of the burden of questioning that went with living with a woman who knew that *heretic* meant to choose, and *heathen,* someone who lived on the heath, on uncultivated cow pastures. As Theo had said, I wasn't the easiest student.

Perhaps, too, Jae-Moon had clinging to her some aura of his grandfather and father, those early upright high-collared Taits who'd gone forth across the sea. Something that Eben, old son of old men, had never possessed, one of their missionary-baptized and missionary-raised women?

"You'll be good for him," I told her. "You will make him happy."

I hoped that was the right thing to say; maybe making someone happy was not the issue or even the goal. Maybe I'd been superficial, spoken in the shallow worldly way of the infidel. What was the right response?

"Ruth tells me," she said, taking her eyes from the screen, "that when our S.S.C. is completed, in all likelihood I will be working on land that now belongs to your friend Mr. Williams."

"Working under—"

"We do not work in the tunnel; that is what the magnets will do. Our homes and our laboratories will be aboveground. We will not be a colony of moles. Is that what you think?"

"No, I was just—"

"Making a joke? I am slow to learn." She gazed at my face again, with the spilling-over look. "I am making the effort to find a common ground for us. Do you understand?"

I made my own effort. "The girls are really excited about having a computer here."

"May I say I do not care for 'the girls'? It is a sexist way of referring to them, a designation that essentially refers only to their genitals."

Boy, this was something. This was how she'd got Eben: taking him to task, creating in him that warm-all-over glow of guilt that feels like religion. On me, it had a sort of vaccination effect. I felt a sharp edge of defensiveness nudge my solar plexus. That knowing the Scriptures and helping to wrestle with the mystery of free will didn't count, that being a sounding board for the texts of his sermons didn't matter, that I was still an unbeliever, I could live with. But telling me what to call my daughters?

"What do you call them?" I asked.

"By their names, Ruth and Martha."

"How about 'the children'?"

"Do you call us 'the adults'? That is an age-based designation. That is what names are for, to identify."

I thought of Martha dancing with Drew, her daddy-in-waiting. How could it be wrong to refer to what I had seen as *girl*?

"All right, Jae-Moon," I said. "I'll go with that here; this is your place now." Deciding I'd probably stuck my foot in my mouth on that one, too. Was there something sexist about "your place"? As if the female tended the territory, especially considering that she hadn't officially moved in. If it were a man, what would I have said? 'You're the boss, here.' Ah ha, I had been sexist. "You're the boss, here," I told her.

"We do not think in those hierarchical class terms, Eben and I." She returned her gaze to the screen.

Well, call me a tree stump. I borrowed again from the Bledsoes, helpful etymologists. "Hmmm," I said, looking toward the hallway of what used to be called the parsonage. A term meaning the house of a parson, therefore ownership. Therefore someone who led a pastorate, therefore a leader. All sorts of evil lurking here. I still liked this house. Cleaning their rooms, my daughters? God in Heaven, they could have refinished them by now.

I stood. "Shall I see if Ruth and Martha are ready?"

"Oh, they are ready," she said, rising also. "I asked them to wait so that we might have a talk together."

The Korean riot controllers, the Darth Vadars, were clubbing someone on the head, while in the background another contingent was dragging a body out of the frame. I could sympathize.

Jae-Moon walked toward the hall and lightly, ever so lightly, clapped her hands, as if calling Great Danes to chow. Ruth stuck her head out of the private room, now the high-tech center I supposed. She looked interrupted, but cordial. "Okay."

Martha, braiding her hair, peeked around the door frame. "In a minute, Momma."

On impulse, I put a question to Dr. Song. My tongue was loose and careless because I was full of anger here and elsewhere, and some of it was leaking out. "What was Eben's sermon today?"

Jae-Moon paused, pressed her palms quickly to the sides of her trousers. "A Paradox—" she faltered.

" 'The Paradox of the Judged,' " I supplied for her. It was the third Sunday after Easter. He had explored the question of how can you be judged if you are not free to have made a different choice? Suggested that judgment by definition must imply freedom. "John twelve," I added.

"I would have to check the bulletin," she said, a spot of color rising on her high cheekbones.

Score one small point for the heathen.

I DIDN'T KNOW whether Drew had meant ten-thirty, if that was just frustration talking at Cinco de Mayo, or if he'd meant eleven when Circleburgers opened. Taking no chances, I got there at ten-thirty, about half frantic to see him and about half frantic not to have to hear about it. I had a permanent soft spot in my heart for Jock, for telling me about the birthday party. If I'd come toodling around the circle, thinking about having enough quarters for the jukebox, and heard for the first time that Drew's kin had given him the surprise Four-Oh after all, I'd have been wiped out. Flattened to a smear.

Maybe I'd get him, them, both boys, a couple of real white hats, gaucho version.

A quarter till eleven, Drew still wasn't there. The staff arrived, let themselves in, talking up a storm to each other. All in new-model Japanese cars. I guessed they didn't have to worry about buying American; they weren't going to lose or gain any more customers than they'd always had. Drew said nobody used these converging highways anymore, but he meant nobody he knew.

At eleven I decided to go in anyway, get an iced tea, make myself sloppy sick playing "Second Chances" and a couple of other favorites. But when I got out of the bathroom, he was there, sitting in the same booth where we'd sat before.

"You work here?" he asked, trying to locate a grin.

"I was just checking the soap dish," I said.

"You ordered?"

"I was waiting."

"Just a strawberry shake for me, I'm not hungry."

"Here." I handed him half a dozen quarters. "Play the box."

"What'd you want to hear?" He jiggled the coins.

Bad. Maybe worse than bad. What did I want to hear? What musicians did I like? Did I want easy listening? I ordered us two shakes, a flameburger and a chiliburger, an order of French fries and an order of onions. I figured we owed them some rent for the booth.

Carrying the tray over, I realized that Drew didn't know that I knew about the party. He was probably sitting back in the booth shortening his life span trying to figure out how to tell me. At least I could put him out of that misery.

"Drink this," I said, handing him the strawberry shake. "It's good for postparty shock."

It took him a minute to hear that. Willie Nelson was singing "Blue Eyes Crying in the Rain," a week late, as the sky outside still had that used-up no-color look. As if the weather film was over and they weren't planning a rerun till summer.

"How'd you know about that?" he said, looking surprised. "You guessed?" He had on a shirt and tie and suit pants; his jacket must be in the truck.

I took a swallow of the vanilla shake, having totally lost my appetite. It wasn't that Drew was dressed up, although I hadn't seen him in a suit and tie since the last Easter at Lila Beth's a year ago. But he must wear them to the office when he went, sometimes anyway. But why today? Was he headed for the lawyer's? Were they drawing up a reconciliation agreement? No, it was more the way he was: flat, with an affect bearing the general configuration of west Texas.

"How I know," I said, "is the boys dropped the news."

"Yeah? Saturday? Why didn't they tell me?"

"I don't think they could go that far, get themselves in trouble."

"They tell you all about it?"

"Just that the Dallas contingent had brought down a portable party."

"Jesus, Cile, I don't know where to begin. Shut Willie up, will you—I hate that song. Did you play that?"

"You played it."

"I did?" He looked down at the remaining quarter on the table. "I hope I didn't play anything else."

"How about 'Let's Fall Apart Together'?"

"Let me get a handle on things." He ate the flame-burger in a couple of bites, wiped his mouth. Checked his tie for stains. Nice tie, bright red with blue and green fish on it. Something Shorty might like, but where would he wear it? For his birthday?

"Sure," I said. Willie was still crying away.

"How's your house coming?" he asked, polishing off the rings, again making sure he wasn't greasing up his tie.

How's my *house* coming? It was worse than bad, worse than worse. Last time he wasn't even going to think about me getting a house. Now he was inquiring after its health. A really awful sign. "Fine," I said. I told him about the furniture from Theo, talking mostly to myself, about how I'd really like to get a table and was going to check out the yard sales and garage sales. That I was getting some day help the first sunny weekend, heavy labor types, to remove the tack-up filigreed cuckoo cutwork siding. "I got a phone," I said. Hoping he'd ask for the number; hoping he'd wonder who was calling.

"That's good," he said, attacking the fries. "God, is he still singing that?"

"That's the second time."

He looked at the jukebox as if it wasn't possible.

"Why don't you tell me about the party."

"What's to tell?"

I took a spoon and cooled myself down with a slurp of vanilla shake. "What is to tell?"

Maybe it was my voice, the calm cobra inflection, that finally got past his dazed glaze. "You want to hear about it?" he said, considering the idea.

"As long as we're both here—"

"Yeah." He pushed the tray away. "I haven't got an appetite," he said. "I think I'll just have a cup of coffee."

I got the coffee, two cups, and a couple of peach fried pies with a dusting of powdered sugar.

He broke one, let the steam out, wiped a spot off his shirt, ate the pie. "You want to hear about it?" he asked.

"Drew, are you *in* there?"

"You want to hear about it, don't you?"

"You got up yesterday morning—"

"I got up yesterday morning." He looked like he could do it, with this slight bit of prodding. He brightened at the idea. "I was sleeping in that football field that's a king-sized bed by myself, wrestling with the covers, hearing the Las Bambas playing the lambada over and over like kettledrums on my temples. I thought I had a hangover, but it wasn't from the beer, well, maybe it was, because I had two scotches when I got home. It was frustrating hell out of me, seeing you like that, but then me being back in that bed in that house of hers just like nothing had happened. Emvee up at the farm, my farm, with her Johns. Okay. You want to hear about it?

"I got up. The phone rang, that got me up. It was

Mother. Mother never calls me on the phone, not on Sunday. Sunday she's going to hear her preacher preach, the preacher whose wife has been trifling with her baby boy, so she's definitely not going to miss a single one of his sermons until she's in that pine box. It's my mother on the phone. Sounding like death warmed over."

I pushed the other fried pie in his direction. If this story didn't have a nasty ending, then why didn't he come by and tell me all about this yesterday afternoon? Take me and the girls out to supper and laugh about what chumps, what *consumers* Dallas folks were? I didn't actually want to listen to a story with a bad ending. Willie was crooning out a third rendition of "Blue Eyes Crying in the Rain." Drew must have put in his quarters and kept pushing the same numbers.

"And?" I said.

"She wanted me to come over. She'd didn't want to alarm me, she said, but it was something of a crisis.

"Naturally I thought, first, since she'd been sick in bed with the flu and wouldn't come to the phone—which I'd thought was just an excuse not to talk to me about the land—that she was dying. I thought what she figured I was going to think. I knew the boys were okay; I'd put them down in their air-conditioned hotel accommodation apartments, picked up a beer bottle, and turned out their lights." He interrupted himself. "Hey, they did all right Saturday, didn't they? Taking the lead, getting out there and dancing to that music?"

"They did." I took a bite of lukewarm chiliburger, but it just sat there not going up or down, so I put the idea out of my mind. This was going to take all day; I'd work on my shake, sip at a time.

I'd dressed up, too, without quite realizing it. Not a suit and tie, but a Sunday dress, now that I didn't have to keep track of my clothes, be sure I didn't wear the same dress two Sundays in a row. It was white with real sleeves and a square neck, and I'd put on sandals with heels. The sky was so bright and light, I'd thought I was dolling up to celebrate seeing it back again after a long absence. But maybe it was that I didn't want to get bad news in jeans and a T, in anything that I'd ever worn to the farm with Drew. This one could get recycled to the big downtown Presbyterian, where they had so many members it would take them two years to notice that Grace Church's parson's ex had darkened their doors.

"So I get dressed." He was working up to his story. "I get dressed, more or less. Thinking with one part of my brain that if we had to call an ambulance or do any hospital admitting that they were a lot nicer, quicker, if you didn't look like a milk farmer. So I put on a suit. Brush my hair. I can remember that. Standing there brushing my hair, drinking some orange juice, trying to get it together. I was in a fugue state, I think they call *it*."

" 'Zombie' I believe is the technical term."

"That's it. I debated waking the boys, thought no, hell, let them sleep, thought yeah, wake 'em, they better be prepared, thought forget it, they'll be gone to a tennis match by now. I looked, no sons. Beds made, that's a shocker, tidy boys making their beds. No sign of breakfast stuff in the kitchen. No juice glasses, except mine, which I refill."

I was about to climb the wall. I concentrated on the fifties photos of fullbacks and queens. Wondering whatever happened to fullbacks and why they'd got rid of them. And when *queens* began to have another meaning. Wondering if by now *fullback* did, too. Maybe I hadn't picked up on the change in the language. I'd have to ask the boys or the Bledsoes when they came to help with the Gingerbread.

"I drive over there, this is Sunday morning about ten, no, it's about nine-thirty, maybe it's closer to ten."

"How many times did you play that?" Willie is crying his eyes out for the fourth time now. Not a cloud in the sky and we're hearing this back-to-back. Where was Drew's head?

"Must have been somebody else played it."

We were the only people in Circleburgers, except for the staff, who were standing with their backs to the windows, nothing to see, having a quick smoke and a cup.

"So—" I nudged him along.

"I get over to Mom's, going the short way, not through the park, but up the hill, past those big places that look like only ghosts live there anymore. There're about forty cars on her street. I'm thinking, God, she's died, everybody from the church came over, I took too long. I still don't have a glimmer.

"I park halfway to China Spring and walk across the footbridge, short cut, run along the path, step over the stone wall, charge right in the front door. Mary Virginia, Bitsy, their mom, John, a couple of other Johns, Mother, everyone we ever knew back in bridge club days, parents of the boys' buddies at camp, couples we used to trade dinners with, every single person I ever knew is there. And they all start singing 'Happy Birthday.' Would you believe I started to cry? Pissing my pants would have been better. Tears just running like rainwater down my face—"

Willie and his backup band were singing the chorus.

"—and they're all taking it that I'm so surprised. I've got out a handkerchief and I'm trying to get a grip on myself. I was seeing those sheets of red I told you about—do you think it can be high blood pressure, at my age, would it start this soon?—because I'm thinking that I'm a cooked goose, that I'm not getting out of there. They've stolen my farm and now they've got me at Mother's, and I kind of sit down on the George Three sofa, you know the one in the main living room—" Here he digressed to fur-

nish Lila Beth's George Something room, down to the prize
Aubusson rug, item by item. So I knew we were getting
close.

"Then they're all tugging at me, pulling me to my feet.
Big surprise, brought it all the way from Dallas. Drove it
all the way from Dallas, hint, hint. They lead me out to
the drive behind the house and there with a red bow on it
is—Cile, honey, get this—a *1957 Chevy Bel Air, green and
cream!"*

He gave me a look: crippled boy finds puppy under
Christmas tree; orphan is reunited with long-lost dad.

"You want to see?" he said.

Lord, he'd driven it to Circleburgers? Was Emvee going to be sitting in the front seat, her hair in a flip, roses
in her arms? Singing "The Sweetheart of Sigma Chi"?

I carried the tray to the trash can as we left, giving a
quick kick to the jukebox, from which lachrymose Willie
was still getting wet.

It was a beauty, sure enough. Waxed and shiny, white-
walled tires, all the extras. We walked all around it, then
Drew leaned on it, all but embracing it. "Then Mother
hands me a box—she was actually, if you can believe this,
cutting church for the party. Your old spouse must have
stopped mid-sermon seeing her absent." He seemed tickled
that he'd got his mother away from my husband; had it
not occurred to me there was competition there?

"It was her dad's watch, the one she's had in her safety-
deposit box my whole life. Look at this—" He stuck out
his wrist, showing me a gold watch with three dials and a
moon phase. "Audemars Piguet, can you believe it? These
things go for about thirty gee, minimum, new; this doesn't
have to be reset until the year 2030. I thought maybe she
was going to have it buried with her. She told me, 'I've
saved it for your fortieth birthday; that's how old your

grandfather was when he received it from the bank.' By this time I'm completely reeling.

"Then, the kicker, they've done the whole fifties scene. Out there in the garden where the egg hunts always are, you remember, between the rock walls, above the creek, well, they've got these old geezers playing, sax man who actually played with Tony Bennett, they strike up their theme song, 'Because of You,' and all the girls get mum corsages and all the guys get pennants. People were there I hadn't seen since Adam put on trousers. Johnny Mack Jones, you don't know him, but we were buddies at Baylor, he was in our wedding. They passed around kid pictures of us, because that's what we were doing in the fifties, being kids. It must have taken Mary Virginia a year to set everything up.

"She said the rain drove them nuts, that they brought the Chevy to the farm for safekeeping, they had this vision of it floating down the Trinity—these jobs only happen to cost about sixty grand is all. But you know, Cile, what I couldn't get over? How on earth did she know I wanted a '57 Bel Air? It was like she read my mind!"

"That must have taken a lot of detective work," I said, leaning against the side of Circleburgers watching him, trying not to choke on my words.

"That's the truth. Nobody could have known I wanted one except you, maybe you, I've mentioned it to you a couple of times, right?"

"You have. Mentioned it to me."

"Can you imagine? I about fell out."

I breathed in and out, shut my eyes and opened them. Looked at the Firebird and then at the magic-mobile on its wide wheels. I was working on giving him the benefit of some doubt. Maybe he knew if he left he was going to lose the land; so he was just pretending that it was the car and the watch that kept him there. I ran that by myself, but it didn't fly. I thought, flushing with anger at my foolishness, at the birthday presents I'd given him: the topsoil T-shirt, the homemade pasted-up grass-roots birthday card. I called myself a few names that maybe I'd share with the boys and the Bledsoes when they came over, expand their vocabularies. Vintage words I used, not just old but *old*.

"What now?"

He leaned against the car, not reaching for me, not even seeing me. It was clear I wasn't going to be invited to help him wax the side of the Bel Air; besides, it was already waxed till you could see your face.

"I've got to think it out," he said, leaning down to wipe dust off his dress shoes. "I still want to see you. It's just, I don't know where I am about this. You could have knocked me over, seeing this buggy. I guess I never thought she heard a word I was saying."

"I've got to trot," I said. "Now that I'm dating, I don't like to be gone from the phone too long."

"You're going off mad."

"Now look who's reading minds."

"After they've gone back to Dallas. They're staying with us until the water's gone. It didn't seem like the time—"

"Let me just ask you one thing," I said, getting out my car keys.

"Green and cream," he said. "Can you beat that? Even the colors?"

"How did the boys take it?"

Drew looked around, as if they might be here and he could check it out. "They had to leave," he remembered. "They had a match and had to leave. Before we cut the cake."

"White hats, those boys," I said, wishing they were

here right this minute in their great rowdy T-shirts, with a whole basket of tomatoes to throw on their dad's swanky showpiece auto. Or dressed in their tennis whites, using the Chevy for a backboard, bouncing a few yellow balls off the grille. They were such neat guys, with such great natural moves. I tried to let my mind wander to what they would do if they were here and as mad as I was. I thought about going back inside Circleburgers and playing carhop, seeing how a malt would look dumped on the front seat. But I didn't want to panic the good ladies having a smoke inside by stealing the merchandise.

"You're going off mad," Drew said again, looking at me in a worried way.

"I just want to get a proper look at the car," I said, jingling my car keys. The boys had sent me a nice telepathy message. "You know, the way you used to see them in the rearview mirror, in high school?"

"After they go back to Dallas, we can—" Drew was repeating himself again, his face wearing a troubled frown.

Clearly there was something I was supposed to be doing that I wasn't. What was it? Wishing I'd been invited to the big Four-Oh? Asking if he'd give me a ride? The light went off in my head. Of course; he wanted to give me a spin in the Chevy and show off the engine. Varoom, varoom.

The thought made me hot enough to rev up my own motor and the Pontiac's, too.

"Where're you going?" he called. "I thought we could—"

"Gonna move this heap." I stuck my head out the window, to get the lustrous waxed green and cream expanse in my sights.

"Yeah, okay." He watched the Firebird leap into reverse.

Watched until the last minute when he had to jump

out of the way as I rammed a big sweet dent in the jutting uplift of my competition.

"What the hell?" he bellowed.

"Give it that *old* look," I shouted, throwing him a big 1950s red-lipstick, hip-wiggling sort of smile over my shoulder. Hitting the traffic circle at fifty miles per.

THE ROAD THROUGH City Park had been cleaned up, curbs installed, and a general beautification project put into effect. At Miss Nellie's Pretty Place, wildflowers bloomed along marked paths. On the columned terrace, Pacific Rim ladies set out orange and green tablecloths for a civic luncheon. I parked and took one of the lower loops through the flowers, reading the tidy signs, getting the common names of plants I knew by sight from spring drives to the farm: butterfly weeds, winecups, Engleman daisies, golden wave, Mexican hats, black-eyed Susans. The leached-out morning sky made the oranges, purples, greens and yellows bright as watercolors.

Driving up the hill, I saw black and white senior citizens at tables set out under the live oaks, having what looked to be a bridge tournament; and at the wooden jungle gym, two blond young men held hands and watched three toddlers climb.

It wouldn't have surprised me to see a horse-drawn buggy round the bend up ahead, so restored did the park look. Turning from what once were bridle paths and now were paved streets, I reckoned that it had been an amount of time beyond counting since I'd had my flat and crept to this halfway point on the hillside, riding on a rim because of worrisome elements on the grounds above. Times had changed in a decade; the world had mixed itself and tidied itself, and, on the whole, improved itself. It appeared to me now as if this once grand City Park might just truly be a park for the whole city now.

The intent of my trip wasn't retrospection, although any visit to Lila Beth had that as a result. My trip today was not that different, really, from the one I'd made so many years ago on the day after Easter, hoping for a glimpse of Andy/Drew in front of her house. Risking losing her for a chance to find him again. Only this time it was more out in the open. She'd made it clear that my wanting him, my seeking him out, might cost me both of them.

Today I could sense the rivers beyond the leafy trees (some change in the quality of light), here on this hill high above the junction of the North Bosque and the Brazos, and this time I did not get lost, did not turn down a dead end or end up at Lovers Leap. I knew the turnoff, now, from the old road to her house, knew just which branch of the fork to take: a circle with picnic tables off to the right, her street off to the left.

She would be home; I counted on that. Because Drew's birthday party had to be cleaned up after; because she'd only recently been down with the flu; because she was always home on Mondays. She'd be dressed; I doubted she appeared any other way. She'd be alone, because I had need of that. And if she wasn't any or all of those? I didn't know. Then I would turn and wend my way back down the hill again through the park, across the bridge, maybe back to the horseshoe pits. I would not be brave enough to try again.

I parked on the street, not quite having the nerve to

turn onto her property, cross over the creek, pull my familiar, doubtless unwelcome, Pontiac into the driveway in front of the house, the gravel and caliche drive which had a small block-lettered sign saying PRIVATE to discourage strangers.

She answered the door. "Cile." She seemed surprised, then quickly recovered.

"May I come in, Lila Beth?"

"Of course, my dear. But where is your car?"

"On the street."

"Do you want to pull it in here?"

"No, that's all right."

"How nice you look." She took in my white church dress and heels.

"I dressed up to meet your son." I let my breath out slowly. "He was dressed up himself."

"You've come to talk about Andrew." She sounded resigned, yet, as ever, cordial.

"No, I've come to talk about my mother."

She sighed and led me into the George Everything room, where she raised the shades on the back windows to let in some of the rained-out daylight. She moved a vase of roses to catch the sun; straightened a chair. "Shall I make us tea?" she asked.

"That would be good."

So we had our tea ceremony once again, in tall crystal glasses complete with mint from her own backyard and lemon slices see-through thin. I told her how well City Park looked. Yes, she said, since they'd put in the nearby probation center the city had gone all out to prove the grounds were more safe rather than less. I said I'd stopped at Miss Nellie's Pretty Place to see the hillside of flowers. The coreopsis must be out, she said, and the rudbeckia. How were my daughters? Did Ruth plan to try for the Academy program next year? It saddened her, she said, her grandson Trey being shipped off before he had a chance to enroll.

At last she put down her tea glass and asked, "Shall we talk about your mother, then?"

I'd rehearsed so much, gone over the story so many times, that I was temporarily at a loss where to begin.

I'd remembered the look on Lila Beth's face that Easter so long ago, her tone of voice, surprised and dismayed, when she'd asked, "*You* were Celia Winters?" using my mother's name. I'd faced up to the difficult truth that one reason I'd kept Shorty and Theo at arm's length all those years was so that I didn't have to learn what they knew about my mother and Dr. Williams. I'd recognized that Lila Beth's turning against me was because she had first lost her husband to my mother and now was afraid she was losing her son to me. Still, it was hard to talk about it, even to broach so tender a topic, here, in her house, in the presence of her unfailing hospitality. "I'm not *her,*" I began defensively. "I'm not my mother, and Drew is not his daddy." I met her eyes. "We're not them, and however mad you were at them, you can't take that out on us."

She looked unsettled, stopping to choose her words. "Were you aware my husband was seeing your mother at the time?"

"No. Not then. Only recently."

"I suppose one sees only what's presented at that age. Eighteen, you were." It was not a question.

"You think I'm like her—breaking up Drew's marriage the same way she tried to break up yours. But it isn't fair to your son to take out your revenge on me."

"Oh, my, is that how you see it?" Lila Beth closed her eyes, pressed her fingers to her temples. She was such a fine-looking woman, trim, tanned. "May I speak my mind, Cile? Will you hear me out?"

"Yes," I said. Relieved to have it in the open between

us; afraid of what she was going to say. "If we don't talk about it, nothing will ever be all right again." My voice faltered. I was unable to keep the hurt and anger from it. "I owed you, Lila Beth. You were like a mother to me. I hardly spoke to my own folks for wanting to impress you, to have you approve of me."

"May I speak?" She took the tongs and put extra ice in our glasses, refilled them from a frosted silver pitcher.

"I'm sorry. Please." I bit my lip, having confessed too much.

"I held him fully responsible for your mother's death. It was so needless, so pointless. She was such a beautiful girl, so full of life. Married to that man—everyone knew that Shorty Guest was likely as not to be in his cups at any hour of the day or night—not noticing what was right under his nose. But that is not to excuse my husband. 'How could you have let her make that trip?' I asked him, when he was grieving, wanting sympathy. 'Why couldn't you either have married her or let her go?' But men, they do that. He couldn't come to me and say there was someone else, he was leaving. I could have handled that. I knew I was not the most—companionable of women. I could see a man might prefer someone more *available*. I'm not using that in a pejorative sense at all, but as the word is intended. Do you understand?"

"Yes." I was wadding up my thick napkin, about to bite down on it. How could it be that nobody else in the world remembered my mother but Lila Beth Williams?

"He had excuses. He hadn't wanted to hurt me; his practice; her child. Not convincing. We were more than comfortable. There was ample to go around. I'd have returned here in any case; my roots were here. This is my home. How *could* he have let her drive out into that flood warning?"

I used the napkin on my eyes instead.

"They were to meet in Wimberly. He said he'd left word at her house that the 'meeting' or 'clinic' or whatever term they used, had been canceled. But that she had already gone."

"His office called me."

She looked pained. "He could have telephoned her the night before. He could have gone to your house and stopped her. The truth was, he wanted your mother and he wanted his life the way it was. He didn't want to change one thing." She put two fingers against her lips, as if to steady them. She looked away and sighed.

I waited.

"Don't you see, my dear, I was not going to have that happen again. I'd cried my eyes out for that poor youngster, motherless, with nobody but Shorty Guest to raise her. I saw that it was my fault as well; I could have seen what was under my nose, walked out, brought the matter into the open. I could have prevented it. I had my own burden connected with Celia's death, you see. Then, when I learned that the girl Andrew was so crazy about was that daughter, my only thought was to get him out of town. To put a stop to that in the fastest way possible. My husband could hardly object to the move; he had his own conscience to deal with."

"You left Austin because of *me?*"

"It was more than I could bear, later, here, when you, Cile, turned out to be that girl, that motherless Guest girl. I was sick in bed for a week. It seemed to me one of those awful cruelties found only in literature: the man rides all night to escape death, who awaits him in the town to which he's fled. Do you understand me?"

I nodded.

"I watched and waited, fretted, questioned Andrew.

Then it seemed to me that I had worried for nothing. That he and you had got past that teenage romance. I relaxed, seeing you each Sunday grow lovelier, become less of a girl, more of a woman, raise your young daughters, handle the congregation without being devoured by it, handle that dour Scot husband of yours with a light touch. The past seemed erased; put to rest. When my husband died, whether by accident or choice in that ice storm I'll never be sure, I'd felt the earlier death had been atoned for, that it was behind me. Behind us all. Then, as your youngsters and Andrew's grew, and there appeared to be no rekindling of the attraction between you, I felt that danger was behind me as well, and rejoiced." She rose, carefully setting down her glass of tea. "You will have to excuse me for a moment."

I wiped my eyes, blew my nose on her white damask napkin, wheezed (getting more like Shorty every day). How I had worried that first time I came to call, that the babies or I would spill something in this fine room; that we'd never be invited back again.

"I must watch my blood sugar far too carefully," Lila Beth said, placing a plate of cheese and apple slices for us by the pitcher. The plate itself had green apples glazed on its center.

"May I continue?" she asked.

"Yes, I'm all right."

We smiled at one another briefly over this small transparent social lie.

She began again. "It became apparent to me in the last two years that my son was spending time out of town on a fairly regular basis, on the Tuesdays, in fact, which happened to coincide with my daughter-in-law's much publicized weekly trips to Dallas, her attendance at that putative exercise class. His office reported that he was checking with the foreman of the properties, meeting with grain representatives about increasing the number of head per acre, attending meetings with concerned citizens about the government's plans for north central Texas. I hoped it was not you; I prayed it was not you. But when you could not be reached by phone, when your car was not at the church or at the parsonage, I began to grow concerned. Pressed, Andrew revealed what he was perhaps unaware of confiding.

"By the time he got around to presenting me with the fact of your alliance, coming out in the open with his plans for divorce, I was unable to handle the news. I told him that he could get over you; that he'd got over you before. I resolved it would not happen again. My fear was that he was too much like his father. My daughter-in-law had picked out a camp for his sons, and off to that camp they went. She'd selected a preparatory school for them, and the matter was settled. I had no doubt she would have taken this matter in her own hands as well, had the economy not taken a downturn. I'd no doubt she'd had her eye for some time on a bigger catch than our small city could provide; it was hardly a secret she had no love for Waco. But, unfortunately for her plans, it was a seller's market. She played for time."

"Is that why she had her family come down to the farm?"

"No, my dear. That was *my* doing. I knew that you had been meeting Andrew up there; it stood to reason. I also knew that he was giving no thought to the danger of those country roads, the risk of your driving that unsafe old car of yours, in an—please pardon me if I am frank— aroused state. I must have walked a path in this rug every Tuesday for the past year. Then, when your affair was out in the open, when you could be more careless still about your frequent meetings, the rains came." Lila Beth stopped, got control. "I went, to tell you the truth, Cile, quite mad. I could see the entire tragedy of your mother's death repeating itself with gruesome coincidence: the same circumstances of weather, the same time of year, the same day even."

The first of May she had died. I thought back. Was that the day I'd been standing in the rain in the phone booth on Lago Lake Drive, getting wet feet? It must have been. Would I have driven up to the farm if Drew had asked me to? Did birds fly south in the winter?

"And you, Cile, if I'm not mistaken, are exactly the age she was."

"Yes." The tears came again.

"I could not sleep for worrying about it. The newspapers and the television carried daily pictures of destruction and fatalities. In desperation I called Mary Virginia and told her to get her family to the farm. They have a deer lease in the hill country; it was hardly a matter of their needing a roof over their heads, far from it. But I insisted they stay at the farm. I became quite adamant. It was, standing idle, I said; there was ample room. It was near the highway north to Dallas and south to us. My daughter-in-law could see the merit of the idea from her own perspective, and so her sister and her husband and their mother were there by sundown. I slept the night straight through for the first time since the flooding began."

I recalled all those times driving to meet Drew in the hail, during tornado watches, through dusters and rain. It would have seemed just one more trip in the chancy old Firebird. She had guessed right.

"I thought I'd got matters under control. Then when I saw that a woman had drowned on a two-lane south of West, and it was four hours before I was sure it was not you—" Lila Beth broke down, seeming to be appalled at herself that she had lost control. She used her napkin to wipe her eyes as I'd used mine. "I took to my bed," she said, "believing that I had let it happen once again."

"Drew said you had the flu."

"No flu bug could survive in this tough hide." She folded the napkin in half, laid it across her knees.

"Whose idea was the birthday party?" I was still stung by the way they had all turned Drew's head with the dream car, the old buddies from way back, the band, pulling all the stops out, tugging every string of his heart. She couldn't have been unaware what was going on.

"My daughter-in-law, as I said, was buying time. Getting her options in order in Dallas. She begged me to let her have the surprise party here; she'd enlisted her family since they were close at hand. She wanted to give Andrew such a fete that he would stay in his marriage long enough for her to get her interests in place. 'I want to give him something he wants more than anything in the world,' she told me. 'That he's always wanted.' " Lila Beth smiled at me ruefully. "That wasn't too difficult to come up with, was it?"

"I saw the Bel Air," I told her. "Drew showed it to me."

"He would." She looked vexed, then continued. "Her friend John knew an old-car dealer who had connections. It had, I believe the story is, been on display at ParkGate, their failed community, back in its heyday when they were selling lots at sky-high prices. They drove it to the farm. Where, I was told, it looked right at home."

"But you sweetened the pot with the Piaget watch—"

"Piguet. I intended Andrew to have that all along. It had been his grandfather's." She compressed her lips. "I had no idea the whole affair would appear an out-and-out bribe. My only thought at the time was guaranteeing your safety."

"He said she was going to sell off all the land if he left."

She put a slice of cheese on a wedge of apple. "I told my son that if he planned to divorce Mary Virginia he must consider that she would take every acre available at the present inflated price. I wanted him to know the probable cost."

I drank some tea, ate some apple and cheese. Lila Beth was right: food helped. "Then you aren't trying to stand in his way?"

"No, my dear, not now."

"May I tell him?"

"Let Andrew make the decision for himself. He has to claim his own life. Grow up or grow old: those are a man's choices. I would hope he has more backbone, more determination, more decency than his father." She reached into the pocket of her gray shirtwaist. "You must excuse me," she said. She put a tiny tablet in her mouth. "It was not you who drowned on that road." Her eyes filled. "The rest of it—doesn't matter anymore."

I picked up a crumb of cheese from the rug, still worried that I'd spill something, still wondering if she'd selected apple and cheese because neither would stain the fabric of the sofa. "I've bought a house," I said.

"I hear this from my grandsons."

I hesitated. "An old place, on Huckleberry."

She supplied the street number. "I know the house. I know every old house in town. That used to belong to—" She gave me the history of the Gingerbread, naming names and dates. "I have never had the pleasure of seeing the inside of it," she said, looking at me as if afraid she'd been too forward.

"My home is your home," I told her, beginning to weep in earnest.

"And mine is yours."

Then, awkwardly, timidly, as if all manner of things might break at the touch, Lila Beth comforted us both.

THE TOTALLY CLOUDLESS
sky continued, a blue chambray shirt
after a thousand washings. The still-
ness made me uneasy. It was the rule in our part of Texas
that weather was a sort of cosmic grandfather clock, each
extreme followed by an equal pendulum swing in the op-
posite direction.

For example, the year Eben and I moved to Waco, with
two toddlers, was the year of the worst heat wave on record.
Sixty-three days that summer the thermometer registered over
a hundred degrees; a hundred thirteen in Dallas. Then, when
everyone had got back what was left of their soil, sorghum,
skin, yards, rivers, lakes, the region was gripped in the "big
chill," the bitterest winter on record in the twentieth century, with fifty days of temperatures below thirty-two that
froze solid winter crops, livestock, cisterns and ponds.

I was in hopes that the ferocious flash floods across central Texas did not mean a summer drought equal to that
of the thirties, fifties and seventies. My house had ceiling
fans but no air conditioning. I hoped the walls, thick because old, would provide insulation. But my worry was not
for myself or the girls, but for the students I might be tutoring. Any kid, I figured, whose parent was paying one-
on-one hourly rates for a good score on the SATs, was
going to come from a house that went from cool to frigid
in the summer months. It might be that I'd have to offer

my sessions at Circleburgers. Not a bad idea, actually, getting the student into a friendlier, less academic atmosphere. A little jukebox wailing in the background.

In this frame of mind, then, I didn't take it amiss when the next weekend a warm front rolled in on a fog the likes of which I'd not seen before. The girls and I stood in the yard, holding up our hands in front of us, amazed, truly, that we could not see them.

We joked that people should say potato soup fog instead of pea soup fog, as this looked a lot like what we were going to have for lunch.

I called Shorty, to give him a chance to bitch about missing out on his fishing, the river levels having finally fallen enough to set out lines again. I said it wasn't foggy under the water, and anyway, if it was, the fish wouldn't be able to see the hook, just those luscious goggle-eyes. He said it wasn't the fish had to drive across the bridge.

It might be we all needed an excuse to lie low, stay in, do nothing. That the fog was weather's way of redressing the griefs and damages of the previous weeks. A downy compress to bind the bereavements of May.

THE NEXT WEEKEND, with the sun out and the wind nice and steady, house stripping was the first item of the day.

I'd rented ladders, borrowed a set of heavy-duty tools

from Shorty, and got six T-shirts, extra large, printed up in purple letters on maroon, saying SAVE THE GINGERBREAD. Those, plus promising to fetch the state's third best barbeque for lunch, constituted my wages.

Daddy Bledsoe had dropped his girls off Friday night so they could be on site for breakfast. He'd given me a sly wink, as if to say he'd seen this separate-dwelling business coming ten years ago.

At eight o'clock in the morning, I was standing at the curb, in cutoffs, my straight hair held back with combs, in an old white shirt, no makeup, taking "before" photos with my Polaroid, when a silver Riviera snaked up to a full stop. Behind the wheel sat a Dallas girl.

"Hi, Cile," she said. "Hope we're not too early. Boy, was I glad to see you standing out front. I told the boys that you'd be asleep and they'd just have to sit on the steps and talk to the paperboy. Carrier we say now that they're girls, too, don't we? But it was now or never, bringing them. I'm in the middle of a million last-minute moving chores. You can't believe how much stuff—"

"Hello, Mary Virginia." It seemed the most natural thing in the world, visiting with her at the curb. We'd always dealt about the kids, and here we were doing it again. If I felt anything at all, it was that I hoped we'd be doing it for a lot of years to come. And not feeling too certain about that. Once hers were officially Dallas boys, welded into their tennis whites, I might never see them again. This might be our last Play Day.

"Listen— Get on out, guys. Let us talk here a minute, hear?" She punched the button that opened the back doors.

Trey and Jock exited the silverado, wearing black shorts, black hightops, and shirts worn wrong side out. I allowed myself a smile. Trey had his gaucho hat in hand, very unobtrusive; no doubt Jock had tucked a rubber band for his hair in his pocket. They gave me high fives and strolled over to inspect the job.

"You're not mad or anything, are you, Cile? About that birthday party stuff?"

"Looks like you'll be settled in Dallas in plenty of time for *your* big Four-Oh in December," I said. I wasn't so much avoiding a direct answer about Drew's party as lost in trying to imagine what sort of complete-with-snow-flown-in-from-Aspen, skiing-down-reconstructed-Swiss-slopes-in-the-Park-Cities kind of party she might have. Deciding she must have been frantic to get this move accomplished before her birthday; terrified she'd be stuck here with some small-town picnic at the horseshoe pits or backyard neighborhood cookout.

"This has been such a mess," she confided, "this whole spring. I thought I'd go out of my mind. But everything has worked out, I have to say. The Japanese—one industrialist, actually, not even a consortium, can you believe that?—bought ParkGate for sixty-one point five. Million, I hate to say. The papers reported it billion. Too bad. *Nueva Osaka* we're calling it. That's a joke. Started out we thought we were getting seventy thousand an acre. No way. But John—that's my friend, not Bitsy's John—says he lost his shirt but not his shorts, and at this point that's great news."

"Good for you." Bending over to talk to her, I saw her dark hair was highlighted with a silver color not far from the car's, that she had little diamond studs in her ears, a nice gold belt on her yellow linen shorts, half a dozen beaten gold bracelets and, on the seat, a yellow leather bag. Definitely a Dallas girl.

"You always were the greatest with the boys, Cile. I swear, I don't know what the Lord was thinking of—I guess I don't have to watch myself around you anymore, do I, about all that—when He sent me boys. It's so great that John, my friend, had brothers; I mean it will make it so much easier. He can talk to boys just like they were anybody. It's a gift."

"You'll be glad to move, I know."

"I have to say I don't mind getting out of this antediluvian town, although Dallas is sort of *anti*-diluvian now, if you get the joke." She repeated it. "I won't mind, I have to say, living where you can see a few dozen buildings taller than 'the largest skyscraper west of the Mississippi and south of Kansas City.' " She laughed. "That still fractures me; they can't believe it up there. I won't mind, either, hearing somebody brag about something besides 'six Confederate generals and three and a half governors.' " She looked up, embarrassed. "I don't mean to offend you." She gestured toward the campaign sign in my yard for the woman candidate, courtesy of Theo.

"I'm glad for you," I said. And I really was. People should end up where they want to be.

"You tell those big girls of yours I said 'hi.' I missed them Easter."

"We missed you."

She turned the ignition on. "I'm going to leave them with you, then. Bring them back whenever you get tired of them. The good thing is that in two years they'll both be off at school and I won't have to carry them back and forth. John, my friend, plays hard on the weekends and he likes me to be free to play with him. It won't be the greatest move in the world for the boys, leaving their friends. But I guess they'll be doing that anyway, when they go off, won't they? At least they have their tennis. Dallas is definitely a tennis town."

"They'll do fine," I told her. Smiling about her sweet boys.

"And summers, they'll have the farm. Outdoors and all that, although you do have to watch out for Pasadena tick disease, I know. Drew's up there right now. He couldn't wait to go. I think he thought we were going to turn the farm into a weekend resort." She pushed her shades up on her frosted hair, stuck her head out the window as she started to pull away. "I guess we'll keep in touch, one way or the other, won't we?"

"Sure we will," I promised. "It'll be just like Baby Days all over again, only now they're big enough to pack their own pajamas."

T HE ALPINE-AWFUL siding was coming off, with the greatest of ease, tacked up apparently by cheap labor in a hurry. When Theo called, the six kids, my basic family unit, had stripped the whole front, except for the part under the eaves, down to the original. Small wonder; how could anything long resist the combined tugs of two Taits, two Bledsoes, and the two Williams boys with their outrageous Ts turned right side out?

They had a cassette player blasting out the music of their generation, a pitcher of lemonade on the porch and three sacks of Eva Lee's smoky pit-barbequed pork and ribs waiting in the kitchen.

"We're unveiling the Gingerbread," I told my old teacher on the phone. "No cream cheese and olive today.

Besides, I'm on a twelve-step program to give your specialty up."

"It's your daddy," she said. "His heart."

"I thought he'd be baiting out, hours ago."

"He's here."

"Is this serious, Theo? What are we talking about? You want me to call an ambulance?" At Shorty's age and weight I wasn't going to give him odds.

"Just come."

"On my way."

The assembled day labor seemed glad to see me leave; there was a lot of exaggerated yawning and stretching. Maybe they'd take a long lunch break, they said. Maybe they'd get wild and drink Coca-Colas instead of Dr. Peppers; the Bledsoes had brought six-packs.

"I won't be long," I told them. "If there's real trouble, I'll call." I had to tear my eyes away from the house. "Did you know it would look this good?" I asked Trey and Jock. "When you first decided it was siding?" How had they known they'd uncover these beautiful old dark colors, stain soaked deep into vertical boards? What a gem I'd found—they'd found for me.

It was foolishly hard to get in the Pontiac and leave them there. I was having an attack of fear-of-loss I guess, a springtime virus. But looking at the sextet of them, all of whom were a part of me, all of whom were making this old eyesore into a dream, I had a moment of panic they might disappear if I drove away. That maybe they were a mirage, like Cow's Party at the farm; Cile's Family on Huckleberry. Something I'd been looking for forever that was going to recede from my life when I turned the corner.

Not true as it turned out.

Not true that Shorty was on his last heartbeat, either. I'd been set up. When I pulled onto Night*ingale* (in the center of Birdville, quick as you could say W-L-G, Where Lives Guest), there was Drew's Chevy pickup right there in the drive. The sight of which caused a deep flutter of excitement to run right up my legs to my stomach.

He was at the kitchen table, and I'd never been so glad to see anybody in my whole life.

"What're you doing here?" I asked him. "I thought you'd be out waxing your birthday present."

"I'm having a Garden of Eden," he said, holding up a gummy peanut butter and butter on wheat, an oil-ruffled lettuce leaf daintily dripping out one side. He had on boots, his longhorn belt, his birthday T-shirt—STOP TOPSOIL DE-STRUCTION—and was grinning at me like crazy.

"Boy here came to ask for your hand," Shorty explained with his mouth full. "I said I thought you were going to need both of them to keep the wolf from the door." Wheeze, wheeze.

"A man's supposed to ask her daddy for her hand," Drew said. "The book says."

"Man's supposed to ask her first." I pulled up a chair. I still looked a mess, but I had got my face on and a fresh white shirt.

"That's right? It didn't say that, book I read."

"I saw Mary Virginia this morning," I told him.

Drew began to whistle "All My Exes Live in Texas."

"What happened?"

"I went by your house—"

Theo, looking like the canary who killed the cat, pushed half a cream cheese sandwich into my fingers, which were still sticky from a strip of barbequed pork I'd grabbed on the run.

"Iced tea?" she asked.

"Coffee." I was overcome with Drew showing up in his old truck instead of his new vintage toy. At the sight of his brick red head, his once-freckled farm face. It seemed the most natural thing in the world for us to be sitting here together at this table. I couldn't for the life of me imagine why I'd ever thought he wouldn't get along with my folks. How could he not?

"Your house," he said. "I went by."

"When?"

"You were at Eva Lee's getting to-go."

"This morning?"

"You want to hear about it?"

"I want to hear about it."

Theo handed me a hot cup of strong brew and stood hovering over us. She'd dressed herself in a flowered flour-sack housecoat, the kind that zipped up the front and had lace around the collar, in an aqua print that harmonized with the tablecloth she'd got out in Drew's honor. It was a new concept in accessories: matching tablecloth and clothes. Her chubby face scrubbed, she looked softer, younger. This was the just-us-family Theodora Moore I hadn't seen before.

Shorty was every once in a while giving Drew's arm a sort of tap, not a real shoulder clip, just a sort of punch. A hey-sonny sort of punch. He looked a little like a man who'd just caught a ninety-five-pound big yellow catfish and was weighing it in. (I guess he and Eben hadn't been what you'd call close.)

"I went by the house—" Drew said.

"The Gingerbread."

"The house on Huckleberry."

"How'd you find it?"

"I got a map. You want to hear?"

"You went by my house—"

"I got a load of stuff from the farm in the pickup. A table—you said you needed a table. Did you buy one?" He looked suddenly anxious.

"Not yet."

"And the six Stickley chairs. We don't need them up there, who cares what we sit on up there? We can use the hall benches. Something else, too."

"What?"

"See, so I drove by, and what I saw were these vandals ripping your place apart. On ladders, with crowbars. There were these big black kids and these two hoods in shirts with messages so crude I thought I couldn't be seeing what I was seeing." He waved his arms, trying to act out his story for us. "I got out of the truck and almost ran into that Chinese tallow tree you've got—nice, they've got a lot of trees over there in the Berries—not looking where I was going, and I shouted, 'Listen here, you, get down from there or I'm calling the cops. This is my woman's house and if you touch another board of it, I'll have you in juvenile court by lunchtime.' Naturally, I was forgetting it was Saturday. I was ready to haul them all in."

I smiled to imagine the scene. No wonder my kids had all been yawning and faking stretches when I left. They must have been popping with their secret. Busting to keep it to themselves.

"Then these big girls, linebackers, came over to where I was standing and they *lifted me off the ground*—can you believe that? One on each side of me, bigger than me with their hair up in those rooster combs and wearing stilts, it seemed like. One of them said, 'You must have made a mistake, Mister, no man has been hanging around with the woman in this house.' That put me in my place all right.

"Then a couple of big white girls rounded the side of the house, laughing fit to kill and—you know what's coming—it was Ruth and Martha. You could have knocked me over. Wearing these T-shirts that said COWS 'R' US, that was Martha, looking pretty as ever, and Ruth had one that said MAKE LOVE NOT—" He faltered, trying to recall.

"WAGYUS."

"Yeah."

"That's a kind of cow. Those were belated birthday presents from their momma."

"They came around the side of the house, laughing their heads off, and Ruth said, 'He's trespassing; he doesn't belong here.' And that put me in my place for sure. I still hadn't focused on the kid in the black hat or the other one, with the ponytail, for looking at what was printed on their T-shirts." He turned to Theo, embarrassed. "Sorry, this is not for mixed company."

"Hey, boy, you're talking to a schoolteacher."

"You sure?" Drew gave them the BE A DICK: PLAY HARD and then the WISH YOU WERE HERE, complete with downward gestures.

Shorty wheezed until I thought he might manage that heart attack after all.

Theo said, "I see all these kids with the shirts turned inside out; they think we can't read backward." She was taking in every word, clucking over him as if he was a prize student.

Drew got back into his story. "Then the kid in the black hat said, 'I'll make bail. That's my old man.' You could have knocked me over with a turkey feather. Those were *my boys*, Cile. And I hadn't recognized them. Didn't you about pass out when they showed up looking like that?"

"I'd seen them off the courts before," I told him. "Those boys and I go way back."

"I made them promise not to tell you I'd come by. I also told the linebackers to go easy on my biceps, that I was going to need them for pushing the old John Deere manual tiller up at the farm."

Those sneaky kids, what a good time they must have had.

"I told them I had a surprise for you." He looked pleased with himself.

Theo took the sandwich plates. To me, she said, chiding,

"Andy didn't get lost. I told him R-O-B-I-N and he was here in nothing flat. It's pitiful how you used to get lost."

"Farmers have that sense of direction," I told her. "Like birds."

"Bees," Theo said.

"I had a map. Plus we'd been almost there, after Cinco de Mayo."

"Where's the Bel Air?" I asked him. "How come you're in the truck? How come you're bringing furniture to your old girlfriend?"

"I sent it back," he said, sheepish. "That's after I hauled it out to Experienced Cars and Trucks to get the dent in the front of it knocked out." He gave me an old Andy smile, smacking his fist into his palm in imitation of a collision. "It took all the fun out of it, having it in mint condition, somebody else doing the work. I wanted us to find an old one, you know, fix it up. The way we were going to do with the Firebird."

"You seemed pretty in love with it."

"Go ahead. Rub it in. I deserve it. I guess I was snowed that Emvee had known what I wanted; I thought that I'd maybe been so eager to get out of there I'd sold her short. I asked the boys; they said it was their grandmom who told her what to get. I'd have sent it back anyway; but that was the clincher."

Theo bent over him in her aqua garden, asking, "How about a little banana cream pie, Andy? I made two this morning, knowing you were coming."

"I might try a taste." He took the plate she handed him, finished the piece in four bites, wiping his mouth with the back of his hand.

"How about you, girl?" she asked me.

"Sure." By the time we left here, Drew and I were going to look exactly like the Guests. "How come you aren't fishing?" I asked Shorty. "You didn't have this heart problem at four a.m."

"Matter of fact, I went fishing. Your fellow here called yesterday, and I had an idea he might drop by. I came home when they quit biting. I thought maybe he needed to hear the merits of bait fishing since his old man had passed away and all he'd ever learned was lure fishing. That's no sport. I figure a boy should get fishing education along with his circumcision."

"At two days old?" Theo raised her brows.

"A figure of speech."

I looked at Drew, trying to see if he was really back or only temporarily back, regrouping. "What happened after you turned in the car?"

"You want to hear?"

"You tell me, do I?"

He nodded to Theo. "Maybe I'll have another bite of that pie." He held out his plate, halved the slice in two bites. "I tried to think it out. What the game was; why all of a sudden nobody wanted me to leave. I'd been an unnecessary adjunct at home in the Carpet Palace; a member of the wrong congregation to my mom. Then all of a sudden they're giving me this society-section surprise party with special effects flown in from three coasts. I fell for it; I admit it. But then I started asking myself, What's going on here? I knew it wasn't me they cared about; I knew for sure it wasn't the hundred inches of blacklands soil it took ten thousand years to make. It had to be money."

Shorty gave him a poke. "You can bank on that."

"Some other year, Mary Virginia might have helped me pack, taken the residuals and her jewelry, and moved to Dallas to some Park Cities address faster than you could say *rich*. Now she was dragging her heels. I'd missed something."

I slipped out of my Reeboks and slid my feet up his legs under cover of the aqua print tablecloth.

"I got out the twenty-five-pound, ten-thousand-page environmental impact study that DOE, that's Department of Energy, put out, which I'd been using as a doorstop at the office, and gave it a look-see. I didn't read it through. Nobody is ever going to read it clear through—you know, honey, I'm going to have to get reading glasses, can you believe that, at my age?—anyway, I checked the table of contents, skimming along, and there it was. UNANTICI-PATED EXPENSES. Un-ANT-icipated expenses, ha, ha. What I learned was that the 'unanticipated expenses of fire ants' eating through their cables' was going to raise the cost of the supercollider from the original four-point-four billion to seven-point-five billion.

"In other words, first time around with their estimate they didn't deal with the fact that fire ants can chew right through underground cables like they were eating licorice sticks. There was this line—I'm quoting here—'the fire ant appears to be attracted to electrical equipment.' Doesn't that kill you? How swift the federals are?"

"What does that mean? You won't have to sell?" I slipped my feet between his knees.

"That prices are soft, and that Mary Virginia knew that and was waiting for them to firm up. I did a little homework, called around up there to the swindlers handling the land quotes, got it verified there was no hard money now. Then I sat her down and put it to her straight: it was going to be the next century before they were ready to tunnel under our blacklands. I said she could have the house right now, whatever she could get for it, plus some east Texas stuff. I pointed out that oil prices are going to go back up a lot quicker than it was going to take for Congress to pass a new collider budget that allowed them to build the whole smasher from the ground up from different plans, to ant-proof it. We're talking serious delays, I told her. Decades."

"It must have worked; she was packing, she said, when I saw her." There didn't seem to be any point in mentioning the fat sale of ParkGate to the Asian interests.

"She folded. One thing you can count on, Emvee doesn't like to wait around. Patience isn't her long suit." He looked at me. "What it really means is, nature has a way of taking care of her own. What it means is, we're not going to be losing our grasslands, this century at least. Looks like it'll fall to the boys to be the ones to keep what's left of the land when all that's left is the land. I guess they won't make too bad a mess of it."

"Are you going to live up at the farm?" I tried to sound as if this was a casual question.

"Come on, Cile, I said I'd been suckered. I said I'd been stupid."

"I didn't hear you." I let him guide my feet into his lap.

"I said it. I've got witnesses." He waved at Theo and Shorty. Glancing at my plate, he seemed to be wondering why I'd got pie and he hadn't, and helped me along with mine.

Theo beamed. "Does this mean I'm going to get to be Mom of the Bride?"

"Sure does," Drew said. He looked at me. "Doesn't it? Cile? Come on, honey."

"I didn't get to give you away the first time," Shorty told me, looking as if he was already thinking bachelor dinner with all his fishing buddies included.

"Maybe that's why it didn't take," I said.

"I told them on Huckleberry if we didn't get back over there in a couple of hours, that would mean I'd run into trouble and was going to need reinforcements." Drew checked his wrist, banded in watches.

"You didn't give everything back, I see."

"I'm keeping this." He gestured to the Piguet calendar watch, which wasn't going to have to be set until the year 2030. "Each boy can have a timepiece from his grandfather."

I stood. Kissed Theo. "Heart attack," I said. "That's such a slick trick."

"You can only use it once."

I kissed Shorty. "Get back to your trotlines," I said. "You've done your duty. We're going to tie the knot."

Wheeze, wheeze. He stood up and we had a wet, fairly fishy hug.

Outside, I said, "You follow me out of the Birds."

A block past the Heart of Texas Fairgrounds, I stopped on Hackberry and pulled over to the curb. Drew parked the pickup behind me. I got out and walked over to the truck, getting there just as he got to the passenger side.

His arms all the way around me, we waxed the side of the rebuilt '58, just the way we used to.

"God," he said, "I missed you like crazy."

"Lord," I said. "It's been forever."

"I love you."

"You can fix up the Pontiac, but only I get to drive it."

He slid his hands under my shirt; found my mouth and stayed there.

"Will you spend the night with me?" I asked, coming up for air.

"Where?" He sounded panicked.

"My house."

"Your house? Can we do that?"

"I don't know." I asked him, "Can we?"

"What about the kids?"

"Mine are going to the Bledsoes. Won't yours be needing to pack their tennis rackets?"

"Stay all night?"

"There's a trapdoor from the attic down into the old root cellar."

"No kidding?" He looked down the street. "I guess we could do that."

"What've you got under there?" I pointed to the back, which had a huge pile of stuff covered with a tarp. It looked as if it belonged to a bunch of Okies transporting all their worldly goods.

"Table, I told you. Dining table. The chairs. Six is all we have."

"What else?"

"What else?"

"You said you brought something else." I raised the corner, or tried to, but it was tied down with ropes.

"Surprise," he said. "I'll show you at the house."

"Not much of a surprise, with six kids looking on."

"You're right about that." He began to work the knots. He pulled the stays loose and lifted a corner. Right there, wedged tight with ancient army blankets, on its side, was the white slatted weather station, looking like a beekeeper's hive. "What do you think?" he asked me. "Is it too late to start again?"

I looked at him, Andy, Drew, through all those years, and I said, "I don't think so. There's going to be a lot more weather in Texas."

Then in tandem we drove as slow as the law allowed, down Hackberry to Blackberry to Mulberry to Huckleberry. Rolling to a stop in front of the Gingerbread, we could hear the music blasting away and see our kids bouncing in time just as they had so long ago. *Once upon a time.*

A Note About the Author

Shelby Hearon was born in Marion, Kentucky, in 1931, lived for many years in Texas and now makes her home in Westchester County, New York. She is the author of twelve novels, including *Owning Jolene*, which received an American Academy and Institute of Arts and Letters Literature Award. She has taught in a number of writing programs, including the University of Houston and the University of California at Irvine, and was the recipient of an Ingram Merrill grant in 1987, a National Endowment for the Arts Creative Writing Fellowship in 1983, a John Simon Guggenheim Fellowship for Fiction in 1982 and the Texas Institute of Letters award for fiction in 1978 and 1973. Married to philosopher Billy Joe Lucas, she is the mother of a grown daughter and son.

A Note on the Type

This book was set in Caledonia, a typeface designed by W. A. Dwiggins
(1880–1956). It belongs to the family of printing types called *modern face* by
printers—a term used to mark the change in style of type letters that occurred
about 1800. Caledonia borders on the general design of Scotch Roman, but is
more freely drawn than that letter.

Composed by Creative Graphics, Inc., Allentown, Pennsylvania
Printed and bound by The Haddon Craftsmen Inc., Scranton, Pennsylvania
Designed by Iris Weinstein